Forgiving Patience

by

Jennifer Simpkins

The Patience Series, Book 1

Forgiving Patience

Cover Art by *Diana Carlile*

The Wild Rose Press, Inc.
PO Box 708
Adams Basin, NY 14410-0708
Visit us at www.thewildrosepress.com

Publishing History
Previously published: Secret Cravings Publishing, 2013
First Champagne Rose Edition, 2020
Print ISBN 978-1-5092-2641-2
Digital ISBN 978-1-5092-2642-9

The Patience Series, Book 1
Published in the United States of America

His body shifted next to hers. "Why did you leave me, Anna?"

The words cut through her. They were sharp, heavy, and full of hurt. She could not only see the pain in his expression, but she could feel it. She knew that pain all too well. He'd broken her heart and caused her to cover up that same hurt.

"You left me, Jake. That night in May, you left me." Tears clouded her vision. God, why did she have to cry in front of him? The first tear fell down the cheek he'd just touched.

She turned from him, as she had so many other times during her short two-day stay, and this time he didn't stop her. She had to get away from him and the memories he represented. Why did he do this to her? Why did he kiss her, make her feel things she'd never felt? And why did he have to bring up the past?

"Anna?"

She kept her back to him. She couldn't let him see the tears he'd caused.

"I'm sorry," he said.

She could hear him walk away, leaving behind a broken heart and a storm of emotions.

Praise for Jennifer Simpkins

"Ms. Simpkins puts a lot of interesting layers into her characters. Anna is a strong yet vulnerable woman who has come home to deal with her inner demons. Jake is the quintessential yummy hero, who has demons of his own to fight. They are both like an onion, one just has to peel one layer at a time, to see their true character."

~InD'tale Magazine (4 Stars)

Dedication

Throughout the process of writing this book
I was supported by some amazing people…
My husband,
who never thought for a second I was crazy
for embarking on this journey.
Jennie,
for being my sometimes-late-night writing partner
and always believing I could do this before I even did.
And my sweet daughter,
I hope you remember the dreams you have now as
a child will still be reachable when you're grown.
To my readers:
I hope you enjoy reading Anna's story
as much as I loved writing it.

Acknowledgments

I want to thank The Wild Rose Press for seeing the potential in *Forgiving Patience* and giving it a new home.

Chapter One

"Jackass!" Anna Kelly white-knuckled the wheel of her small convertible and screamed into the wind and exhaust fumes left by the truck of the speed demon who zipped in front of her.

Filled with more rage than fear at the terrifying thought of being killed by what looked like one of those giant green pythons stitched across the front of a Boston baseball player's uniform, she continued driving down the curvy stretch of road toward the home she'd sped away from eleven years before. She should've taken her New York Sparks license plate and shoved it into that Boston truck's ass.

Not that she knew for a fact he was a Boston fan. She just hated pythons, and the truck's ugly shade of green rubbed her the wrong way.

With a damaged heart and soul at the age of eighteen, she couldn't leave October Road fast enough. She'd spent fifteen years of her youth on the lonesome path. Except for Ms. Edna's and her properties, hundreds of acres on the left side of the road were used primarily for farming. Corn grew on most of the lush farmland, the rest left to be cut for hay.

Forcing herself to take in a calming breath, she smelled the sweet scent only freshly cut hay could leave in the air. She exhaled slowly.

The breath was of no help. Her mind still raced

after her near-death experience.

The Lawrence farm was off the main highway, a mile before her own road and leaving no reason for either brother to venture down her way. Unless her spitfire neighbor had a crazy-as-hell grandson, the reckless driver had to be some jerk joyriding in his daddy's oversize truck. She enjoyed driving fast—music loud—as much as the next person, but she wasn't about running somebody off the road.

Welcome back to Patience.

She hadn't wanted to come back here in the first place, and as she'd expected, things already looked bleak.

Finally, just to the right, she could see a clearing. She was almost there, and it would be time to go to work. She'd been trying to pump herself up for the last hour or so, but now that the time had arrived, she didn't know if she was ready. What if she wasn't strong enough for the ass-kicking she was about to put herself through? Why couldn't Em have chosen to get married in Hawaii or the Smoky Mountains? Anywhere else in the world was safer than Patience.

The same post she'd remembered as a child held up a mailbox with the barely legible numbers one, nine, two painted on the side. Anything more than a slight breeze and the rotten wood was going to be lying in her ditch. She made a mental note to have it repaired.

The front of the house was impossible to see because of the unkempt bushes lining the driveway. The smell of freshly cut grass filled her head again—immediately bringing back memories, at least the good ones, of the times she'd spent with friends at the ball field or having weenie roasts in the Lawrence family's field. That particular smell transported her back in time. She gave in to the urge to park there for several minutes, eyes closed and soaking it all in.

She couldn't glimpse the house she hadn't seen since that rainy morning in May due to the four-wheel-drive truck interfering with her view.

"You've got to be kidding me! Python is parked in my drive," she muttered. The idiot who'd come close to ending her life had his big-ass truck parked in her driveway. The guy was going to get a piece of her mind.

A few years ago, she would've avoided the confrontation, but not now. She was no longer a pushover. She'd grown a backbone—well, was in the process of growing one—and this guy was going to see the new Anna. This time she refused to be the same little girl who wasn't allowed to have an opinion or voice when it came to her life. Standing up for herself was the only option she had. She refused to be a woman who lay down and took what was given to her. *Might as well use that backbone right now and show this boy who he'd just messed with.*

After cutting the engine of her car, she peeled herself off the leather seat and swung the door open in one smooth motion. She blew back strands of hair falling on her face as she marched to the truck. What she wouldn't do for a hair tie. Today was just like any other Tennessee summer day, and the air was hot and so thick at times it was hard to breathe. Every part of her felt disgusting. If she got rid of the roadrunner parked in her drive fast enough, she would have time to strip off her clothes, open the bottle of wine she'd brought, and take a long bubble bath. A bath that wrinkled every part of her body.

She rose to the tips of her toes to peer through the mud-streaked window but only saw a soda can in the designated holder, trash thrown on the passenger floorboard, and a simple gold chain dangling from the rearview mirror. Nothing useful.

She stomped to the right and then to the left of the house. Nothing. He couldn't have gone far. He had to show his ugly face sooner or later to get to his toy out front. She would just prop herself up against his door and wait.

She wished she had her Louisville Slugger baseball bat or whatever her crazy aunt called it—oh yeah, *ball buster*. When Anna got her first place in Linden, Aunt Lidia had insisted she get a *ball buster*. She would remind Anna that every woman needed protection from the crazies in the world. If she had one at that very moment, she could use it on the truck and then the guy. That would let out some of her built-up anger.

"Can I help you?" a deep masculine voice questioned from behind her.

She whipped her head around, almost losing her balance in the process, and was met with a man wearing ripped jeans and a white T-shirt stretched around toned muscles. She didn't know much about sex, but she had a feeling this guy was the pure definition of it. At least, what great sex would be like.

Was it getting hotter? For a second she considered fanning herself but used her brain instead and didn't give the man standing in front of her the satisfaction of knowing he was droolworthy.

To top it off, his ball cap hung low over his brow, shielding his eyes from the sun and hopefully, from her uncontrollable stare. A man with a ball cap was a sure turn-on. This was no boy, as she'd first thought. Hell no. He was a full-blooded male. He was sexy as he—

Wait... She remembered the first time she had heard that southern-boy drawl—and the last.

No way! This could not be him. She knew it was, but how could it be? She did her best to stomp down her attraction toward him as she looked at his suntanned, stubbled face.

With just one glance, she knew he wasn't the same guy she'd professed her stupid young love to all those years ago, the guy she'd willingly given her heart to. There was a hardness about him now. If she had to take a guess, she knew exactly when that change had happened. A world of hurt and disappointment was in his guarded stare.

Just as in his younger days, he still could probably get away with pretty much anything, including murder, with those same sinful good looks. Damn Lawrence brothers. They were unnaturally blessed with the kind of good looks that made every woman in Patience, and the two surrounding counties, come running.

"Jake."

"That's what most women call me, but judging by your pissed-off expression, you might have a few other choice names." He leaned a shoulder against one of the front porch columns and crossed his arms over his broad chest.

She forced her gaze from his perfect body and noticed all four porch columns looked freshly painted glossy white. Scanning the rest of the house, she could see—what in the world?—new, black, barnyard-style shutters. She'd expected peeling paint revealing exposed wood. Maybe she wasn't going to have to spend a small fortune restoring the outer beauty of the aging house. How was this possible? The realtor overseeing the property for her hadn't mentioned anything about doing repairs.

The clearing of a throat brought her back to the man. Oh yeah, Jake. She would figure out the whole house thing later. Right now she had bigger things to worry about. Like a sexy man glistening with sweat.

She could do this. He might not have been expected, but she was strong enough to take on big bad Jake Lawrence. Fortunately, she wasn't the same impressionable teenage girl. Like him, she, too, had changed. "Did you not see me back there?"

"Not sure what you're talking about, sweetness."

She let the endearment go because he knew damn well what she was talking about. How could he not? "I find that hard to believe since you rode my bumper for almost a mile. Do you know you ended up running me off the road? I could've been Ms. Edna for all you knew."

"I knew you weren't Edna. The old woman goes American all the way, not some foreign make. She wouldn't be caught dead in what you poke around in."

"Thought you didn't know what I was talking about?"

He smirked. "If I'd wanted to run you off the road, I would have."

"Is that supposed to be some kind of threat?"

"Just stating the obvious."

"You could have killed me." She overexaggerated, but his nonchalance was irritating to say the least.

He lowered his head and kicked off some of the

day's mud covering most of his work boot. What was his deal? Did he make it a habit to go around torturing innocent women because he had the need for speed? Then again, he had a reputation for causing pain and suffering to people who didn't deserve it.

"Come on, Anna," he said after he was apparently satisfied with the look of his boot. "You know your life wasn't in any danger, and I sure as hell wasn't close to ending it." A corner of his lip turned up.

Was that supposed to be a half smile, or was he trying to intimidate her? She refused to let either work.

Whether he was going for the intimidating tactic or not, it was the first time she had heard her name spoken by that mouth in eleven years. She had a plain name. Nothing special. He had no nicknames for her, except for the sweetness comment, nor did he draw out a syllable. Still, he said it like no other man she had ever been around. It took all her strength to stay composed and not get unnerved.

"Do you know what you did to my car?" she asked. "For your information, your little stunt probably scratched the paint."

He only stood there, arms still crossed, looking as if he couldn't give a damn. "Are you hurt?"

"What?" His lack of concern for her well-being pissed her off.

"I asked if you were hurt."

"No, I'm not hurt. Does that make it okay for you?" She, too, crossed her arms, taking a strong stance against the man using his long legs to leave his position on the front porch and approach her. She expected to see a limp or even a wince of pain as he walked. There was no evidence of either. To a person who didn't enjoy America's pastime, he would look like a perfectly healthy man, a man who had never experienced excruciating pain. But she knew differently.

Even though she was a New York Sparks fan through and through, on a quiet night or lazy Sunday, she would find herself searching the channels for an Atlanta game. If Jake had played for Boston, there would be a lot more hostility going on right now. Supporting him was something she'd never admit to anyone.

It had been a clear July night. She'd ducked out of the office an hour early and curled up on the sofa, gripping the remote as she watched what was unfolding on her television screen.

As Jake rounded second base and headed to third, his childlike grin faded to stone. Even through the pain, his concern never wavered from the game. He headed home against the third-base coach's instruction and came face-to-face with Carlos Lorenzo. The only hope Jake had at being safe and getting the assurance run was to charge the two-hundred-and-something-pound catcher.

Lorenzo successfully caught the ball bulleted from centerfield, planted both feet, and guarded his plate. Back in the day when there weren't as many rules, Lorenzo was the type of catcher who didn't mind being trampled over. Jake gave it all he had, and after colliding with the man, he collapsed on home plate, grabbing his right leg.

The television cut to commercial too quickly for her to comprehend what had happened. At first, the manager and his teammates tried to downplay his accident, but Anna knew in her gut it wasn't going to be okay for Jake. She had cried for him that night—another thing that remained a secret.

He stopped an arm's length away. She took a calming breath and stared at the magnificent man. He had all the classically charming looks. His hair was still russet, dripping with sweat and curling out from under his ball cap. A slight dimple was centered on a strong chin, and the blue eyes gone dark were unreadable and stared into her, weakening her stance.

He kept in shape probably out of habit more than anything. She imagined that if he rolled up his sleeves, he would reveal a farmer's tan. That day's grime covered his clothes and boots. He smelled of sweat and dirt, but under all that, she could faintly smell the cologne he'd applied that morning. The mixture of scents flowed to her through the gentle breeze provided by Mother Nature.

"You don't have anything broken. You're not bleeding. Did you happen to hit your head?"

She instantly reached to rub a palm across her forehead. "No."

"Then we can rule out a concussion, so I don't see what the big deal is."

"The big deal? You want to know what the big deal is? I was driving down a usually deserted road, my road, only to be run up on by a reckless jerk and forced off. That is the big frigging deal."

"Sorry, but I'm not seeing how this is my fault—"

"I see you haven't changed." She stopped him midsentence. She already knew he wasn't going to cop to it. Taking responsibility for anything wasn't his style.

"What makes you think that?" he asked, still sporting his "I don't give a damn" expression.

"You don't care what you do or who you hurt, just so long as you get what you want."

She was showing him the backbone she hadn't had all those years ago. Liza, her good friend from Linden, would've been proud. She'd worked hard for this backbone. It was nice to finally put it to good use. He couldn't break her heart, run her off the road, or anything else he desired. He could take his charming looks and stick it. She wasn't falling for it.

"What are you looking at?" She watched as his sapphire gaze ran up and down her body.

"I'm just picturing your cute little ass." Like a switch being flipped on, his somewhat half grin spread out to a full-on smirk.

My what? Did he just comment on... "You haven't seen my b..." Shut up, she scolded herself. She'd just walked into that one.

"So you like the idea that I like your rear."

"No. I couldn't care less about what you like or don't like for that matter. Now can we get back to the part where you apologize?"

He ignored her. "You don't even want to know how I know you have a nice ass?"

It was time to regroup and hold whatever comments to herself. Her backbone was getting her into all kinds of trouble.

"You have some damn fine, sexy curves you used to not..." His voice went low, and her stomach fluttered. "By the way those jeans look from the front, I can picture the view from the back perfectly in my mind. Just fair warning, when you do actually turn away from me, because well...you have a history of running away, I will be staring a little too long for your comfort."

She remained focused on one thing at a time. But she'd had a good reason for leaving him. The day leading up to her departure still stuck with her. "I will not be turning away until I hear an apology, so you'll have to find some other willing woman to gawk at, because it won't be me if I can help it."

"Wanna bet?"

"I don't have to prove anything to you."

"Kinda figured you'd say that."

She didn't realize the type of trouble she was in until it was too late to prevent his strong arms from gripping her shoulders and swinging her backside toward him.

"Are you crazy? Let me go, Jake." She said everything her mind was screaming, but deep down she wanted to see if she still felt the same way in his arms. Over the years she'd wondered if what they'd had was real or just some hormonal crush, although crushes didn't stick with a person for eleven years.

And it was just as she'd expected—intense. Wonderful. Her attraction and need for him were still almost too much to put in words. And given how tightly he held her, he had to feel something familiar too.

Still, feelings or not, she was not letting him off easy. She tried jabbing him with her elbow, but he anticipated the blow and stopped her midmotion.

He pulled her up hard against him, and her breath became ragged. She tried putting up a small fight, just for show purposes, only to be yanked back, fitting nicely against his rock-solid body—a body that even under these circumstances, she could appreciate.

"Not a chance. Not only can I see your ass, I can

feel it right…there." He placed a hand on her midsection and pulled her up as close as she could get, making them practically one person.

Her body settled at his thighs. Oh God. She could feel…him…there.

"I have to say it feels better than it looks, if that's even possible." His voice was low and thick as it vibrated against her exposed neck.

Even though the temperature was well above ninety degrees outside, with a heat index of a hundred, a chill slid down her spine, and lower. Wait. No, what she was feeling lower, like between-her-thighs lower, was not a chill. It was something she hadn't felt in so many years she couldn't remember the last time.

She was sure he could see the goose bumps popping up, revealing he had more than just a strong hold on her. He also had her reacting to him. She desperately tried not to tremble.

Her jumping heart now resided in her throat.

Anna wanted to demand that he release her immediately but was afraid her weakening knees wouldn't hold her up on their own. As if sensing her near faint, he shifted one hand from her waist to trace his index finger up her neck. He was killing her insides.

"It makes me wonder what other assets look and feel this damn good."

"Please stop," she pleaded to keep up the pretense of really not wanting him.

She couldn't think about much else. The only sounds she could make out were those of her pounding heart and Jake's steady breathing in her ear. She could've been in Times Square, and it would've sounded all the same to her.

"You sure that's what you really want? From where I'm standing, you seem to be enjoy…" She lost her ability to hear his whispering words.

The motions of his gentle finger gliding up, down, and up again left her in a trance. Her eyes involuntarily closed. She tilted her head to one side, giving him better access to the spot she hadn't known could be so sensitive, only to be zapped back to reality.

She was held up by only her own strength and will. What the hell had just happened?

Just like that, his touch was gone, vaporized. A tingling sensation was the only remnant he left behind.

Her back was still to him. "Wha…what in the hell are you doing?" Had she just imagined his hard, muscular body holding her, touching her, making her want to cry out in need? No, of course not. It was real. It felt real.

"You don't look like the kind of woman who will have sex on the front lawn, but I can keep going if you'd like."

She took a second to pull herself together before turning to face him again.

There were probably other women in town who would agree to front-lawn sex, especially after feeling those hands on their bodies and seeing sweat running down his throat, pooling at the neckline of his shirt. Not her. When he lifted his shirt to wipe the sweat beads running down his face, showing a well-maintained stomach, she felt nothing.

Get real. She'd just experienced firsthand how he could cause any woman to respond to a simple touch. Except that simple touch was lethal.

"You'll never know what kind of woman I am."

"Mmmm." He acted as if he were mulling that over. "You sure? I don't think you can afford losing another bet to me. You still look pretty rattled after the first one."

"It's always a bet with you, Jake. Isn't that how we got started in the first place?" Her voice broke slightly. He was bringing up memories she'd been trying to shove aside for the past eleven years. Their entire history had started with a stupid bet. What did that say about their past relationship?

"Lighten up. There's no need to be hostile. I'm sorry. Okay?"

She took a small, calming breath. "Watch yourself. I haven't touched on the hostility I can dish out. I wasn't expecting to see you here now, but I will hash out our differences if that's what you really want, or you can get the hell out of my way."

He stepped back and held his hands out as though he were surrendering. She turned from him, not bothering to give him another glance.

After opening her car door, she heard him holler, "Nice license plate." She turned and glared while he stood there looking all sexy and cocky.

She didn't have to look at what he was pointing at on the front of her car. Jake had always hated the Sparks, and he would ride her ass about it every chance he got.

"Bring it on, Lawrence," she murmured.

He apparently didn't hear her, but that was fine. She ensconced herself in her car and slammed the door. He stood in place with his arms crossed and a smirk plastered on his face. What a jackass.

Why couldn't he be a Boston Pythons fan? It

would be so much easier to hate him if he were.

Chapter Two

Anna made up an excuse about needing to drive into town for supplies. The necessities were right beside her, neatly packed in her suitcases, but given her state of mind, she had to get away from Jake. A bottle of cheap wine she'd bought before entering Patience's city limits sat in the passenger seat. She had enough food and clothes, so she was prepared for a long couple of weeks.

She was furious with herself for allowing Jake to make her think things, feel things, and touch her affection-starved body. She was insane. He'd had her almost moaning at his gentle touch. He'd clearly mastered that technique on plenty of other women since the last time she'd seen him.

She cranked up the radio, allowing the unique voices of her favorite alternative rock band to blare through the car speakers. They did a poor job of blocking what had just taken place with Jake and the thoughts that snuck up and plagued her mind lately. Usually, music was an escape. It made her feel as if she were somewhere else, doing something else, or even being someone else, but right now no amount of music could take away the demons she'd have to deal with for the next couple of weeks.

Her childhood home contained enough pain to fill an endless pit. Coping with the memories of what had taken place there was going to be the hardest challenge because of the secrets no young girl deserved knowing or experiencing. Forgiveness was out of the question, but maybe she would be lucky and eventually forget. In her book forgiveness was overrated. How could anyone ask her to forgive someone like that? A person who was so dark and cold that their soul was blacker than black. No—forgiveness was not going to happen. Ever.

Some days were good. Those days she could go without thinking about the late-night visits from the devil himself. Days like today, she wasn't so lucky. She'd awoken this morning in drenched nightclothes, taking a minute too long to remember she wasn't being smothered with the smell and look of her small childhood bedroom. Awakened with thoughts of being back in that hellhole was always frightening, but she was adjusting to the frequent night terrors. At least that's what she told herself.

Then she had Em's wedding, her main purpose for passing the city limits sign. She cherished her best friend. She'd come back to help and to be a part of what she hoped would be one of the happiest days Em would ever remember. Em was the best part about Patience.

While she was thrilled at seeing her childhood friend, she couldn't wait to get back to her current home, Linden. It matched Patience in size, but what was important was that the people were different. She loved that she was anonymous and got the privilege of supplying the little bit of information she wanted to make public rather than having everyone know everything about her.

Most people in Linden only knew she'd grown up a day's drive away in Patience, Tennessee, had come to spend time with her mom's sister, had never married, and that she'd decided to stay because she fell in love with the quaint town. When her mother had moved to town several years ago, people got a little nosier. They got more curious about Ms. Kelly and what had made her suddenly move away from her home to live in a new place with new people at her age—which was only fifty—but when they noticed that the frail woman was sick, they were respectful and only helped if they were needed. Anna really did love it there. She had good friends, an aunt she adored, and the dream of opening her own small coffee shop and bookstore. Life was good there. It was quiet, simple, and most of all safe.

She didn't want to go to Em's just yet. It was going on six o'clock, and Em would already be at the banquet hall for her party. She would have to wait to talk to her nosy friend there. Maybe Em would be able to shine some light on the whole Jake situation. No, it was not a situation. It was a full-blown crisis.

She needed to make a quick stop at Garrett's realty office and see what was going on with the house. He'd been the one dealing with the previous renters and whom she planned to have list it. He wouldn't clear enough from selling the house to make up for everything he'd done, which was a lot more than she originally thought. He was the only one who could've had the house painted to its former glory. It looked better than she remembered from her childhood memories. Was that all he'd done? She had been a little too preoccupied to have a good look around, but first thing in the morning she was going to survey the property and make a list of all the repairs she needed to have done. She hoped the repairs wouldn't put too big of a dent into her already-diminishing bank account.

Great, it looked like Garrett was still working, judging by the two vehicles in the parking lot. She pulled in behind a compact car and a late-model Mustang with two different colored doors. The office was on the small side but looked cute on its corner lot. If she remembered correctly, it had once been a home. It reminded her of a country cottage, something that should be sitting in some coastal town. The yard was neatly kept, the driveway was paved, and two rocking chairs sat on the porch and framed a large window. The rockers were a fixture found on most front porches in Patience. A small building that matched the office perfectly sat where the drive ended.

A sign that read *Garrett Tillman Realty* hung above the door. Before she could ring the doorbell, the door flew open and a petite woman stood just inside it, looking about to burst with excitement. Anna didn't know if she had to pee or if she'd just won the lottery.

She looked to be in her early twenties. The bumble-bee-yellow dress with matching earrings fit the woman's mood and bubbly personality. Her stylish, sleek bob cut made her look almost childlike. Instead of heels, she wore white canvas slip-ons. The shoes would be an odd choice because they seemed boring, and *boring* wasn't the word to describe the person in front of her.

"Oh, you must be Anna. I've been waiting to meet you. Come in." The woman squealed with excitement, clapping her hands at the same time. "Do you need anything? Juice, soda, water?"

Anna was finding it difficult to get a word in. Where was this woman's enthusiasm coming from, because it couldn't have something to do with her being back in town? "No, I'm fine. What's your name? I don't think we've met."

"I'm sorry. I always forget to tell people that. I moved to town about a month ago, so nobody knows me very well yet. I'm Georgia McKinnley. I was raised in Georgia, so my mama gave me the name. It's kind of cool, I guess."

Georgia could have been Garrett's girlfriend, but Anna doubted it. In high school, he'd always been soft spoken and most of the time, stayed to himself. Why he became a realtor, she didn't know. She'd never thought of him as a people person.

"It's very nice to meet you, Georgia. Is Garrett around?"

"Yes. Let me get him. He's in his office. Be back in a sec." Georgia scurried to the back of the office.

The front room was neatly furnished. A small desk with two chairs in front of it sat by the door. A couple of more high-backed chairs sat off to the side with a small end table that held a lamp and a few magazines. No pictures hung on the walls, but a few were grouped together on a small secretarial desk. They appeared to be of Georgia and her family. Georgia must work for Garrett. Now that made more sense.

In one frame there were seven kids with an older man and woman. If Georgia had just moved to Patience, as she said, Anna figured the separation from family had to be hard on the woman. A pang shot through her gut. She'd always wished for a big family. She was thankful when she heard footsteps. They brought her back to reality. She stood up straight, not wanting to seem as if she were snooping.

Garrett entered the room with Georgia. "Anna, it's nice to see you. I wasn't expecting you for another week or so."

"Em and Tommy's bride-and-groom party is tonight."

"I met Em about a week ago, needed to get my hair done and all," Georgia chimed in. "She was just going on and on about her wedding. She said something about a friend coming for it, but I didn't know she was talking about you. You must be so excited. Me—I love weddings and all. They're so romantic." She brought both hands to her chest, her round face lost in the thought of love.

Anna couldn't help but smile. Georgia was like a ray of sunshine, inside and out. Even though Anna didn't believe everyone found love and happiness, she liked the woman's childlike outlook on life.

Garrett stood with his arms crossed. Anna swore she could see a tick in his jaw. Annoyance rolled off him in waves. Was it because of her unexpected arrival? Or did it have to do with Georgia's talkative nature?

"Yes, Em is my best friend. You know what? Why don't you come to the wedding, since you love them and all? I know Em wouldn't mind. In fact, she would insist that you come. You two seem like you would hit it off. You can be my date." Anna didn't know why she'd just invited someone she didn't know to a wedding that wasn't even hers, but she liked Georgia and wanted her to feel welcome. Plus, she wasn't lying; she did think Georgia and Em could be friends. The only problem would be they both would be talking so much they probably wouldn't hear what the other was

21

saying.

"Are you sure? I don't want to impose since I just met Em and you and, well, everyone."

"You wouldn't be imposing. Like I said, you can be my date. It will save me from being the only girl going alone. The old women around here like to talk. At least now they can't say, 'Oh, look at that Anna Kelly. She came here alone. Must not have found her a man yet.' Now they'll just think I'm into women. That makes for more interesting gossip."

A giggle escaped Georgia. "Well, if you insist, consider me your plus-one. I think you and I are going to be good friends."

"Me too," Anna said. The woman seemed genuine, and she liked that.

"I must have forgotten about the party," Garrett cut in. "You want to come back to my office? I figure you have a lot you want to discuss. That is, if you have time?"

He sent Georgia home for the day and showed Anna to his office in the back. His personal space looked similar to the front area Georgia occupied. A few plaques displayed his accomplishments, and his state license hung on the beige walls. A desktop computer and the usual office supplies—a stapler, tape dispenser, cup of pencils, and lots and lots of sticky notes—sat on top of his desk. A houseplant that had seen better days sat in one corner of the room, but everything else would be found in most business offices. The office held nothing more than what was needed.

If—no, scratch that—*when* she got her own office, she wanted to be wrapped in the solitude of green walls with splashes of burnt oranges, reds, and chocolate browns. She envisioned a simple black desk, although nothing as massive as Garrett's, a built-in bookshelf housing all her favorite novels so that on late nights when she needed a break from paperwork, she could pick up a romance novel and lose herself, and of course, she needed a couple of filing cabinets and some actual office supplies. She wanted to feel at home there. A place that represented her.

Garrett took his seat in an executive-style chair behind a large walnut desk, while she took the guest chair across from him.

"How was your drive? It's a scorcher today."

"It wasn't too bad. Just long."

"Have you been by to see Emilee yet? I know she's looking forward to your visit." He arranged a few pens in their holder and straightened his desk phone so it was situated at one corner of the desk.

She could tell he was making small talk, but she'd play along. He looked nervous, and she felt sorry for him. "No, I'm going to see her tonight. I wanted to stop by here before I go back home and throw myself together."

"Oh…right. I forgot you mentioned the party."

"It's going to be over at the banquet hall. I think everybody Mr. and Mrs. Bradshaw have ever talked to will be there. Of course, Em always likes having the excuse to throw a big party. I think she just loves the attention."

"You're probably right. She's always struck me as a woman who loves to be the center of everything." As if realizing he had just described how vain Em could sometimes be, he stopped. Sweat settled in the creases of his forehead. "Sorry. I just mean—"

"It's fine. I know how Em can come across. Don't worry about it. Don't tell anyone, but I've thought the same thing a time or two."

He let out a long breath and settled back in his chair. She was glad. He did not need to get all worked up over a comment most people likely thought and maybe even said directly to Em's face.

"How's your aunt?"

"As crazy as ever. She definitely keeps my life exciting."

He tapped a pen on a notebook pad, barely looking her in the eyes as he asked his array of questions. Something wasn't feeling right. It was more than him just being nervous. In all the years she'd known Garrett, he'd never asked about her personal life. Why would he take an interest now?

"What's going on, Garrett?"

"I take it you've been by the house," he finally said. "It's the only reason I can come up with why you're here on a Saturday afternoon when you have other places to be."

"Yes, I've been there. I had to get away. Jake happened to be there, and I needed to take a drive. I ended up here." Wait. Why was Jake at her house? And why was she just now asking herself that question?

"I'm really sorry, Anna. I was going to tell you. I wasn't expecting you this early." The rosy-cheeked guy wore a sheepish grin. He pulled at his necktie.

"Tell me what? I wanted to come by and tell you I was in town and get an update on the house. Plus, I wanted to thank you for the new paint job. It looks beautiful. Is there a problem?"

He frowned. "I take it you didn't look around the rest of house? Did you happen to go inside?"

"Oh, I looked around it when I wanted to beat Jake and his truck with a *ball buster*."

Garrett's eyes went wide. "A what?"

With a wave of her hand, she eased the troubled expression paralyzing his face. "It's nothing. We were just getting reacquainted. So what's up?"

"Well, I don't know how to tell you this, but remember I was thinking of you when I agreed."

"What is it, Garrett? You're killing me here. Just spit it out."

"Jake lives there." He released a gush of air.

"Excuse me? Please don't tell me what I just heard you say is right, because I think you said the cocky, now-brooding Jake Lawrence is living in my house."

"He made an offer you couldn't refuse."

"I'll be the judge of that. It's my house, and I get to decide what's best." She put both elbows on the desk. "What was the offer?"

"Please don't be mad."

She wanted to reassure him she wouldn't, but that would've only been a lie. Something was going on here, but she couldn't exactly put her finger on it. Jake in her house? "What did Jake offer?" She no longer cared about how uncomfortable she made Garrett.

"He said he would fix up the property if I let him live there for one year," he said slowly, clearly dreading every word coming out of his mouth. "When his lease is up, he said he would leave."

"Why would he want to do that?"

"I'm not sure. After he was injured and his mom died, he seemed restless and angry at the whole world.

He started drinking way too much, which resulted in him getting into a lot of bar fights. I don't know why he wanted to stay at your place, but after he moved in, he became a different person. A man who changed for the better."

"That's what guys do sometimes to let off steam, Garrett. They drink, get loud, and fight." Except Garrett didn't look like a man who would do any of those things.

"Not like this. He was getting into fights every other night of the week. He was out of control, to the point where Bradley couldn't even tame him."

This had to be a painful time in Jake's life, as well as his brother's, but that didn't give him the right to involve her. She had her own set of problems, and she sure as hell didn't—or wasn't—involving him in them.

"Well, I want him gone. Tonight." Anna didn't know what made her madder. Was it because Jake was in her house or because he and Garrett had decided what was best for her without her knowing? She refused to let a man take care of her and tell her what she needed to do. She answered to herself—no one else.

"Anna, he signed a lease. You can't kick him out. And just so you know, he signed the lease before you informed me you were planning on selling the place."

Her first day back in Patience and Jake was already invading her life and recruiting Garrett in the process.

"Well, what am I supposed to do now? Go live at the inn? Did you ever think of that when you were looking out for me?" She couldn't stay with Jake. She knew that the first time she saw him again. The two of them together equaled danger.

"I have a small studio apartment behind the office

here. I lived there when I first opened my realty business. It's fully furnished and move-in ready. I had it thoroughly cleaned for you, and you can move in right now if you like."

"You thought of everything, didn't you?" She was in control of her life, not Jake and not Garrett. Jake was moving out of her house, no matter what she had to do.

****

Jake took a long pull on his first beer of the night. After today his aching and worn body screamed for the scald of a shower. The aging house, above other things, had kept most of its water pressure. The need for relief forced him to enjoy his beer at the same time.

His body felt the strain he put on it daily. But he had to keep busy. He was working on finding and keeping that inner calm, something he'd found so effortless while he was getting to play out his little-boy dream.

A maximum of two or three beers in one day was his limit nowadays, though he wished that commitment had been made *after* today. It would be so easy to skip the party he was required to attend, go to Ollie's, and order the hard liquor that brought a strong-stomached man to his knees and worshiping the white throne the next morning.

Yeah, that would make him feel good for the night, but it would be a boneheaded move.

He'd promised himself, and some other overbearing people, that he would no longer self-medicate with alcohol and ass-kickings. That meant no more liquor to sooth an aching heart and a broken body and no angry bar fights with big-ass motorcycle guys who were double his size and sported grim-reaper

27

tattoos. It was time to face what had been taken away from him. It was time to quit taking the easy way out.

He wanted to be that man who found it satisfying to be able to rocket a ball over the fence in left field when hitting it with the meat of the bat. He wanted to believe in his ability to ground a ball and make a smooth play to first base like the best of them. And shit, he wished his legs moved as fast as they once had so he would be able to beat out the ball being bulleted home and score the game-winning run in walk-off fashion.

Tonight he had to go to a party and support two of the best people he knew. Tommy and Em had helped take care of him when the drapes stayed shut for days at a time and sleep overtook his body after an all-nighter spent guzzling a bottle dry. Tommy had woken at least one night a week to come pick his drunken ass up at the bar after last call was announced. And Em—well, what could he say about that woman? She hounded him and would've kicked his ass before any of the guys, but really, she couldn't kick him when he was already down with no intent to get up. She did, after all, have her moments of sweetness.

Bradley had mentioned picking him up and riding to the banquet hall together, but Jake knew the guy wouldn't be alone. He'd decided against that idea altogether. He didn't feel like playing third wheel to his brother and whichever woman he would be with for the night. Ideally, his companion was always a different woman every night. The guy's motto was *no need to wear out a good thing*. Jake was sure Bradley would have run out of women after the past ten years.

Not yet.

He also didn't want to hear Bradley ragging on his

ass all night about how he was a disappointment to the Lawrence family name. For the most part he let his kid brother talk because he'd saved his sorry ass more times than Jake could count over the past two years. Bradley was the only family he had left, and even though Jake didn't deserve him, the guy always had his back.

No matter what Bradley thought nowadays, Jake had no problem getting women—after all, he did have the Lawrence charm to his advantage. He just hadn't wanted to screw the usual unattached woman in a roach-infested room above Ollie's lately. Yeah, attractive women dressed in scanty miniskirts showing long, tanned legs and big breasts covered with only thin tops just didn't do it for him anymore.

What was he thinking? He was becoming a sorry excuse for a man.

Maybe he wasn't feeling the bar scene because he was still recovering from a hard-on caused by the hysterical blonde from earlier. No matter what everyone else thought of him, if one woman caused his cock to rise, he didn't go out and stick it in some other willing woman. Unlike his brother, he had some standards.

A woman with long, honey-blonde hair replaced the imaginary short brunette. Sea-green eyes a man could lose his soul in, high cheekbones, and full, kissable lips on milky skin made up most of her gorgeous face. The hourglass flare of her hips made her jeans fill out in all the right places—accompanied by her swelling breasts filling out her thin, snug T-shirt— and made his shaft harden and push toward the zipper of his jeans. She was natural, a woman who had come into her own.

Jake had almost been too rough earlier. He could hear the shock in the ragged breath that escaped her wet, waiting lips. He had to feel those sexy curves pressed up against him. Her skin was smooth, much as he expected, and her sweet smell invaded his head, making him forget about everything that had sucked in his life. Not wanting to hear about how he purposely meant to run her off the road, which he hadn't, he'd pulled her into his arms. And he sure as hell didn't want her to bring up his failure to take responsibility.

But she was out of the question. He wasn't into serious women. His type was simple: uncomplicated. Anna Kelly could never be that woman. His best bet was to stay clear of her. She was better off without him around.

She was here for her best friend, and he had no right to interrupt her plans. Except he had. He was surprised when she didn't ask why he was there at her house. For a brief second, he caught a glimpse of surprise wash across her face when she first noticed him. Nonetheless, she was so wrapped up in the shock she never wondered why he was standing on her front porch. She probably ran off so quickly because of the rattling effect he had on her. She would find out about the deal he'd made with her pushover realtor soon enough.

Her wrath would come down on him again when she heard about him living in her house, but she was kind of cute when she got all demanding and tested her take-charge attitude on him.

It was wrong, but he couldn't shake the feeling that tomorrow wouldn't be another dreary day, which normally left him feeling hopeless and watching those around him live out their lives. He had to see her, even if it was only for a couple of weeks. For the first time in years, he felt something he'd thought was lost forever, and it was because of her.

Fuck.

Time to party.

He allowed himself to linger a few more minutes in heaven before stepping out of the shower and dressing in the clothes Em had demanded he wear. Damn woman. He was a grown-ass man. He'd been dressing himself for a long time.

He grabbed his keys and let the new screen door slam behind him.

Chapter Three

The party celebrating Em and Tommy was a true reflection of the love they shared. Photos of the happy couple were situated on a table in one area of the room, chronicling their love up till this point. Anna got teary-eyed at seeing everything she'd missed in Em's life.

"Anna Lynn Kelly."

Anna knew who the voice belonged to. She turned from the table. "Ms. Edna." Her fiery neighbor was dressed in a blue skirt and matching suit jacket paired with black, sensible flats she imagined the simple woman only brought out for special occasions. Her gray hair was swept back in a low bun, and she wore little makeup to cover her gracefully aging face. She looked exactly as she had eleven years ago. In Anna's eyes she was pure loveliness, even though the old woman made it nearly impossible for anyone to actually love her.

"Ms. Edna, you look exquisite tonight."

"So the lost sheep finally decides to come home."

It was just like the stubborn woman to ignore a good compliment when it was given and to not even offer one in return. Anna hadn't kept in touch with her neighbor and only knew through Em that Ms. Edna still worked five days a week at the salon and was exactly the same in spirit. To most, she came off as hardheaded and borderline rude, but Anna loved that about her. She was true to herself and couldn't care less what anyone else thought.

"Yes, I'm back for a little while."

"Why?"

"I wouldn't miss Em's wedding for anything. I'm the maid of honor." She hated that anyone—particularly a person she respected—would think she wouldn't come home for her best friend's special day. Had everyone been so surprised to see her back? Of course, she hadn't really been jumping at the idea of returning and dealing with the town and what it represented. She couldn't blame Ms. Edna for doubting her friendship duties. She only hoped Em hadn't doubted her too.

"You missed a lot of other important things around here, child. When Emilee said you were coming back, I didn't believe her. You know how the girl talks. I don't think she believes half the things that come out of her own mouth."

Anna could hear the motherly tone leaking out. Ms. Edna was disappointed in her for taking too long to come back. Her mother hadn't lived in Patience for years, so other than Em, what reason did she have for returning? Had the woman missed her? After all, they had known each other as long as Anna could remember. For the first time, she wondered if not coming back was a mistake.

Ms. Edna didn't have any family, so Anna's mom had made it a secret tradition to set aside one day a week to spend a couple of hours with their cranky neighbor. Ms. Edna would've resented a pity visit, so they made up reasons for visiting—such as needing a cup of sugar—which she saw right through and sent them packing back across the field.

"Em was telling the truth. I'm here for a couple of

weeks."

"Where you stayin' since that older Lawrence boy is shackin' up at your place?"

Anna was trying to forget Jake and their little run-in for just this night. "Garrett offered me an apartment behind his office."

"Good. I would tell you to stand up for what is yours, but it's best you stay away from Lawrence. He and his brother skirt around with every floozy in town. Just look at that Bradley. He's practically having sex right there on the dance floor with some girl he probably picked up last night—"

"Ms. Edna!" Was this outspoken sixty-year-old the woman she'd grown up living next to? She did not want to be talking about sex with Edna. It was just…wrong.

"What, child? You think I don't know about sex? I might be a single woman, but I was young once. Those rotten li'l devils are sure nice to look at, but they are t-r-o-u-b-l-e if you ask me. You stay away." The older woman pointed a stern finger.

"I'll keep that in mind, Ms. Edna." Anna tried not to blush.

"Well, I gotta go over here and see when Louise wants to come in and get her hair fixed. Don't be a stranger." Edna gave her one harder look, as if to make sure Anna was really there and not a ghost. Even though Anna wanted to give her a hug, she decided against it because Ms. Edna wouldn't like the sign of endearment—especially in public.

Nonetheless, Anna was glad to be done with the odd conversation. She couldn't erase the picture of Edna as a young girl, skirtin' around with all the single handsome men. Why hadn't her dear neighbor ever married or talked about an ex-lover? Ms. Edna in a relationship? Did she have any family in or around Tennessee? The many questions intrigued Anna.

Before she could start feeling sorry for herself and replaying her bizarre day so far, she eyed the room, looking for Em. If anyone could distract her, it was her lively best friend.

Because of the lack of time, she'd thrown herself together in a frenzy. After the irritating conversation with her realtor—and she now used that word loosely, because of the position he had put her in—she'd had just enough time to reapply her deodorant, add some powder to cover up her sunburnt face and mascara to her eyelashes, run a brush through her hair, and slip on her previously chosen dress paired with red heels. The sleeveless black cocktail dress had a high neckline just for mingling purposes. When she knew there would be a big party she needed to attend, she'd intentionally packed this dress because it covered the splotches of red on her neck if she got too nervous.

A knot formed in her stomach at the thought of having to socialize. So far she'd gotten by with just a few hellos from other passing guests and the short, nerve-rattling sex talk with Ms. Edna. She was anxious about meeting Em's friends. She hoped they accepted her as the maid of honor. While she took Ms. Edna's lead and told herself it didn't matter what anyone else thought about her, deep down she wanted Em to have a wonderful wedding. Em didn't deserve to have her Patience friends and her best friend, who lived what seemed a million miles away, to be at odds and uncomfortable with one another.

She took a deep, calming breath and gave herself a

mental pep talk. This was not only important to do for Em but also to prove something to herself. She caught Em just as she was leaving one group of people for another.

"Hey, stranger!" Em pulled her into a hug. "Are you having a good time?"

The faint smile she used to cover her true feelings didn't fool her friend. Em knew her too well. Em took her hand and gave it a little squeeze. Anna looked down at their joined hands and was comforted. She also figured Em didn't want her passing out and taking all the attention away from her and her party.

I have missed this.

"I haven't talked to the other bridesmaids yet." Anna guessed volunteering to actually interact with people was a good start in the right direction.

"Come on, then. I was just making my way over to them."

They approached two women—one of whom she recognized from her high school days. The woman looked out of place at the lavish party. Her short black skirt with a white baby-doll tee and flip-flops were a far cry from what Anna expected to be worn at such a fancy party. Her simple brunette hair hung loosely past her shoulders. A to-die-for tan left her needing little to no makeup. She came across as looking the part of the girl next door, but there was a toughness about her.

"Anna, this is Jessie Daniels, Tommy's li'l sister. I don't know if you remember, but she was a couple of years behind us. And this is Jill Wright." Em pointed to the woman standing next to Jessie. "She works with me at the salon and was two years behind Jessie in school."

Jill had dark, curly hair springing out in every

direction. Anna wished for hair like that but knew it had to be a nuisance to deal with every day. She was about Anna's height and blessed with a naturally tan complexion. The spaghetti strap dress she wore was modest and cut just above the knee. The minty-green color looked amazing against her bronze skin.

"Yes, I do remember. You played on the softball team. It's nice to see you again, Jessie. And it's nice to finally meet you, Jill." She gave both women a friendly handshake.

While Jessie could be the spokesperson for a strong-willed, confident woman, Jill seemed more conservative.

"Yeah, softball days were the good ol' days. Now I'm stuck playing with all men." Jessie didn't look that upset at the idea. "I'm glad to have backup." She rolled her eyes at Em. "She's driving me crazy with all this wedding stuff. Stuff I know nothing about. You have to help her—help me...p-l-e-a-s-e." She clasped her hands together.

"Em, are you really being a bridezilla?" Anna looked at Jessie. "I have your back, so don't worry. Between the three of us, I think we can take her."

"Good, because I was about to boycott the wedding altogether."

Anna didn't doubt Jessie was telling the God's honest truth. "What does Em have you doing?" she asked, feeling surprisingly comfortable.

The woman tucked a piece of her dark, shoulder-length hair behind her ear. "Well, let's see. Last week it was buying the groomsmen's and bridesmaids' gifts, which I think is absurd. This week..." She turned to Em as if asking her what her chores were, even though

Anna could tell Jessie knew exactly what she was supposed to do. "Oh yeah, I have to send out invitations for her bachelorette party, a party she won't allow me to throw. I feel like a grunt. Jill doesn't do anything."

"Hey, don't throw me into this." Jill held both hands in the air. "I volunteered to help, but she won't tell me anything. Don't blame me. I've tried."

Anna liked the friendly banter between friends. These were the people closest to Em. In some ways, she felt like an intruder on a life she hadn't been a part of.

"Jill is busy at the salon till dark five days a week," Em chimed in. "And works half days on Saturday. You are the most available person, Jessie, so stop being a terrible sister-in-law."

The comment sounded harsh, but the smile that spread across both women's faces told Anna this was normal talk between them. Em obviously loved Tommy's sister, and even though Jessie would probably deny it, she loved having Em around.

"You saying I have nothing to do? That I can drop everything at the store to go and rescue your ass?" Jessie asked Em. She turned to Anna. "Jill only works four and a half days a week. They're closed on Mondays."

"Good grief, Jessie, can you be a lady for one night?" Jill scolded. "Have some manners. You are at a party that doesn't consist of beer kegs."

"Fine. Just for you, Jill, I will act like a lady," Jessie said sarcastically. "I won't say another damn word. Oops. Sorry, I guess you don't approve of *damn* either."

"Forget it. Anna, it's so nice to meet you. I hope we get a chance to spend some time together while you're here." Jill gave a pointed glance in Jessie's direction and turned on her heel. She headed toward an attractive man seated several tables away from where the bride and bridesmaids stood.

Okay, what is up with that? Note to self—watch the language around Jill.

"Well." Jessie broke the unwelcome silence that hung in the air.

"Jessie, do you always have to do that? Why can't you play nice with her?" Em crossed her arms.

Anna wasn't sure what was going on, but as maid of honor, she needed to channel the waters in a different direction. Things had been going so well with meeting Em's friends. No need to ruin the atmosphere. Em would thank her later for taking charge of the situation and turning the focus off Jill and her abrupt exit.

"Em, you should feel bad for sending one of your bridesmaids out to buy her own gift. That crosses the line."

"I paid for the gifts. Now that you're here, Anna, I can entrust you with some things. As you can tell, Jessie isn't into all the wedding stuff."

"I'm never getting married, so I don't need to know anything about how to throw a wedding. I'm glad I only have one sibling. I don't think I can go through this torture again."

"Well, I hope that plan works out for you, but for now, you're mine. So until I walk down the aisle and your brother says 'I do,' you're stuck with me." Em turned to Anna and smiled. "You come by the house tomorrow so we can catch up. It's crazy here, and I want to be able to actually talk."

Em sauntered off, leaving Anna with her comrade.

"Is she always like this?" she asked Jessie. "I mean, when did she get so bossy?"

"You haven't seen anything yet. Sometimes she is just downright scary. Weddings do not bring out the best in people. That's for damn sure. Come on. Let's get a drink."

They took a seat at a table situated in the middle of the room. Jessie stopped a tray-carrying waiter and grabbed two glasses of wine. She handed one to Anna and tossed back hers in two hefty gulps. *Wow.* Nothing like alcohol to calm the nerves. Anna could learn a few bad habits from her.

"What do you do?" she asked. "Em said you were the most available."

"I split my time at the family hardware store with my dad and Tommy, but I also work on our farm. We're setting tobacco, and for some reason Em thinks that's easy and I can just drop everything because I don't have a clock-in, clock-out job."

"It must be nice to be your own boss. I want to open up my own coffee shop someday. I hope to experience the same feeling."

"I would hardly call it being my own boss. I have to deal with an older brother who thinks he's in charge of my life and a father who thinks I'm still five." Jessie grabbed two more glasses of wine and passed one to Anna. "And I do work hard."

"I'm sure you do." Having a family, no matter what their flaws, must be rewarding. Even though Jessie was complaining, she sensed the woman adored them.

Anna had always wished for a brother or sister, someone she could experience life with. The closest thing she had to a sister was Em, who was indeed sister material. Em had sworn her to secrecy many times and given advice about boys. They'd even had the occasional fight. Overall, she was thankful to have her bossy friend in her life.

They sat and talked about high school. Jessie asked what it was like to live somewhere other than Patience. Anna told her small details about Linden and how at first it felt strange to be in a town she hadn't grown up in but soon grew to love.

She couldn't help but notice Jessie's gaze wandering several times as they talked. She was looking to her left at a man slow dancing with a long-legged redhead. They were the same couple Ms. Edna had pointed out earlier, during their need-to-forget sex talk. Bradley Lawrence was holding the woman close while they swayed to the newest country song. He looked ruggedly handsome—much like his older brother. Instead of the typical suit and tie, Bradley wore the snug-fitting jeans that most men in Patience sported on a workday, with the sleeves of a plaid, western-cut dress shirt rolled up to his elbows. His cowboy hat was pulled down low, allowing him to only zone in on the woman he was grinding on. She doubted he noticed anyone else was in the room, including Jessie.

From the look on Jessie's face, she didn't appreciate the couple or their dancing skills. A look of hatred mixed with love filled the woman's eyes.

"Is that Bradley Lawrence?" Anna approached the subject lightly.

The soft color filling Jessie's cheeks told Anna that the usually confident woman was embarrassed at being caught watching Bradley and his date. "Yeah, that's him. Same old, same old with him."

She didn't know exactly what Jessie was referring to, but whatever was going on, a discussion about a Lawrence brother wasn't a topic she cared to embark on at the moment. Still, she couldn't resist being a tad curious.

Someone tapped on her left shoulder. "Excuse me, miss?"

Anna turned in her chair and came face-to-face with Kevin Costner.

****

"How's the house coming along?"

Jake shifted his weight off his bum knee to his left leg without making it obvious to Tex. He'd grown up with Tex, and it wasn't as if his buddy didn't know he was in pain a lot of the time because of the old baseball injury. But he didn't want anyone to look at him and think he was some washed-up ex-ballplayer.

"It's coming. I finished up the exterior painting this week."

"I stopped by there a couple of days ago and saw the side porch you were adding. If you need any help, just holler."

Jake only nodded because he and Tex both knew he wasn't going to ask for help. Lately he was out to prove he could do all the repairs with minimal assistance. Every day he pushed himself a little harder and was now finally getting his life somewhat back together. He was far from normal, but he was better than he'd been not too long ago.

"That sexy blonde sitting with Jessie looks familiar."

Jake took a swig of his second beer of the night.

"That there is Anna Kelly."

"Wow. When did she get back?"

Jake's jaw tightened at the thought of Tex scoping out Anna. The guy was not harmless when it came to beautiful women—and Anna looked positively beautiful. Her honey-colored hair hung loosely past her shoulders. Every now and then she would sweep a tendril falling in her face back behind her ear. Her sleeveless black dress showed off her milky, smooth arms, and the crimson heels showed she was definitely not boring.

She looked like a mixture of a levelheaded woman who wanted to look presentable at a fancy party and a wild cat burning to come alive.

He knew she had a wild side because he'd seen a little bit of it earlier when she'd laid into his ass. He usually didn't enjoy being handed his rear, but it wasn't so bad with Anna. She made a good butt-chewing downright sexy.

He had every right to be concerned for any woman who was in his friend's line of vision.

"She rolled into town today. Claims I tried to run her off the road."

"Let me guess? You didn't, though?"

"No, I didn't try to run her off the road." Jake gave the other man a hard look.

"Come on, Lawrence. We all know you have become obsessed with speed."

He couldn't say much. It was true. He loved to feel free and get that adrenaline rush while going almost ninety down a country road. But he wasn't out to hurt anyone. The loss of his dad in a car wreck caused by a drunk driver taught him to always be aware when driving. It was pure coincidence that he had driven up on Anna. Why did she buy a sports car if it was only to poke around as if she were in the middle of a school zone? A car like that was meant to be driven hard and fast.

"Why, look at that. I lost my darn chance. Another brave guy is making a move on Ms. Kelly," Tex said, not looking too upset. The guy would have another woman to dance with in a matter of seconds.

Jake snapped his head over to stare at the older man standing by the table where Anna and Jessie were seated. The man bent to brush back strands of hair that had fallen into her face. He whispered something in her ear. Whatever the man said made Anna blush and glance toward her new friend. Stupid Jessie—of course she would be the one to sway her toward a man who was almost twice Anna's age. He had to be close to fifty. How dare that old man prey on a pretty woman he didn't stand a chance with—besides this one dance.

The geezer took Anna by the hand and led her to the dance floor. Jake could tell by her stiff posture she was uncomfortable, but probably because she was nervous. Then a smile broke out on her face, followed by loud, carrying laughter.

Well, this is just damn perfect.

He set his beer bottle on an empty nearby table, fearful he might break it with only his grip, and clenched his fists at his sides. His knuckles turned white. Anger was a feeling that could carry a man away and swallow him up. He didn't like the emotion, but he couldn't exactly wish it away. If he could, he wouldn't have spent years of his life drowning in it.

What to do now? Only thing to do was wait and see

how long this dance lasted. The guy had to go back to his table of buddies sometime. The party wouldn't end for another several hours. Good plan—just wait.

What was wrong with him? Why did he care who Anna danced with? Right now he just had to be content with watching her. If he were honest, he would have to admit he'd watched her most of the night. In the beginning she looked almost scared at being around all the people she hadn't seen or probably talked to in over a decade.

Her entire face lit up at the sight of her—well, technically *his*—elderly neighbor. Anna had an unspoken bond with Edna, which had been hard to form.

He had tried visiting the grouchy woman, but all she'd had to say was "Lawrence," which amused him and forced him to reply "Edna." When she hadn't said anything further, he'd given her a friendly wave and headed back across the field. The woman actually scared him a little.

Anna looked more relaxed after sitting with Jessie. Probably because of the glasses of wine Jessie kept handing her. Anna didn't look like a woman who drank much or who could hold much alcohol. Jessie should've known she wasn't like her. Jessie was one of the guys—sort of—though she didn't look like one of the guys. She was tall, slim, and she could drink any guy under the table and beat 'em at a game of pool at the same time.

"If you want it that bad, why don't you go over and interrupt the dance?" Tex gave him a wink and small push. "If you don't, I just might."

Yeah—that wasn't happening, but while Jake

would love to walk over there and send the geezer back to his table, he wasn't sure how Anna would take it. But honestly, he didn't care. He couldn't stand by and watch her with another man any longer.

"You know, Tex, that might be the best thing to come out of your mouth tonight." He picked up his beer from the table next to him and took a long gulp before setting it back down. He walked around a couple of older folks slow dancing before he crept up on Anna and her dance partner. "Can I cut in?" He didn't give Anna much of a choice because he put one arm around her back and his other one cut in between the couple, letting them know he was indeed interrupting their dance.

"What are you doing, Jake?" She pinned him with a pointed stare.

"We've got some unfinished business to talk about. I'm sure Gee—I mean your new friend wouldn't mind cutting the dance a little short."

"I mind, so move your arm," she protested through gritted teeth.

"Sorry, but I can't do that." Jake narrowed his gaze on Anna. "We need to talk. Now."

"This isn't something I want to get in the middle of. Ms. Kelly," Geezer interjected. "It was nice to meet you." He leaned across Jake's arm and was barely able to lay a kiss on Anna's cheek.

Jake tensed at the kiss, but he was satisfied he sent the guy packing. He would never let some guy step in while he was dancing with a woman—a smart and sexy woman, at that. The guy didn't deserve to be dancing with Anna if he couldn't even defend his right to be with her.

"Uughhh…" Anna stomped one of her crimson heels. "What is your deal, Jake?"

"Did you really just stomp your foot at me?"

Chapter Four

Anna couldn't believe what Jake had just done. She was having a perfectly normal time with Kevin Costner—*normal* being the key word. He was sweet and interesting. It had been a long time since she'd enjoyed another man's company, and she didn't mind sharing a dance or two with him. And good grief, he looked just like the man she watched in the movies. Did he know he resembled Kevin Costner? He had to. No man could go through life and not know he looked like the man who played in *Bull Durham* and her personal favorite, *For the Love of the Game.* Which brought her full circle to the man now standing in front of her.

"Yes, I just stomped my foot at you. Why did you run Kev—I mean, Cam—off like that?"

"Cam? You're already on a short name basis?" he asked. "You never gave me any nickname."

"His name is Cameron, and we were having a nice time, at least we were until you rudely interrupted. And I have plenty of names for you, but for the sake of Em and Jill, I will refrain from—"

Before she could finish, he had her hand tucked tightly in his, dragging her from their spot on the dance floor. "Let me go." She tried keeping her voice controlled, but she had a feeling she was failing. "Where are we going?"

He didn't stop until they were out of the party

room and right outside the double doors. Although it was nightfall, the humidity had stuck around.

"Now…" He ran his gaze up and down her body, stopping at her eyes, just before he pulled her close for a private dance. "I have you alone."

His smile caused her stomach to flutter, and she hoped he couldn't see her uneasiness. After all, she was furious with him for so many things. He constantly made her life difficult. Between him just being him, the whole house situation, and him invading her privacy just now, she had no reason to find him sinfully sexy. Cam was uncomplicated. Jake was difficult, cocky, reckless, and unnaturally good looking.

Add all that up, and she had a very complicated, sexy-as-hell man. Not what she needed.

She had full access to his devastating stare because of the dim lighting outside and absence of a ball cap shielding his eyes. The intensity caused her thighs to ache. He cleaned up damned good. Instead of the stained and sweat-drenched jeans and T-shirt he'd had on earlier, he now sported a black dress shirt, with the sleeves rolled halfway up his arms, topped with a black tie tucked behind a gray-and-black vest. A narrow black belt circled his waist, securing his tailored black pants, which fit him just as well as the grimy work pants he'd worn earlier. Did he always have to look so good? What would it feel like to run her fingers through his sun-streaked hair curving just above his shirt collar?

Don't you dare move those fingers. Control yourself! She needed to get it together. Jake was off limits in so many ways. Better yet, she was off limits to him. What purpose did he have for running Cam off? Did he actually enjoy throwing her for a loop? What a jerk.

"I have to say you look stunning tonight, Ms. Kelly."

"Quit trying to change the subject."

"Which subject might that be, Ms. Kelly?"

She stared at him long enough to remember why murdering him was not a suitable solution to her problem. "That you just invaded my privacy again. And dragged me out here against my will."

The double doors remained open, making it possible for her to hear the band starting a new song. She should have recognized it since she faintly heard the crowd cheering, but her mind was too busy rummaging through other things—especially the man running his hands up and down the snug fabric on her back.

She was somewhat confident wearing her simple black dress and favorite red heels. While the dress was tight fitting because of some extra pounds she'd gained, she had to admit it made her feel sexy. She wished she'd had more time to reapply her makeup and do something with her hair, but the dress and heels made up for what she lacked in the hair department. She might have had to wear a high neckline, but instead of overbearing amounts of cleavage, she showed off curvy hips—something Jake had complimented her on while he had her backside pressed up hard against him, having her fight through the heat for air.

He pulled her closer, while she kept her hands on his shoulders and tried to lessen the closeness, if that was even possible. She fit comfortably against his hard thighs. Her face heated at the memory of their earlier encounter. In one day, he had already pulled her up against him twice, forward and backward. Having to look at his suntanned face while being grasped tightly was a little too much. All the blood rushed to her head. She gripped his shoulders a little tighter by squeezing his vest between her fingers, fearful of making a complete fool of herself. He must have taken the touch to mean she wanted to get closer, because his hands left her back before he took both of her arms and wrapped them around his neck.

She fought her instinct to squirm away. In fact, she refused to allow him to see just how much he got to her. "And you can stop calling me Ms. Kelly now."

He cocked his head to the side. "Why? You don't like it?"

"No."

"You liked it when Cam said it."

"Well, maybe you should have taken the hint and bothered some other woman."

"But I have you."

Anna sucked in a breath and let it out slowly. How could this man make her want to kill him in his sleep one minute, and the next cause her heart to skip a beat?

"I'm furious with you at the moment."

"What for, Ms. K…sweetness?" he choked out.

"Don't act dumb with me. You know damn well why. How could you take my house from me?" She hadn't meant to sound so desperate, but the throbbing in her throat leaked out before she could swallow it.

"I didn't take your house. I'm renting it from you. There's a big difference."

"You purposely hid that you are renting it from me. You could've told me earlier."

He shifted her in his arms until she rested perfectly

at his midsection. He bent down and spoke low and thick in her ear. "Since you brought it up, I have to say I'm truly, truly sorry for, well, you know."

No, she didn't know. What was he sorry for? Was it because he ran her off the road, because he took her house without her signing off on it, or because he had her wanting to have sex right on the front lawn? Or was he sorry for all those years ago when he crushed her heart?

"I'm just saying you could've told me I wouldn't be staying at my house while I'm back in town," she said frostily.

"If I said that, it would be a lie. You are more than welcome to stay at the house."

"What?"

"You can stay at the house if you want. There are two bedrooms and a lumpy couch. Although only one of the bedrooms has a bed. You're welcome to either the bed or couch."

"Okay, I'll have to say that's a no. I will just stay at Garrett's until I get you out of my place."

He smirked. "So is that your plan? To try to wiggle the house away from me?"

Was he challenging her? She knew he never backed down from a bet. "Honestly?" Anna asked.

"That's the only way."

That was a lie if she ever heard one.

"Yes, that's my plan. I came home to live in that house, and I expect to before I leave, regardless of whether you have a rental agreement or not."

"If you hadn't rushed off earlier, you would've noticed all the improvements I've worked my ass off on."

She'd noticed some of the changes he—instead of Garrett—obviously had done. He probably was the one who mowed the grass too. Thing was, she didn't want anyone's help. It was her house now, and she needed to be the one to take care of the improvements. She didn't have the money or skill to make it look like a house of its era should, but she was responsible for it, not Garrett and damn well not Jake.

"They're not your improvements to make. You had no right. Don't you have better things to do, like help Bradley at the farm?" Why wasn't he living at his brother's farmhouse? The Lawrences had a pretty sizeable place to care for, and it had taken both brothers plus a close family friend to keep it running after their dad's death when Jake was fifteen and Bradley thirteen.

"I have time for both."

How could he do the work required for running a farm and remodel her house at the same time? His knee had to give him some problems. Otherwise, why else had he left baseball?

They continued swaying to the soft country music. "So what was so important that you couldn't wait to talk to me?"

"We'll get to that in a minute. Right now I just want to enjoy this. Before long someone will be out here to rescue you. You know we're now going to be town gossip?"

"And whose fault is that?"

Although her patience was running thin, she let him think he was in control by continuing this little song and dance. She could turn from him anytime she wanted. She was sure of it. "I saw Bradley on the dance floor earlier. Is he married to that woman he was dancing with?"

Jake laughed. "Bradley? Shit, no. That guy will never settle down. That woman he's here with tonight is probably someone he met last night at Ollie's."

"Ollie's?"

"It's a bar that opened about six or seven years ago on the outskirts of town. Not something you would be into, but it has cheap beer and sometimes live music."

"What's that supposed to mean? How do you know what I am into? I'll have you know I am no prude. I have been in a bar before."

"Honey, I never said you were a prude. You just don't look like the type who would enjoy hanging around a watering hole like Ollie's."

God, if he only knew how *good* she was and how much she wished to be bad. For once in her life, she wanted to be free of her past and allow herself to live. She wanted to be careless, make rash decisions, and live out her impulses.

"What's going on in that li'l head of yours?" He bent his head so he could peer into her downcast gaze.

The brief concerned look was the hottest thing she'd ever seen. The softness of his eyes left her insides trembling—at least she hoped it was only her insides. She was feeling a little more relaxed, probably because of the extra wine Jessie had insisted on plying her with. She knew Jessie offered some useful bad habits. The wine was probably a bad idea since she hardly ever drank more than one glass at a time, but right now she was thankful for her fellow bridesmaid's persistence. She could handle this dance with Jake and anything else that came along. Not that she was thinking about anything else. This dance would be it. Speaking of dancing, it was time to end it.

"Can you tell me now what was so urgent and the reason you needed me alone?"

He snorted a laugh. "What? Ready to leave me already?"

"Start talking."

"Okay, okay. Well, like I said, we have some unfinished business to discuss. I figured doing it now is just as good as later."

"What business do we have? Are you moving out of my house tomorrow?"

"No."

"Well then, it's settled. We have nothing to talk about. I listened. I danced." She tugged against his hold with little luck. He kept a tight grip on her hand.

Even though he was becoming impossible to deal with and he was a pain in the ass, she couldn't deny her attraction to him.

His smile turned mischievous. "I have a proposition for you."

She didn't want to hear his proposition. The expression on his face told her everything she needed to know. He was up to something, something she wasn't going to like. Probably something that would make her life even more complicated.

"You don't even want to know what I'm suggesting? I can see your curiosity is winning out. Why not just ask?"

"Fine. I'll bite. What are you suggesting?"

"Let's just say, *suggesting* can mean so many things."

"Just get to the point," she bit out.

"The way I see it, we have some things we need to

work out that are way overdue. You go on three dates with me, and I'll move out of your house, not asking for a cent of the money I've put into it."

"Are you serious?"

"Dead."

He had to be joking. Right? Blackmailing wasn't the right word, because he had nothing on her. Hostage negotiation, that's what he was doing. He was holding her house hostage unless she did what he wanted.

"We have no business together, if that's what you want to call it. What makes you think I would ever subject myself to you again?"

"Because you want your house back."

"I could just wait until your lease is up."

"Now, we both know you won't do that. You've probably already been to Garrett trying to find a way to get me out. You want that house right now for some reason, so you will go on three dates with me. Want to tell me why it's so important to you now?"

She pulled her body from his hold with more strength than she thought she had. "You're an ass! I'm through listening to all your crap. If you want to be a stand-up guy and keep my house," she said sarcastically, "then so be it. I can't stop you. But I will fight you every step of the way. As for this little idea you have in your pea-sized brain that I will go on *a* date—let alone, three of them—with you, well, let's just say *no way in hell*." He gave her a major headache, but at the same time the depths in his eyes caused her heart to beat rapidly. "I'm guessing you expect me to sleep with you too?"

"I was just coming up with a way for you to get your house back." He took hold of her arm, as if knowing she had been about to turn away. "And I'm not opposed to the second."

"How generous of you." She wrestled her arm free and resisted stomping her foot again.

"Anna, will you please listen to me for one damn second without throwing some hissy fit?" He raked a hand through his unruly hair.

"*Hissy fit? Hissy fit?* Do you hear yourself when you actually talk?"

"Can you be calm, please? I was just thinking we could go on a couple of dates. You're the one who brought up the sex."

She narrowed her eyes. "Well, screw you, Jake. And not in the good way."

This time she did walk away from him. He was smart enough not to follow. Before reaching the parking lot, she glanced back. "And I'll never sleep with you."

Three dates? Sex? What was he? Some genie granting her three wishes? Hot damn, she was the lucky girl who got to spend three dates and probably some great sex with the wonderful and talented Jake Lawrence.

She didn't think so.

****

"Oh, Anna, it's about time you got here." Em dragged, hugged, her into the house. Her model-perfect friend, eyes growing wide, was giddy at the sight of the friend she didn't get to see often enough. Anna had never seen her happier, and that was saying a lot because Em had a contagious smile and was a total optimist. Her long blond hair looked like silk, the sides swept up in a butterfly clip, complementing her bronze skin. To top off the look, she had pink manicured nails and a flawless face.

The perky woman quickly had Anna parked in a stylish leather chair situated on a zebra print rug—and Em looked ready to get down to business. Anna just hoped it was about the wedding, running a marathon, or even the rise of gasoline prices, anything other than whom she had seen since crossing the Patience city limits.

"What? I don't get a tour of the new house?" she asked, trying to bypass the Jake conversation. Em had always been a big J-Ann fan. More than once she had tried smoothing over the blowup that had happened a decade ago, but Anna didn't want to hear it. She'd moved on with her life and didn't want to be reminded of the hurt he'd caused to her already-vulnerable heart. After a few unsuccessful tries, Em gave up on the issue. Anna was thankful.

She had a bad feeling about Em's giddy attitude. "Nice rug." Bringing up the subject of the unusual print for a living room might've been her only chance to delay the subject she had been dreading since yesterday. Em and Tommy had worked hard so they could buy the Cape Cod house. Talking about it should be her saving grace. It was like talking about a new baby with a proud mother. Em couldn't resist the opportunity to brag about her accomplishments.

The unusual prints intrigued her. Em was daring and bold when it came to décor. She brought everything together and made it look strangely beautiful. If Anna ever got to open her coffee shop, she would love to ask Em to help decorate it. She had always envisioned it as bold and colorful, a welcoming place to spend an hour or two writing or just sipping coffee with a friend. One day her dream would come true.

"It took me two months to talk Tommy into allowing it in the house. It's pretty rockin', isn't it? Now stop stalling. We have some girl talk I'm dying to catch up on. So spill." Her gossipy friend meant well, but she worked in a hair salon and thrived on the ins and outs of everybody else's business.

Anna offered a weak smile. "Spill what?"

"Don't give me that. You know damn well what I'm talking about. You lived in this town once. You know how the gossip mill runs. Patience might look small and move slow, but when something juicy happens, the phone lines start humming. I'm just mad you've made me wait till"—Em glanced at her watch, frowning at the time—"almost three o'clock."

"And me coming back is juicy?"

"What you came home to find in your driveway is juicy. You and Jake dancing at my party is juicy. You coming home is just way overdue and long expected. I've been talking about it for weeks. So what took you so long today?"

"Sorry. I didn't sleep much last night."

Anna didn't want to tell her friend that insomnia was an every-night thing, that sleeping until noon was common when she didn't have work, and that she operated better when the sun set for the day. If she said all those things aloud, everyone would think she was taking the new vampire phase to the extreme.

Em all but rubbed her palms together, waiting on the juicy news that wasn't going to be revealed. Anna's lack of sleep had everything and nothing to do with Jake, but not the way Em thought. Yeah, there had been some heavy breathing and weakened knees involved both times she'd seen him, but most of their contact was arguing. Em's mind was going in a whole different direction—a direction Anna was not traveling.

"That explains the pale face and dark circles. You don't waste time, do you? I know Jake is good, but, man, I expected you to at least wait a week or so before you let him get you into bed."

Anna stared in shock. She couldn't care less about the insult to her appearance, even though it drove home the thought that no matter how long she stood in front of the mirror she could never pull off Em's looks. She was more concerned about how Em knew Jake was good in bed. Maybe she didn't want to know. The thought was just wrong…unfathomable.

"God, no, I didn't mean I know from personal experience," Em quickly added, as if she could read her mind. "It's just…word gets around."

Anna guessed that fell into the juicy column for the town gossip. He was a guy, and all guys who looked like GQ cover men were bound to have multiple partners, but that didn't mean she wanted to subject herself to the specifics.

She recovered from the shock and changed the topic to something not involving Jake. "What do you need me to do to get ready for your big day? You better be careful because Jessie seems very tempted to quit the whole thing."

"I'm really not going to get any details? At least tell me if his running you off the road is true," Em begged.

Good grief. Patience had to be the most gossipy town. "No. You don't get to hear anything since you just happened to forget to tell me he was living in my house," she said with a pointed stare.

Em crossed her arms and scrunched up her face. "Fine, I will just have to get my gossip from Tommy. And I am not sorry for not telling you. If I had, you probably wouldn't have come back for my wedding. You can call me selfish, but I wanted my best friend here."

Shit—that stung. She was a horrible friend. It made her regret her time away from Em and her life. They didn't see each other enough. Twice a year hardly qualified as enough time spent with your best friend. Em had never asked Anna to visit her in Patience over the past eleven years, but Anna could have gathered up enough courage to set her own demons aside and come back to see her cherished friend. Em had a whole life Anna knew little about. She had friends, a job, and a future husband who Anna was just now actively becoming familiar with. A pain settled in her gut and forced her to see the reality of her best friend's life she'd mostly only heard about.

She abandoned her chair to kneel in front of Em. "You listen to me, Emilee Bradshaw. No amount of Jake exposure could keep me from your wedding. Got it? You are my best friend, and I'm sorry if I made you feel you weren't important enough for me to haul my ass to Patience." She forced a tear back. She couldn't afford to let the waterworks go, because there was a possibility they'd never leave.

Em reached out and hugged her friend a little tighter than she had earlier. "Oh, don't make me cry. I know you've had your reasons, and I understand them, believe me. I've just missed you, is all."

"Well, I'm here now, and I plan to have lots of girl talk."

Em wiped away the beginning of tears about to run down her perfectly made-up cheeks. "Good. Now tell me about what's going on with you."

"What do you mean?" *Please don't let it be any more Jake and sex talk.*

"About your coffee shop and bookstore. Have you told Jake that you need to sell the house so you can use the money for a down payment on a building?"

"No. The building I had had my eye on sold about a month ago. They're putting in another auto-parts store."

"I'm sorry, Anna."

"I'll find another spot, but it's none of Jake's business what I do with my house. One way or another, I will get him out. He has no right to be there. It was a lowball move to make this deal with Garrett."

"You know I'm on your side…"

"But?"

"Don't be mad at me. I'm just saying that house has in some way saved Jake from his destructive self. When he first came home, it was no happy reunion. He was cold, hard, and furious with the world, and that included everyone around him. There were plenty of nights when Tommy was called to pick him up from Ollie's because he was too drunk to put one foot in front of the other. When he moved into your house, that all changed. Maybe it was because of the butt whippings from Bradley, but mostly it was because he threw himself into something again. I know he's worked hard to straighten up in his life. To be the Jake we all remember—the fun, arrogant, confident, and slightly cocky guy."

"Well, he sure is getting back to his old ways. Every time I've seen him, he's been a complete jackass."

Her friend's eyes grew twice their size. "So you have seen him more than once? You did find him in your driveway?"

Anna laughed. It felt like old times to sit, talk guys, and let her guard down with someone she'd missed terribly. Even though she felt exhausted from lack of sleep, which had more to do with her sweet dreams of the old Jake she'd known as a stupid kid. She didn't remember him the way Em had. To Anna, he was uncaring and made promises that in the end he couldn't keep.

"Okay, what I'm about to tell you doesn't leave this room. No shoptalk or pillow talk. Got it?"

"Deal." They shook hands, hit their knuckles together, and made their hands into the shape of guns. They'd made the handshake up as kids. For the most part it was the only thing that got Em to keep her big mouth shut. Whenever Em was about to reveal the sacred information she had been told not to mention, she would think back to the handshake and change her mind.

"I know you saw us last night. Well, after he all but carried me outside, he tried making some ridiculous deal with me. A deal I will not be taking, by the way."

"What was the deal? You sure are making me beg today."

"It's fun watching you when you're starved for information. You really are a junky when it comes to gossip."

"Shut up and just tell me what Jake asked you, please."

Anna couldn't help but smile. "Okay, he said he would give me my house back if I went on three dates with him, and he won't ask for any of the money he's sunk into it."

"I know this isn't something you want to hear, but it sounds like a good deal to me. I mean, three dates with the *famous Jake Lawrence*—most women would fight you for that chance. Plus, you need to sell the place. If he's done a lot of work on it, you can gain more profit out of it. That will be good for your future business."

"I don't want his money, Em. I can take care of myself. I shouldn't have to subject myself to anyone to get my own damn house back."

Anna's entire body tensed. While it was good to let things off her chest, she didn't want to take her frustrations out on her best friend. Deep down she knew Em was only looking out for her.

"Quit being stubborn, Anna Kelly. If the guy wants to put all his money into a house that isn't even his, then that's his stupidity. You should just chalk it up as good luck."

"Luck? Being around Jake is not something I would consider as luck. I came here for you"—and other things, but Em didn't need to know about the nightmares—"not to date Jake Lawrence. Besides, I'm sure he has some girlfriend on the side he's not telling me about."

"Nope, no girlfriend since he's been home. He doesn't date. I've never even heard him talk about a woman in years. Not that he's celibate. He is a hot-blooded male, but he hasn't had a serious relationship since, well, probably you."

Good God, her? That was eleven years ago.

She knew at her core he probably didn't have a significant other right now. She was just trying to get information from Em without coming right out and asking for it. Even if she wasn't interested in him, she could still be curious. And now her interest was piqued even more, because to go that long and not have a serious relationship was just unheard of. Of course, she hadn't had but a couple of dates in all this time, but he was a professional baseball player. He could get any woman he wanted, and he'd had nobody.

She didn't understand what she was feeling, but for some reason a weight had been lifted off her shoulders.

"Well, I'm still not dating him."

"Have you ever thought that it might actually be fun? It might make your time here even more interesting—not to mention giving you a break from helping me plan my wedding, which, by the way, is not fun. It's stressful and a lot of hard work dealing with me on a daily basis. Having a hot affair with a man would make your time here memorable."

"I will not be having an affair with any man. I'm not interested. Looks like I'm yours until the minute you say 'I do.' "

Em's expression turned serious for the first time since she dragged Anna into the house. "You do whatever you want, and I'm always here for you. Jake did you wrong after so many others had before him. You look good now: strong, healthy, and a little happier. You have to hear me when I say this—you are not your mother. You will never be her. Stop comparing your life with hers. You need to start living a life that is not shadowed by her mistakes."

Chapter Five

The sun had not yet set. It was that time in between day and night. The night was her favorite time, which didn't make sense, but the darkness was somewhat comforting. Sleep would not come for several more hours, so after leaving Em's house, Anna drove to a place that always allowed her to think and pass time—the walking track.

It was isolated from the rest of the town, and besides the one couple walking, it remained lonely. To her mind, it was perfect. As a teenager, she'd run and walked many miles around this track, and being here brought back the memories of her youth. She didn't realize she'd missed the feeling of normalcy the track brought. She and Em had gone there several times a week to gossip about the latest boy her picky best friend was dating and to make plans for the upcoming weekend. Anna mostly listened to Em's comparisons between J.J. Thompson's and Cal Michael's kissing abilities. She didn't have much to offer to the conversation, but Em was content with doing most of the talking.

She didn't have a place like this in Linden. While she did take late-night walks around her apartment complex, between the barking dogs and the comings and goings of other tenants, it was impossible to savor the quiet. But Linden was safe and didn't hold the past that still haunted her and held power over her life, control she still fought to get back after all these years.

The abuse she'd endured as a child remained with her every day, reminding her that she needed to continue using her inner voice and stay in control.

Even though it was almost eight, the humidity in the air made it feel as if it were still way above ninety degrees outside. Summer brought predictable afternoon storms, and she could see and hear the enormous thunderclouds that threatened in the distance. As a child, she had cried for her mother's comfort when the gray clouds started their rumbling. Now she enjoyed the sounds of God moving furniture. She couldn't explain the turnaround. Maybe it was because she'd grown past the part of being that scared girl, maybe it was because she recognized it as something she couldn't control, or maybe she really still thought God was moving his furniture. All she knew was the sounds made her feel alive.

The beat of her favorite ska punk band set the pace. Her breathing intensified. She was out of shape, but damn, she couldn't even walk a lap without her heart beating wildly in her chest. She didn't give up. She slowed her pace just a tad as the music in her iPod changed. She could feel the sweat running off her back, smell the rain that was bound to come, and see the sun start to set. If she wanted to get a few miles in, she needed to start jogging. If she remembered right, one mile was two laps. She had done one mile and had every intention of accomplishing two. Her legs were heavy, but the faster she could bring them to move, the better she felt.

The elderly couple holding hands was up ahead,

venturing off the track and probably leaving to beat out the storm that was brewing. The sight of them from behind looked reassuring, indicating that sometimes love worked out and people did stay together for the long haul. She instantly thought of Georgia and her bright outlook on life and love. Those were good thoughts to have since she was a bridesmaid for her best friend's wedding. She needed to have zero negative thinking when she was helping plan a life-changing event. She gave a short wave before passing the couple and continued down the track.

Twilight was starting to set in, and just like eleven years ago, only the light poles that lined one side of the track worked. She was the only one left, which meant she was isolated in the dark. The thought should've frightened her just a bit, but instead, it made her feel alone, and that was something she didn't mind being.

Every part of the track was vivid in her mind—every dip, incline, and the darkest spot that made her pick up speed. That part of the track hugged the woods, and on some nights the wind whipped through the trees and caused sounds that made one jump and curse the parks and recreation department for not fixing the broken lights. Anna had intentionally left her music blaring to block out the rustling of leaves and picked up what speed she could muster. Her legs and chest burned from the strain she was putting on them. That's when something grabbed her from behind.

A strong arm reached around her waist, bringing her to an abrupt halt, throwing her iPod to the pavement, and ripping the earphones from her ears. A scream settled in her throat.

Oh God, what's happening? Her body jerked in

every direction possible. Sucking in whatever air was available, she prepared herself to fight. Her right leg found balance and kicked back until it came in contact with her assailant's body. That broke his grasp long enough for her to slip out of his muscular grip. As his callused hands scratched across her midsection, a chill shot through her and caused a tear to fall down her already-damp cheek. She knew he was actually a man, but the trace of his hand made the thought seem more real. More tears fell from her eyes, blurring her vision. The attacker slowed, but only for a second. She started running, her legs feeling weak. But she didn't have far to go. The exit was in her sight, and she just needed to make it. She had to. Her pulse beat in time with the movements of her legs, or at least that's what it felt like. She wanted to scream, but nobody was around to hear her cries. And she needed to save what air she had for whatever happened next.

The thudding of shoes meeting pavement coming from behind her was moving closer. She refused to doubt herself, and she was not going to be a victim. That outcome was unacceptable. She could hear hollering, or maybe it was the sound of her blood pounding in her ears. She took the chance to glance back and stopped dead in her tracks.

She knew the man. He stopped running when she turned. He was bent over and obviously in some kind of pain but trying not to show his weakness. Strands of his dark brown hair were wet from sweat. When she had secretly watched a few of his games, watching him sweat in the scorching heat, seeing him lunging after a grounder was her favorite part. Men in those types of pants should be considered illegal.

Tennis shoes, running shorts, and a faded gray T-shirt clung to a well-formed chest that would be considered a dream to any woman alive.

She wanted to scream at him, but the intensity in his eyes had her holding her breath. Instead, she swallowed the words. He looked dangerous, but not in a run-for-your-life kind of way. A pointed stare sent a chill up her spine, and she trembled. Her feet felt bolted to the asphalt, forcing her to face the man she'd thought was attacking her.

He walked with the slight limp she'd expected to see the first day she saw him. Oh God. She'd kicked him, and now he was hurting. She wanted to force her legs to move and rush to him, make him sit and rest, or insist he go to the hospital to get an X-ray. The injury to his knee had cost him so much. The anger, her fright, and the hundred other emotions running through her veins were gone, because now she was only concerned about Jake.

She let him make his way to her. He would only resent her for recognizing his weakness and rushing to his side anyway. He had pride and didn't want to show any weakness. And in her own way, she understood. She wouldn't ask him about his injury; she wouldn't ask him if he was hurt or how he'd recovered from it.

"Are you okay?" he asked, composed and apparently recovered from his pain. "Did I hurt you?" He sounded genuinely concerned.

"No, I'm fine. I just thought you were someone else. I'm good now." That was somewhat of a lie—she didn't like that she still cared so strongly for him.

A working light pole shone above him. She couldn't make out the color of his eyes, but she already knew they were sapphire blue, and right now they looked dark and hard. His features couldn't hide the emotions residing behind them.

She recognized the look of fury, hurt, and confusion. She saw it in her own eyes when she looked in the mirror most days. It was frustration at not being able to change the situation. Only the end of his baseball career could make Jake feel those kinds of emotions.

"What are you doing here by yourself?" he asked through clenched teeth.

"I've been coming here most of my teenage life. It's always been safe. It still is, unless you were really trying to attack me."

A slight grin formed. "I'm beginning to think I'm just your go-to guy when you need to blame someone. First with the whole car incident, and now me attacking you."

"Maybe you should quit giving me reasons to make you my go-to guy."

"Yeah, I guess I could do that, but you look so damn cute when you wrinkle up your forehead and try to take charge." His eyes softened and looked playful in the light. "What is wrong with you? I yelled out your name several times."

"I had my iPod. Which you ripped from my ears." She pointed down the track, where her iPod probably lay scattered in a thousand miniature pieces.

"I would say that wasn't my fault, but I don't feel like listening to you rant about me and responsibilities again. So what I will say is—if your iPod happens to be broken, I will buy you a new one. Deal?" He gave a gentlemanly bow. He knew how to work his charm.

"I say that's smart."

"I say it's way easier than arguing with a stubborn woman." He ran a hand through his unruly hair, pushing long, unkempt pieces out of his eyes.

"If you weren't here to attack me, then what are you doing here?"

She hated that she was foolish enough to be spooked so easily. But what was she supposed to think? It was getting dark, she was alone, and someone grabbed her from behind. Any sane person would have reacted the same way. While Patience had been a small, "sit on the porch with a glass of sweet tea" town when she'd lived here, things changed. How was she supposed to know it was Jake behind her?

"Just the same as you—running, enjoying the fresh air, killing time. I come here a couple of times a week. This body doesn't keep up on its own."

She'd figured out the hard way that a body required healthy eating and exercise to stay in shape. She found it irritating to see him fit and strong, while she was way out of shape. That was it. She was making it a goal to get her butt down to the track a couple of times a week herself. No more late-night chocolate. Women around the world were being told a complete lie—chocolate was not a girl's best friend. She needed a new best friend, and that was going to be running, or at least brisk walking.

Of course, why else would someone come to the walking track? She remembered a time when they'd come here together. Did he remember those night walks or early-morning runs?

"Why are you?" she asked.

"Why am I what?"

"Why are you here past dark? Most people come down here before sunset."

He looked at her from her feet up to her chest, but his gaze stopped there. Crap. She'd forgotten she only was wearing a faded piece of fabric called a sports bra under her large vintage T-shirt. Just great. Why couldn't she have worn something a little bit more presentable out in public? Now she was paying the price.

"Well, I have to say this look on you comes in a close second to last night's dress. While the shirt is oversized, the shorts leave little for me to imagine."

Along with her T-shirt, she wore cotton shorts that might have been considered too tight, but that was only because of the weight she'd gained. They had not been deliberately bought to show off her legs.

"Is this you trying to be cute?"

"Not at all. I love the look."

"Well, I don't care what you like, or don't for that matter."

Though it was hard to turn from those piercing eyes, she did. Heat started at her neck and worked its way upward. Damn curse. She couldn't hide her irritation, attraction, or any other passion she secretly felt, except it couldn't be a secret because it literally showed all over her face.

Jake grabbed her arm before she could run away again. "What have I done, Anna?"

Her gaze dropped to the part of her arm he held firmly in his grip, but only for a second. "The list is too long, Jake."

His hold weakened just a bit, but she could feel he wasn't ready to let her go. "Jesus Christ. I was simply stating I don't mind your sexy clothes, and whether you want to admit it or not, you do care what I think. You forget I can read your face." He used his other hand to point to the face blazing with emotion.

"Let. Me. Go."

"You going to run again?"

She didn't exactly know what time in her life he was referring to, because she'd run from most of it. For his well-being, he'd better only be talking about a few minutes ago. When she didn't respond, he did the smart thing and released her arm.

She yanked her ponytail down, only to fix it and put it up again. "You're impossible. At times, you're a complete asshole and—" She stopped to think of another word. "—reckless."

"You know you love it, though."

"Oh, let's not forget cocky. Did the baseball groupies stroke your ego so much that you've forgotten you're not as charming as you think?"

The biggest grin spread across his face at that moment. He actually thought he was God's gift to women. "You would be shocked at what they stroked, sweetness."

Wow. That was not what she was expecting. She had to pick her jaw up off the asphalt to even remotely try to respond to his crass comment.

Knowing that what she was going to say next was a low blow didn't stop her one bit. If he was going to fight dirty, she would too. "Did a baseball ever hit you in the head and cause foot-in-mouth syndrome?"

His expression only wavered for a second. She could almost see his mind going back to the baseball he'd hit, causing him to try to make it home from first base, only to be rewarded with his career ending. If she wasn't waiting for the change in his facial features, she probably wouldn't have noticed. He recovered nicely, seeming unscathed by the dig and memory.

"I'm just telling you like it is. I'm an honest man."

"Well, if that's not a lie in itself… You don't have to go making up stories just for my benefit. I will still think less of you."

He laughed. "I have all the proof to back up each and every one."

"I'm sure you do. I bet all the women at that bar I wouldn't be caught dead in know all about you, huh?"

"Sure do. Maybe you should go down there some time while you're in town and ask around. The stories will make your thighs tingle and your cheeks flush. About like they are right now."

"Wow. You are something, Jake Lawrence. I've been back for two days, have dealt with you running me off the road, stealing my house, trying to bargain with me to get it back. Now you scare the living daylights out of me, and you still are an asshole. And don't even say that none of this is your fault. I've never slapped anyone before in my life, but I don't mind you being my first."

He was most likely telling the truth about sleeping around—a baseball career had nothing to do with that. Em had even commented on it during their visit earlier. Besides, he'd known how to do that eleven years ago; he just hadn't been so damn cocky about it. Well, she really didn't know if he was cocky or not because she didn't stick around to find out. Back then he'd had sense enough to hide it. Now he was just being cruel.

"So what about those dates? You want to come

over for dinner at my house tomorrow night and make the first one official?"

"It's my house, and no, we will not be dating."

"Why?"

She crossed her arms over her midsection. "Because you're a jackass."

"You should really work on your self-control. It causes a frown line right there." He brought his hand up to rub the center of her forehead.

"Don't touch me." Instead of stomping away, she racewalked toward her car. She was not out of control. Just showed how well he really knew her.

She didn't hear any footsteps from behind, so she could only hope he wasn't following her. A clap of thunder shook the ground, startling her. She'd forgotten about the storm brewing. A fat raindrop landed on her cheek and slowly slid down her face. She'd trustingly left her keys in the car and was steps away when she heard gravel crunching.

Another clap of thunder boomed in the sky. The storm was getting closer and ready to show its ugly face. Maybe she would be able to sleep tonight with the soothing sounds.

She was opening her door when Jake reached around her and slammed it back into its closed position. "What do you think you're doing?"

"This…"

His words were lost against her lips. She was pinned between her car and Jake, left to either fight him or allow him to invade her mouth. This was not a tease. This was him being greedy. She brought her hands up to protest, but her defenses went unnoticed. He braced himself up by placing his hands on the car, on either side of her, pressing his body even closer. Her body had found a welcome home nudged between his thighs. She could feel all of him behind his running shorts. If she wasn't careful, she could get lost in his smell, his touch, and the strongest of the three—his taste.

She had to stop her hands before they fumbled their way over his tempting head of hair. She opened her mouth enough so he could slip in and take over like a man who meant business, a man who wasn't afraid of what he wanted. Their tongues tangled as he let out a groan she could feel rumble in his chest.

To her surprise, she felt strong and sexual. Something she'd never experienced with another man or allowed a man to make her feel. He ran a finger down her cheek, leaving a path of sizzling heat. There was no escaping him and the feeling of need.

The light pole above gave off a soft yellow glow, and with the help of the moon, she could see his eyes go a shade deeper. He stopped his hand on her chest, broke away from her trembling lips, and spoke softly with his lips still touching her mouth. "I can feel you."

She said nothing in return because it wouldn't have sounded anything close to what she was feeling. She was inexperienced, so instead of words, she took a ragged breath and stared into those dangerously sexy eyes, searching for more emotion, more connection.

"The way your heart is pounding right now, mine is doing the same. With every thud, I want you even more." His eyes brightened as if recalling something special. "Do you remember that party we were at, the one where we spent half the night talking by the fire?"

She smiled. "Em was so excited because it was the first party she'd thrown and a lot of her boyfriend's college friends were going to be there." Anna remembered being so nervous that night. Even back then, she hadn't done well in large crowds where she was forced to mingle. Her solution had been to drink. Looking at the man in front of her, she was still trying to decide if that was a good idea or a bad one. "That next Monday at school, everyone was saying how it was the party of the year."

"It was pretty memorable. It will always be one of my favorite nights—but not because I got to hang out with some college freshmen, but because I got to spend it with you." He moved beside her and leaned against the car. "Within five minutes, I knew you were something special."

"Was that five minutes before or after the bet you made?"

Jake burst out laughing. "You've never really gotten past that part, have you?"

In all honesty, it had never been a big deal that Jake only waltzed up and talked to her that night because one of his friends bet him he couldn't get to second base with the *sweet girl from school*. And she'd probably easily gotten past that part because not once while they were talking had he tried to kiss her. They'd spent the entire night getting to know each other. He'd asked how long she and Em had been best friends, and she'd asked him endless questions about the following year's baseball team.

She tried to cover her smile. "I just like reminding you how it really happened."

"Well, then"—he nudged her—"let's not forget about the two wine coolers that ended up down the front of my shirt and jeans because *someone* couldn't

79

handle their alcohol."

"Fair enough. We both made some mistakes."

"What I did wasn't a mistake." His deep tone had Anna turning to look up at him. "I would gladly take on another bet if it got me you. The only thing I would like to do over is the way the night ended. If I'd known it was going to take you two months to understand that I really was into you and wanted to go out on a date, I wouldn't have let Em drag you away so easily without getting a goodnight kiss."

And if she hadn't been semidrunk at the time, she might not have been so easily pulled away. She recalled lying in her bed after Em drove her home, wondering if maybe she had lost her chance to be kissed by one of the most popular boys in school. But then the following Monday he seemed to be everywhere she looked. After every class her stomach would flutter, just thinking that he might be waiting for her outside the classroom door. At the end of the day, he asked if she wanted to come over and have dinner at his house. He claimed his mother made the best fried chicken, which later Anna learned was true, but because she started overthinking what dating a guy like Jake would mean, she ignored his advances. She was sure he was used to having occasional sex when he dated someone, and it was a hang-up for her.

After two months of him never giving up and her desperately wanting to say yes, she agreed to a date. One double date with Em and her boyfriend led to another solo date until it was known all over town they were indeed a couple. It had been the best year and a half of her life.

His body shifted next to hers. "Why did you leave

me, Anna?"

The words cut through her. They were sharp, heavy, and full of hurt. She could not only see the pain in his expression, but she could feel it. She knew that pain all too well. He'd broken her heart and caused her to cover up that same hurt.

"You left me, Jake. That night in May, you left me." Tears clouded her vision. God, why did she have to cry in front of him? The first tear fell down the cheek he'd just touched.

She turned from him, as she had so many other times during her short two-day stay, and this time he didn't stop her. She had to get away from him and the memories he represented. Why did he do this to her? Why did he kiss her, make her feel things she'd never felt? And why did he have to bring up the past?

"Anna?"

She kept her back to him. She couldn't let him see the tears he'd caused.

"I'm sorry," he said.

She could hear him walk away, leaving behind a broken heart and a storm of emotions.

Chapter Six

Anna slammed the door of the studio apartment and threw her keys and purse down on the small table closest to the front door. "Home sweet home."

Her newfound temper bubbled over, bordering on hysteria. She wasn't familiar with this new emotion. How was she supposed to handle it? Was it okay to scream and let valuable breakables fly across the room? What was the correct protocol? She'd seen many tempers flare as a child, but her mom's boyfriend's temper stemmed more from hate and evil.

Taking a much-needed calming breath, she flopped onto the small sofa centered in the middle of an area that could be considered the living room.

Men. Who did they think they were? Egotistical, arrogant sons of bitches. She was twenty-nine years old and a woman capable of making her own decisions when it came to her life. Jake had no right blaming her for leaving Patience. If things could have been different, she would have wanted to stay. She'd dreamed of staying here and building a typical white-picket-fenced family. She'd wanted to be one of those girls who lived and died in the same zip code.

She fisted her hands before relaxing and raking them through her messy ponytail. Why couldn't things have been uncomplicated? She'd been back for less than two whole days, and already her time had been spent either being run over by a man or arguing with a man. The whole weekend would have been a bust if it wasn't for seeing Em and making a couple of new—at least she hoped—friends. She liked both Jessie and Georgia.

Anna slumped back on the sofa, instantly wanting to throw her feet up on the coffee table, before noticing it didn't look like something feet were supposed to rest on. She took a long look around the sparsely decorated beige room. A flat-screen television sat in front of her, flanked by two bookcases. The kitchen was small but offered a stainless-steel stove and refrigerator, so there wasn't much to complain about there. Frozen dinners were all she had on the menu for the coming weeks. The bed was hotel chic with its leather headboard and heavy taupe quilt.

Overall, it was a step up from the childhood home she'd expected to be sleeping in. It looked very similar to the office Garrett occupied. The one negative was the overwhelming lack of color. The only splashes in sight were two pink throw pillows oddly out of place. She'd tossed them off the bed the night before, refusing to accept Garrett's apology. He seriously owed her more than a few frilly pillows to make up for his error in judgment concerning Jake and her house.

She wished she could pinpoint exactly when everything had gone wrong. This was not what she had planned in her head. She was a planner; that's what she did with everything in her life, and this was definitely not the way it was supposed to play out.

For starters, she wasn't supposed to see Jake this early in her trip back to town. As soon as she saw those charming good looks, her first response should have been to run back to her car, forsaking the apology. He was dangerous to her system.

Why hadn't she put up more of a fight when he grabbed her? Why did she let him touch her and bring on these sudden lapses in judgment? At least now, maybe her nightmares of the past would be replaced with a new set of dreams, dreams that were a nightmare all in themselves.

Right now, she was supposed to be in her house, going from room to room, facing down the demons that resided there. Demons that still haunted the six-year-old girl who remained buried deep inside her. Girl and woman both deserved freedom. She was finally ready to take control of her life, free that scared girl, and Jake stood in her way. Whether he knew it or not, he prevented her from being able to move on.

Reliving the pain that was permanently attached to the house wasn't something she was looking forward to, but it had to be done if she wanted to move on with her life back in Linden. Instead, she was sitting in a beige room, emotionally exhausted from her close encounters with Jake and from finding out he was sleeping in her house—probably her old room.

Nothing good could come from her seeing Jake, dancing with, or kissing him. Oh God, had she really just kissed him? He'd instigated it, but she had definitely kissed him back. What a moron. She no longer was safe around him.

The thought of him inside the same walls she'd lived in for most of her life made her feel embarrassed and surprisingly turned on at the same time. Boys had never, under any circumstances, been allowed in her room—not that she had really wanted them to be—but imagining Jake stretched out on a bed in the purple room warmed her body. What was wrong with her? She didn't want him in that sinful room, that evil house.

Men had never made her panties wet. Yeah, she could appreciate them from afar, but not to the point that she was picturing them in bed, maybe sleeping buck naked.

Really, Anna? God—stop, no more thoughts. He was just unexpected, and seeing him again was weird.

She was furious at him. She'd be smart to forget all about Jake Lawrence.

There was nothing she could do tonight about Jake stealing her house or his kissing her. What she really needed was a bath and sleep. She stripped off her clothes, folding each piece and placing them on top of her suitcase. She walked into the bathroom that was nestled between the bedroom and kitchen and welcomed the warm breeze that filtered through the open window, bringing the scent of flowers, rain, and nature. It was comforting and familiar.

A clap of thunder boomed, startling her, but then caused her to laugh at how foolish she was being.

After taking out her contacts, she jumped into the stand-up shower since there was no bathtub. She still fumed about not being able to take an actual bath. The sunburn she'd known was coming had arrived yesterday, making it hard to stay in the shower for long. She pat-dried her sensitive skin and slipped on a camisole and matching panties.

All she could do was take her meds and forget all about Jake, at least for the night anyway.

She stared at the little blue pill before she placed it on her tongue. She hated taking medication, especially the kind that took over her body, giving her no control over her actions. But if she wanted to sleep, the blue pill was her only hope. Tomorrow she was going to figure out a way to get him out of her house, and if she wanted to be completely honest, out of her mind too.

To pass the hour or so it would take for her meds to cloud her mind and ease her eyes shut, she picked up a new romance novel she'd gotten at a bookstore between Linden and Patience. Her friend Liza had recommended it, saying it was hot and heavy and to be prepared to need the touch of a man.

Speaking of—crap. She still hadn't emailed Liza to tell her that she was okay and not falling apart at the seams, which was a complete and utter lie.

Liza was one of the few people who knew her past and knew why coming back to Patience was going to be difficult. She was also a therapist and as a counselor, understanding. But if someone hadn't actually lived it, there was no way in hell they could completely understand the loss.

She got out of bed to retrieve her laptop. She fired it up and started typing.

Liza,

Sorry I haven't been in touch. It's been a crazy weekend. My plans have changed a little. Instead of staying in my childhood home, I'm staying at my realtor's apt. Sit down! Are you sitting? Brace yourself—Jake is staying at my house. Yes—Jake the rat bastard. He's been fixing it up for some lame reason. Don't worry. I'm already thinking of ways to get him out.

Hope everything is good back home. Please check on Aunt Lidia and make sure she's taking all of her meds. You know how she can be. I'll be in touch.

Luv ya,

Anna

After she was satisfied with the email, she hit send, put her laptop away, and picked up her book. It might not have been what she needed at the moment since her love life was nonexistent and she wouldn't be getting touches from any man. She needed some hot and heavy in her life, and getting it from a book was s-o-o-o much safer. Plus, the man in the book couldn't care less that she was wearing ten-year-old glasses, no makeup, and had her wet hair piled up on her head. It was perfect.

An hour later, before even getting to the good parts, she drifted to sleep, still in an upright position with her paperback resting on her chest.

****

The door creaked open, and through her squinted eyes, she could see a dim light spill into her room. Her tiny heart started thumping at the trepidation of what was to come. She tried to remain still and hoped for once that pretending to be asleep would stop the devil from touching her. But just like every other time, it didn't. The door closed behind him, shutting out all light and hope. It was only a matter of seconds now. The smell of cheap cologne mixed with beer filled her small room. She should scream. *Why can't I scream?*

Anna jerked up on the bed with her heart racing. She gripped her chest and forced her beating heart to calm. She dropped her head on her drawn-up knees until she got her breath back. Over and over again she told herself, "It was just a dream. It was just a dream. It was just a dream."

****

Jessie sat in Em's salon chair, her head tilted back in the groove. Her hands gripped both armrests until her knuckles were white. "Ouch! Good grief, Em, be easy."

"Well, you're getting your eyebrows waxed. It's going to hurt a little. Quit being a baby and let me do my job." Em applied more hot wax and a removal strip to Jessie's brow. When satisfied, she ripped it off. "We need to get all three groomsmen and Tommy to pick up their tuxes. My cousin Melanie will get the outfit for Sam, my little ring bearer. I'll send Tommy to get his final fitting. Anna, can you deal with the groomsmen?"

"Sure. Just let me know how to get in touch with them." She was happy to help. It would be best if she stayed busy.

"Michael is my cousin's husband, so I assume she'll get him, but if you can, get in touch with Bradley and Jake."

She had gone most of the day without thinking about him. Of course most of that day had been spent asleep in bed, but he had still been off her mind. Was her contact with him ever going to end? It didn't look like it. As long as she was in Patience, Jake was bound to be in her life. With fewer than three weeks left of her visit, she needed to get him out of her house. And after Em's wedding, he would be out of her life. She just needed to get through the next two weeks.

"Okay, I can do that," she said softly, hoping the other two women didn't notice her uneasiness with the simple request.

"Mama is having the last meeting with the caterer. We're also going to get the band that played at the party Saturday to play at the wedding. They were surprisingly good."

"I saw where Jake interrupted your dance with that hot guy from the hot-guy table," Jessie chimed in. "Such an asshole, if you ask me."

Anna didn't know Jessie had been watching her and Jake so closely.

"I saw y'all leave together. How was the reunion?" Em asked, obviously hoping for any bit of information she could try to sneak. She wasn't the least bit subtle.

Anna didn't answer.

"Come on," Jessie said. "We're between the sacred walls of 'everything gossip.' If you can't spill the beans in the hair shop, where else can you?"

That's what Anna was afraid of. She didn't want her gossip to leave the shop and be the talk of Patience. The only other person who knew about the kiss was Jake, and though he could tell Tommy, which would result in Em finding out, she had to hope Jake wouldn't talk.

She sat in her chair, ignoring Em, Jessie, and their prying while she flipped through a styling book.

"All done," Em announced to Jessie.

"Thank God. Do I have any eyebrows left?"

"I suggest you stop complaining unless you want to start paying for your waxings and cuts." Em glared in Jessie's direction. She cleaned up her mess and came back to sit by Anna, drinking one of the diet sodas she'd offered everyone earlier.

"So did you and Jake get it on after my fabulous party or what?" A big smile spread across her face.

Em was dressed down for her day off, but she still looked as if she could replace her running shorts and baby doll tee with a flashy dress and be ready to walk down a runway in an instant. She kept her white-blond hair straightened and makeup flawless, with lips painted pale pink.

Anna would have felt inadequate if it wasn't for Jessie sitting there in overalls, wearing only a sports bra in place of a shirt. Jessie's body was toned and tanned. Even though she farmed most of the day, which was what probably kept her in top shape, a farmer's tan didn't mar her body. Maybe instead of opening a coffee shop, she should get into the farming business. She was never one to want to flaunt her body, but she had to admit that if she had Jessie's, she would have worn just a sports bra to the walking track instead of her extra-large T-shirt. There was no telling what Jake would have said about that.

"No, Jake and I certainly did not get it on."

"So what was the rush to get out of the stuffy party?" Jessie asked.

"Hey," Em cut in, "my party was not stuffy. You just wouldn't know class if it was a snake and snuck up and bit you on the butt."

They went quiet before Jessie broke out in laughter. "Really, Em? Did you just say that? That was undoubtedly the worst overused line ever."

"Why don't you just shut up? How is that line?"

She considered laughing with friends a good way to spend part of a day. At least that's what she hoped Jessie was starting to think of her as. The woman was fun to be around and kept Em on her toes.

"Now instead of making fun of me, let's get back to Anna." Em eyed Jessie.

Jessie stood, pulling her John Deere cap down low. "You may as well just spit out your news. Otherwise, this one"—she pointed to her future sister-in-law—

"will just pry it out of you anyway."

Anna knew she wasn't going to make it out of Cut & Curls without having to spill her guts. She didn't know if she wanted, or needed, to keep it to herself anymore. Maybe it would be best if she asked what they thought about the whole situation. She'd gone over it in her head for most of the night and still had come up with nothing remotely logical, unless she counted the idea of sneaking in his back door and smothering him in his sleep with his own pillow. If she didn't talk to someone, she was liable to kill him.

She closed her book. "This doesn't leave these sacred walls, got it?"

"Got it," they answered in unison.

She took a steady breath. "Okay. I didn't rush out of the party because I couldn't wait to have sex with Jake. It was him who kidnapped me. We danced alone outside, followed by him making me a proposition. I refused."

She had never seen Em speechless, but at that moment her best friend couldn't muster up a single word.

"What kind of proposition?" Jessie took the lead.

"You already know this part. Remember, Em? He said he would give me my house back if I went on three dates with him." Anna left out her sarcastic comment about them hitting the sheets. Nobody was hearing that piece of the conversation. Em and Jessie could beg all they wanted, but they were not getting that little bit of juicy information.

"Oh yeah," Em recalled.

"Dickhead," Jessie added.

"What else?" Em asked. "Has something else

happened I don't already know about?"

She should've guessed her friend would know she was holding something back. She had never been a good liar, having nothing like Em's abilities.

"After I left your house yesterday, I went to the walking track just to clear my head and try to shed these twenty pounds I've packed on. I had earbuds in my ears, so when someone grabbed me from behind, I thought I was being attacked—"

"Wait? You weren't, though, were you?" Em's pale green eyes enlarged.

Anna placed a hand over Em's. "No, it was Jake."

Em was the only person besides her mother, Liza, and her aunt who knew about her past. She was thankful for her constant friendship. Em had been there from the beginning, and if it wasn't for her, Anna didn't know what she would be doing right now. Em and her family had given Anna a way out of hell when she was a child and defenseless. The lump forming in her throat made it nearly impossible to finish her story. She was touched by the thought of someone being worried about her. When Liza talked to Anna, she would try to use facts and research to provide comfort. Her aunt couldn't help but feel uncomfortable. Anna didn't blame her; child abuse wasn't exactly something anyone would enjoy listening to or want to be reminded that such evil remained in the world.

"Jake?" Em asked, clearly confused.

"He said he tried calling my name, but I couldn't hear him because of the earbuds."

Her iPod—she'd forgotten all about it. It was still on the track somewhere. After Jake had brought up their painful past, her only thought had been to get as far as she could away from him.

Em and Jessie continued staring at her, waiting to hear what happened next. "We talked—most of it not civilly—and when I had heard enough, I turned and booked it to my car. The only problem is that he caught up with me and stopped me." Anna swallowed. *Can't stop now.* "He kissed me, and I'm pretty sure I kissed him back."

At this, both women were speechless. They were not going to be able to keep this juicy gossip to themselves. Great. Why had she opened her big mouth?

"So let's backtrack, just to make sure we're all on the same page," Em said.

"Good idea, Em," Jessie said. "We need to make sure we haven't missed anything."

"So for Jessie's benefit, Jake interrupted your dance so he could ask you out on three dates, and if you accepted, he would move out of your house for good. Then last night y'all happen to be at the track at the same time. You think he's attacking you when really he was trying to get your attention. Then he kisses you, and you kiss him back. Does that cover it?"

"Well, I kicked him when he was chasing me."

"Right on, sister." Jessie cheered while giving Anna a high five.

"In the knee," Anna added in a subdued voice.

"Oh," both women said at the same time.

"I know. I never would have done something like that to him, but in my defense, I didn't know it was him."

"Is he all right?" Em asked.

"He looked like he was in pain at first, but then he went right back to being a charming asshole. So I'm thinking yes, he was hurt but had too much pride to show it."

"Men." This came from all three women.

"What are you going to do?" Em asked.

Anna assumed she was talking about the dates and the kiss since that would be the only thing on Em's mind for years to come. "I'm not going out with him, that's for sure. As for the kiss—I can't lie, it was nice, but it was a mistake for me to kiss him back. I'll deal with him for the sake of the wedding, but afterward I'm done."

She didn't feel the need to volunteer the information that Jake blamed her for leaving him. That was a hit to the gut, and the memory was still raw. She didn't know what to say or even think about that. It wasn't her fault, at least she didn't think so. Maybe she had blinded herself by blaming him for everything that was wrong with her life. Except she didn't blame him for everything. He got blamed for the part he was responsible for. The rest of the responsibility resided with others, herself included.

Jessie didn't look all that convinced. "Are you sure it will be that easy?"

For some reason Anna remembered the way Jessie had looked at the other Lawrence brother. Something deeper was going on there, more than just a woman checking out a man, and she was intrigued. Why did Jessie stare at Bradley as if he was more than a nice male specimen? Did Anna look at Jake like that? No…no, she certainly did not. She wasn't sure what Jessie's deal was, but her situation was different.

"It's no big deal," she lied. "We had a thing eleven years ago and shared a kiss last night. Nothing more."

Em smirked. "I think it's more than that, Anna. Jake was a big part of your life before you left, and now here he is stirring up those feelings again. If you ask me, you should beat him to the punch."

"What do you mean?"

"Don't let him decide what happens between you two. If you want to have sex with him, have sex. If not, don't let any opportunity pass by without showing him how badly he royally screwed up." Em spoke more quietly than usual, as if she were telling her darkest secret. Who was this person? First, she was speechless, and now she was talking quietly and meaningfully. Her friend had evolved.

"I can't do that. I don't want to do that."

"Sure, you can," Jessie said while jumping to her feet. "I gotta get back to the farm, but it was a nice chat, girls. Listen to my future sister-in-law, Anna. She might be crazy as hell most of the time, but this time she might just be right."

"Jessie…" Anna trailed off.

"I know, I know. I won't say a word. Promise."

"Thank you."

"No prob. See ya," Jessie said as she walked out the door.

"So," Em asked, "what do you think of my idea?"

"I think you're out of your ever-loving mind."

Chapter Seven

Jake kept busy day and night for the next three days. It was a good thing he worked by himself. He hadn't seen anybody else in days and decided that was for the best. After all, he was in a sour mood and would have been just as happy kicking someone's butt as he was hammering nails. The house saved him. Since coming back to Patience, he had been bordering on becoming a drunk and a man who had a reputation for wanting to pick a fight with every bastard he came into contact with. He had the tendency to go after the biggest guy in the bar, and while he missed the adrenaline rush, his body was thankful for the absence of beatings it had been given on a nightly basis.

In the blazing sun, he tried sweating out his frustrations. Building a porch was damned hard work, especially with a one-man show.

He welcomed the sun and the heat and humidity it brought. It beat on his bare back, probably leaving it a little pink. He pulled a blue bandana from his back pocket to wipe away the buckets of sweat dripping from his face.

He loved the outdoors. What wasn't there to like? A couple of years ago, he'd eagerly worked outside most days and nights. It was the best time of his life. For four short years, he'd gotten to be someone who most young boys could only dream of being—a major-league baseball player.

Now instead of hearing the roar of thirty-thousand fans while he rocketed a ball over the left field wall, he had the pleasure of playing with the same group of people he'd first learned to love to play the game with. His old job was just a really vivid dream, and his job for today was to build this damn porch.

Singing along with the high-pitched Aerosmith front man, Steven Tyler, he beat nails and wiped sweat away for the first part of the day. He should've given in to his impulses and gone out on the lake. Fishing would've been more relaxing, but he didn't have the patience for it. He needed the sweat and sun today, even if his knee was crying out in agony. That would just have to be something he dealt with later. A hot tub would be nice. That would cure a lot of his problems and add value to the house.

Not that he was counting, but he hadn't seen Anna in three days. Touching her was a mistake he now suffered through. Just the thought of her made him instinctively go hard. The tears she had been trying to hold back were what he fell asleep seeing every night since then. He'd pushed her too hard. Fuck, he really was a jackass. Why couldn't he ever get anything right with her? He didn't need or want this right now. His motto over the past couple of years was to keep his sex life simple and easy. The only problem with his great plan was he hadn't even been inside a woman in months.

"What's up, bro?"

Jake turned down the radio and looked over his shoulder, only giving Bradley a slight nod that said, *nothing, but I'm not in the mood to be fucked with.*

"What? I don't get a 'Hey, how's life been since I fell off the face of the earth?' "

Bradley knelt, rubbing a hand over the two-by-four boards Jake had just measured and cut, looking happy as a fool. The guy never got down on life, and it pissed Jake off. His brother lived a single, simple life, and nothing pleased him more. Why couldn't Jake be that carefree? For the summer, Bradley's hair was buzzed short, and to shield him from the sun's rays, it was covered with a straw cowboy hat. His eyes were a few shades lighter than Jake's—a feature he had heard all the woman went wild for. He was years younger, which as a kid, only gave Jake the upper hand at whooping his butt every now and again.

His brother continued running his mouth, and Jake considered doing the same thing right now. Bradley just didn't know when to shut his trap.

"You not talking today?" Bradley asked.

"Do you ever shut up?"

"What crawled up your ass?"

Jake only gave him a warning stare. He was itching for a fight, and it wasn't going to take much for Bradley to be the lucky victim.

"You've got woman problems, huh?" There was nothing his brother loved more than women. Jake had once witnessed him making a teenage schoolgirl and Edna blush at the same time. And that was saying something, because Edna hardly ever smiled. It only made sense that this would be his first explanation for Jake's piss-poor mood.

"No."

"Now, don't lie to your little brother. You're my role model."

Jake should've punched the cocky grin right off his face. He was sure the guy deserved it for something or other. "I don't have women problems."

"The way I hear it, it's because you don't have any women. It's really sad. You're a major-league baseball player, not to mention a Lawrence. You should have women bringing you casseroles every day of the week."

"Ex. I'm an ex-ballplayer, and I don't need advice about women from you." It took everything inside of Jake not to start pounding on his brother right then.

"I think you do. When's the last time you got laid? By the looks of you, I say…two, three weeks, if not more. If you're getting rusty, I can always help you out. I've got more women than I can handle. You can take one of mine. We'll call it an early Fourth of July present."

"You don't give presents on the Fourth of July, you dick. And I don't need your leftovers. I can pick my own women, so butt out of my life, and I won't say anything about yours."

"Don't turn this around on me. Nothing's wrong with my life. All is perfect with the Bradley show."

"If you say so."

"You know what? I know why you're in a foul mood. Anna's back, and you can't stop thinking about her. You're mad you screwed up with her all those years ago. That's it, isn't it?" Bradley's grin widened.

"Watch it."

"I saw her at Em and Tommy's party, and I ran into her just yesterday, and, man, she is as fine as a Georgia peach. That fair skin…and all that blond hair is enough to make any man die of a hard-on. If you don't do something about her, I will. I think I just might ask her out."

"Fuck you."

Jake was accustomed to being quick on his feet, giving him the upper hand. He fought through the pain coming from his knee and attacked. Bradley never saw it coming—the blow landed right on his jaw and knocked him hard to the ground. When he sat up to ask what in the hell was going on, Jake pounced on him. They moved together, matching hit for hit. They gave blow after blow before a jacked-up black Chevy kicked gravel around the driveway, throwing a cloud of dust behind it.

Neither brother stopped to give the third man a glance. The man jumped from the truck, not even slamming his door.

"What the hell? You want to tell me what this is about?" Tommy pulled Jake off Bradley but didn't have the strength to hold him for long. Jake shook Tommy off like a pesky fly—which only proved how angry he was, because Tommy was a stocky guy—and had Bradley pinned to the ground again. Bradley met the pin with a punch and bloodied Jake's lip in the process. Using both hands, Jake shoved his brother's head hard against the grass, sawdust, and dirt.

"What the fuck?" Tommy wrapped an arm around Jake's neck, putting enough pressure on him that Jake was forced to release his brother. "Break it up. Now."

"Let go of me, Tommy," Jake said.

"You goin' to stop this?"

When Jake didn't resist after a couple of minutes, Tommy released him, shoving him down on his ass at the same time. Jake dabbed at the blood running down his bruised chin.

"What's your deal, dude?" Bradley asked, chest heaving.

When Jake didn't answer, Tommy took a swipe at his side with a pointed cowboy boot.

"Nothing," Jake grumbled.

"It's sure as hell something with you two. I pull up, and all I see is arms, legs, dust, and blood flyin' everywhere."

"I said it was nothing. Now drop it."

Tommy must have noticed a certain look in Jake's eyes because he didn't push Jake any further. "Fine. You two shitheads want to ruin those pretty faces, then be my guest. I just stopped by to tell you Knight needed to change the game time to six thirty instead of six. Something to do with one of them having to take his pregnant wife to the doctor. You comin'?"

"Yeah, I'll be there." Jake wanted to be pissed about the change in time, but that would only prove how big of an ass he was. And some of the guys on the team were already complaining about his competitiveness. This time he kept his mouth shut.

"Okay," Tommy said.

Jake stared at his feet until he heard the engine fire up and back down the drive. He didn't want to look at the damage he'd done to Bradley's face. Hell, he didn't want to look at the damage the kid had done to his. But he had to admit he'd taught his brother well. The guy gave out a good punch. Any older brother would be proud.

"Sorry."

"What?" Bradley wasn't going to make it easy for him.

"I said I'm sorry. It's been a lousy couple of days,

and I didn't feel like hearing your smart-ass mouth."

"So you just decided to sucker punch me?"

"Yep."

"Well, okay, but you owe me. Or is it the other way around?"

Just like that, it was over. Bradley let it go as Jake just having a few bad days. God, the guy could piss anybody off. Why was he so damn happy? Bradley rose to his feet, cleaned the dirt from his shirt and pants, and held out a hand. Jake stared at him for a second before he took it, pulling himself up to his feet. He grabbed the shirt he had yanked off earlier and tossed it to his brother to clean up the bloody nose he'd caused. Both brothers wiped the blood and dirt from their bodies for a few minutes before either one spoke.

"You need help with this porch?" Bradley asked.

"Nah, I got it. You've got enough to handle."

"You're worse than a woman. Quit being stubborn and let me help. It will save on time."

They worked in unison for the rest of the day. After several repetitions of an Aerosmith CD and a six-pack of beer, the small porch was finished.

****

According to Em, Thursday nights in Patience were meant for softball. Anna had vaguely remembered some softball games going on between the adults when she lived here, but she'd never been to one. At first she'd resisted coming, but what else was she going to do? She'd spent the last two days cleaning Garrett's apartment, walking at the track, and one day she'd had dinner with Em and Tommy. Her body was too sore to walk another lap at what was now considered the never-ending walking track, and plus, Em would be at the game.

The breeze blew in from the west. A lot of balls were probably going to sail out of the park. The outfielders would be busy trying to keep them in. She wore flip-flops, jean capris, and a Sparks T-shirt with her man's number on it. Jax Dalton was a legend. When he did decide to play his last game, he for sure would be going to the Hall of Fame. And besides his skills at shortstop, he was gorgeous. She was proud to wear number two on her back. She'd mostly raise a few eyebrows since the entire town started and ended with Jake Lawrence, number twenty-five, playing third base for the Atlanta Rockets. But she couldn't blame the town, or Jake for that matter. He gave the townsfolk something to believe in, gave them someone to cheer for and say, "Hey, that kid is from right here in Patience, Tennessee." Even she was proud of what he'd accomplished.

Being from a baseball town, she couldn't remember a time she didn't love the sport. There had also been a time she too cheered for the Rockets. The day she left Patience had also been the day she abandoned its beloved baseball team too. She'd never doubted that Jake would someday play for his favorite team and she wouldn't have the strength to watch. So instead she'd started following his nemesis, the New York Sparks. It hadn't been until later in his career that she tortured herself by viewing a few of his games.

Both sides of the road and the parking lot were full of cars. Luckily, she found a spot as someone was leaving. A Little League team had just finished a game. She closed the roof of the car, shut off the engine, and placed her keys in the console.

She made her way to the home team's bleachers while kids scurried past her.

"Come on, guys. Let's go see Jake before it starts." With full-face grins, the eager group of young boys continued to dart through the crowd. It was important for all kids to have role models. And it was good Jake had cleaned up his act.

"Anna, over here." Em waved a hand and motioned for her. "About time you got here. It would have started already, but one of the guys from the opposing team wasn't here yet, and the umpire wasn't finished chalking the field."

"Sorry. I had trouble finding a parking spot."

"Liar. You probably just rolled out of bed. You need to go see a sleep doctor. I've haven't seen anyone else past the age of eighteen who doesn't get up till noon every day."

If only her friend really knew she actually got less than five hours of sleep a night. A sleep doctor wasn't going to help what was wrong with her—she needed a vacation from her mind. Her problem was that it never shut off, never gave her a long enough break so she could fall asleep and stay that way. She hated taking medicine for her disorder, if that's what it was, but it was the only way to remain sane and not be a crazed wacko.

"It's after six," Anna said after taking a look at her watch.

"Well, just saying, it wouldn't surprise me."

Anna stared through the lenses of her sunglasses out onto the field to see the same group of kids who'd just about run her over surrounding Jake. He was demonstrating a good batting stance and swing while *squishing the bug,* as those in the baseball world liked to call it. Though she didn't want to, she smiled. Her heart seemed to grow a couple of sizes larger than her chest allowed. She was starting to respect him for how he'd lost everything he loved and yet still turned his life around. Those kids down there worshiped him because deep down he was a good person. Maybe she was being a tad too hard on him. He was a human who had made mistakes, and all he could do was try to live a better life.

Sunday night at the walking track was the last time she'd seen him. And it had surprised her how he'd stayed away. She thought he might try to use some excuse to come by and see her, but he hadn't. She didn't know if she was disappointed or elated that he'd finally gotten the hint she didn't want him around.

"Who's playing?" Anna asked.

"We're playing Knight." Em took a draw of her soft drink.

The Patience team was dressed in fitted, gray uniform pants, white-and-red shirts, and solid red caps with the letter *P* stitched in the center. They all looked the same. The names on the backs of their shirts were the only way she could tell who each guy was.

Wait.

"Is that Jessie out there?"

"Yeah. She plays second base."

"That's right. I do remember her telling me she plays on this team."

"Tommy hates it, but that's only because she's better than him. She's one of the best players on the team. Well, besides Jake."

Good for her. She liked that Jessie more every day.

She recognized more people. Besides Jessie, she also knew Bradley, Tommy, and Tex—a guy she'd gone to school with. She'd seen him at Em and Tommy's party, but she had been a little too preoccupied with Jake and Ms. Edna's sex talk to make a point of talking to him.

She was watching Jake chase the kids off the field so the game could get started when Em asked, "You trying to be a rebel?"

Anna frowned. "What?"

Em pointed to her Dalton shirt and smiled. Anna guessed she was being some type of rebel. But it honestly didn't matter to her. Originally, the shirt was meant to only be worn to bed during her time in Patience, but when Em had invited her to the softball game, the time seemed right to shake the wrinkles out and wear it outside the house.

She shrugged. "What—my shirt? It was the only baseball attire I had, and I'm at a ballgame. What else was I supposed to wear?"

"By the looks of the old men from the top of the bleachers, you were supposed to wear anything but *that*." Em pretended to be disgusted.

She hadn't meant to, but she took a glance back to find four older gentlemen giving her the eye, as if to say "child, who do you think you are, wearing that piece of trash?" Oh well, if they didn't like it, they could stop staring a hole in her back.

It was already the fifth inning. She cheered when it was appropriate and booed the opposing pitcher when he tried to pick off one of Patience's guys on first. As she'd predicted, the outfielders had to stay alert for the many balls carrying as far as the fence. Tex played centerfield, along with left- and right-fielders she didn't know.

While she was seated on the first-base side of the field, she unfortunately couldn't hear but could see Jake yelling from his third-base position at Bradley, who was playing shortstop, about something he was doing wrong. Once or twice Bradley's eyes ventured to the crowd, and she wondered if that was what angered Jake.

A grounder was hit up the third-base line. Jake fielded the baseball and threw it to Tommy at first to beat out the speedy runner trying to get a base hit. He didn't take a moment to enjoy the play he had just made or to take a breather; he was ready for the next batter. His legs were apart, knees bent, and he was fixated on the man situating himself in the batter's box. He was fluid and smooth with his movements, especially considering he'd suffered a pretty bad knee injury less than two years ago.

Anna couldn't help but notice how he seemed to have lost his childlike enjoyment while he was on the field. When he had first started playing in the big leagues, he was like a kid out there. Of course he played hard and wanted to win, but he was being paid to do it. During their conversations as teenagers, Jake had mentioned many times that it was not lost on him how fortunate he was to be able to live out his bigger-than-life dream. Seeing this version of him broke her heart.

Despite his hard and way-too-serious expression, he was sexy as hell. The way he looked in those pants and ball cap were causing wetness that had nothing to do with the damp, humid air. This was bad...really,

really bad.

After the last out, the home-team crowd cheered for their boys and girl. High fives were given around the pitcher's mound. The crowd went their separate ways. It was still a work night, so most had to get up in the morning for their last day of the workweek. The small-town life seemed simple to her, but it was something she'd never minded in the past. She was a small-town girl. It was one of the reasons she'd never tested the big city. New York was a place she wanted to visit but never would she actually move there.

"Anna, you ready?"

She looked up to see Em standing above her. She was the only one still seated on the bleachers, staring at the field and the one player who stood on it.

"You go ahead. I think I'm going to stick around for a while."

"You taking what I said the other day to heart?"

Em was referring to her idea of Anna having sex with Jake. "No. God, no. I just woke up, remember?" she said playfully. "I want to enjoy the night air."

"If you say so. I'll call you tomorrow."

"Okay."

Why in the hell am I waiting on Jake? It had been a long four days since she'd seen him and had time to cool off. Of course she was furious at his comment. And she had every right to be. He'd left her the night he slept with another girl. She might have broken up with him first, but she had good, logical reasons for that. What reasons did he have for jumping in bed with Cara?

She didn't know if Jake knew she was there, but that was fine with her. She was more than satisfied to just watch him pack his bag with several balls, a couple of bats, and his mitt. He handled each piece with such gentle care, as if he were touching it for the last time. It was too sad to watch anymore.

"Hey, slugger, whatcha doing down there?" she hollered.

When he finally looked up from his task, there was pain in his eyes. "Just packing. I'll be up in a sec." He finished with his bag, left it sitting outside the dugout, and walked through the gate and casually up the bleachers.

"Great game." She gave him a guarded smile. Making the first move was new to her. Usually he was the one who tried to sweet talk her into his life nowadays.

"It was a win. A little close because of my dick of a brother. I swear that guy has babe radar. If a single woman is within ten feet, he's going to know about it. He needs to leave the women alone when we're on the field and concentrate. Oh—and nice shirt, by the way." Of course he would have something to say about her Sparks T-shirt.

"I don't want to hear it. I've already had your cheering section all but threaten to have me removed from the ballpark."

He threw his head back and laughed while sprawling out beside her on the bleachers, long legs crossed at the ankles, resting his cleats on the bottom next row. His pants stretched over his strong thighs. His damp shirt clung to his chest. Ringlets of hair curling out from under his cap were dripping with sweat. He was a hot mess, but he was *hot*, even with a puffed-up lip. That must have been a result of the fight he'd had with Bradley yesterday. Em had mentioned Tommy drove up on them rolling around, throwing punches in her front yard. Men.

"He only made an error or two."

"Errors equal runs being scored," Jake said matter-of-factly.

She had a feeling he was a real butthead on the field. It probably had nothing to do with Bradley and had everything to do with Jake. "No harm done. You won the game. Isn't that all that matters?"

"Yeah. But he'd better straighten up, or I'll bench his ass."

"Can you do that? I mean, are you the coach too?"

A mischievous twinkle lit his blue eyes. "No, but I'm his big brother." Humor fading, he hesitated. "I'm sorry about the other night at the walking track. I was the one being an ass, and I had no right to say those things to you."

He didn't apologize for the kiss, and that was a relief. It was never a good thing when a guy said he was sorry for kissing you. In her opinion that meant he regretted it, and she didn't want that. She was mad after it happened and totally out of her mind with confusion for much of the week, but she didn't regret it.

"It's fine, really, Jake. Don't worry about it. I'm not mad anymore."

"No, let me do this. I was a jerk to you, and I want to tell you I'm sorry."

Why did she have a feeling he was saying *sorry* for a lot more than just telling her she left him over a decade ago? No, they were not talking about this tonight. She wouldn't have it. She wasn't ready to tackle the Cara and Jake situation—she didn't know if she ever would be, or ever wanted to. He had been a jerk, and she ran away. Nothing left to discuss.

She shook her head. "Stop. I don't want to talk about it. It's over, so let's please drop it. Okay?"

"Okay," he said, looking relieved.

"I've been thinking about your clever idea of giving me my house back. I've decided to take you up on the three dates."

He stared at her in surprise. "Wait, what? You want to date me?"

"Only for my house. Nothing more, Romeo."

"Romeo, huh? Did you already grow tired of slugger?"

Busted. She hadn't even caught herself on the nicknames she was throwing out left and right. "You caught that?"

"Yep."

"Well, I just didn't want you to feel left out. You seemed pretty hurt when I used my dance partner's short name. Just don't want to bruise your ego, is all."

"Is that so? So what about you wanting to go on a date?"

She held up a finger. "Correction. You wanted to go out with me first. Let's not forget that."

One corner of his mouth turned up into a half grin, as if he was considering the idea now. How had she made this decision without knowing she'd made it? She was just digging herself into a bigger hole when it came to Jake. There was no way she could survive being around him for three dates. He looked yummy drenched in sweat after playing six innings of ball. How was she supposed to handle this clean-shaven, hard-bodied man? While his look was playful, it was also dangerous.

"What about dinner at my…sorry, your future place tomorrow night?"

"That will do, but there will be no sex."

Chapter Eight

Em tapped her foot and stared at her watch at the same time. She was clearly upset about something, and Anna doubted it was because she'd lain down for what ended up being longer than a twenty-minute power nap.

"Hi, Em." Anna had always found it unfair how beautiful and made up Em was. No matter what time of day, the woman looked immaculate. Tonight was no different, except for her coming across as tense and having a scared look that only appeared when trouble loomed. She'd brought many men to their knees with that look. *Oh God. Something had happened, or would be happening soon.* A long time ago, she'd learned she wasn't supposed to get in Em's way when her eyes deepened to a color that resembled emerald, richer than her natural color of pale green.

Em pushed by Anna and walked into the apartment. Her attire consisted of a form-fitting red dress that stopped a little above her knee. Her hair was straightened, as she usually wore it, so it reached the middle of her back. Open-toed pumps and big hoop earrings rounded out her friend's look for hitting the town. Not good. She thought it was about ten o'clock at night—Anna still wasn't sure about the time—her only question was why Em would want to leave her soon-to-be husband to go out to some party or club. And why did she look as if she were out to get revenge on an ex-lover?

"What's going on, Em?"

Em plopped down on the couch. Ignoring the dent-free coffee table, she threw her feet in their high heels up on it before burying her head in her hands. Her falling blond hair covered both sides of her face.

"Em, you can tell me. You know that, don't you?"

After a sniffle, she lifted her head. "It's Tommy. We got into some kind of fight over nothing important."

"If it was nothing, then why do you have tears filling your eyes?"

"See, after the game he told me he wanted to go out tonight with Bradley, and I wanted him to stay home with me. I was going to try to cook some kind of chicken casserole his mama always makes for him and beg until he agreed to watch that new romantic comedy with me. And he…"

Big, whopping tears fell from her heavily mascaraed eyes. If Tommy did anything to hurt her friend, he was going to have to deal with her. Men were getting on her last nerve this past week. She had sympathy for none of them.

"Men are just jackasses sometimes, Em."

"And we love them anyway, don't we?"

Anna didn't know if she would go that far. She didn't know any man she loved—jackass or not. She figured this was Em's time. It was best to just humor her. "Yeah, sometimes I guess women do. What did Tommy do?" If the mood had been lighter, she might have asked what Em had done to Tommy. But Em wouldn't care for the comment, even if it might have been true.

"He walked out," she choked out, eyes brimming

with tears. "Left. He's never done that before. We always talk things through, and then he figures out that my way was actually better. I don't know what happened tonight. Do you know what he said to me? Let me just tell you. He said…he said I was being crazy and that he was leaving no matter what I said."

What could Anna say? The poor guy had to agree with Em all the time. How he did it, she would never know. What was the best way to handle this? Did she break the best-friend rule and side with the guy, tell her she was being selfish? Or did she say *He's an asshole, just give it some time, and he'll figure out what he's lost*? She instead concluded she needed to do what was right. They were not in high school anymore.

"Em, I'm going to tell you this as honestly as I can. I know I'm not an expert on men, but what I do know is that sometimes they have to go out and hang with the guys. Just like we have girl time, guys need to be around other guys so they can pick their noses and tell lies about how many girls they've bedded. It's all innocent fun. You've got to let him make some of the decisions. He is a man, and he is prideful just like the rest of them."

"I know you're right. I just hate the fact that they all go down to Ollie's. You can't even imagine the type of women who hang out there."

"Em, listen to me. Tommy loves you. Only you. He's not going to this Ollie's place to find women. He is there to drink a few with the guys—that's all. Now if he makes a liar out of me, we will get my *ball buster* and beat him with it."

"I don't know what a *ball buster* is, but I already know I like it."

"We'll have to get you one. All women need a *ball buster*."

"Will you do me a monster favor?" A smile formed on her friend's face, softening her dark eyes, bringing them slowly to their natural state.

She was afraid to ask. "What?"

"Will you *pleasssse* go to Ollie's with me?"

"Won't that be like checking up on him? I don't think guys appreciate that too much."

"Not if you go with me. We can play it like you wanted a girls' night out. Please, please…"

"I love you, Em, but I can't. Look at me."

"Don't be silly. If you don't go, I'll have to go down there and make a complete ass of myself. I need you. Please."

Maybe it was due to guilt because she had missed out on so much of Em's life over the past decade, but she could feel her defenses wearing down. "Fine."

"We're going to have so much fun. Now go get dressed. You look a mess," Em said, apparently unaware she wasn't making Anna feel any better about the upcoming events.

****

"Minny, can we get a couple more beers over here?" Jake wanted something stronger than just beer. He wanted Jack Daniels with a splash of Coke, something that burned going down and coated his belly. Not that long ago he had let the amber liquid cloud his mind every night, making all the decisions for his disgusting way of life. His mornings had mainly consisted of strong coffee and sweating through the haze from the night before. But that was no longer an option. He worked damned hard to not get caught up in his self-destructive ways again. Beer had to be good enough.

"Sure thing, Jake." The pink-haired bartender hollered out above the Thursday night crowd. Minny was a cute, strange-dressing girl in her fishnet tights, black-leather miniskirt, and hot-pink T-shirt that was the same shade as her hair. She never hit on him, and they got along pretty well. He liked that she didn't take shit from any drunk trying to catch a feel. She was a tough one, but on nights like tonight, when most men were drinking a little too much and talking about the softball games that had just taken place, he always kept a concerned eye on her. She was, after all, only five three and maybe a hundred pounds. In his opinion, she needed a bouncer around to keep a watchful eye out for her. Drunks could be assholes. He should know because he'd been one for a year.

She placed a bottle in front of him, Tommy, and the willing woman at his side. The sexual vibes she'd been sending his way all night only proved he could have a woman if he wanted one.

It had taken ten minutes of driving around before he realized there wasn't much to do except go nurse a beer and head back home. He was letting the jukebox, laughter, and smell of fried food distract him from whatever was making his blood boil. He had gotten what he wanted. What had brought on his sudden need to sulk? He couldn't believe she'd agreed, but he wasn't going to try to change her mind. It took everything he had to keep his emotions in check.

Garrett's apartment was dark when he'd done a drive-by. He was disappointed and had even thought about moving up their date to tonight. But it was only because he wanted to see her.

Maybe that was what caused his foul mood, because ever since leaving the park, his mood had fallen from bad to *leave me the fuck alone*. Why he had come out, he really didn't know. He couldn't sit in his house thinking about—no, take that back, it was Anna's house. He couldn't sit in her house and brood about everything he'd lost in the past couple of years.

Minny had made it known Bradley had already left with a brunette about an hour ago. At least Jake didn't have to listen to his speech about using the Lawrence charm and good looks to get a woman. He didn't want a woman, especially not the woman clinging to his side.

The day he limped his butt back into town, he'd met Carly at Ollie's. She had recently relocated to Patience. It was the middle of the day, and he'd thought it unfit to see a woman ruining her pretty face, crying over a light beer. He took the barstool next to her and laid on some of that family charm Bradley talked so much about—only to be turned down on his ass. Apparently, a woman like her didn't associate with a drunk, out-of-work nobody. It stung, but it was exactly what he expected. No woman wanted a washed-up ballplayer. Except Carly didn't follow baseball and hadn't known about his previous career. She'd thought he was just another unemployed Joe who hadn't amounted to much after high school. Every day since, she'd bent over backward to try to apologize, make him feel all better, and do whatever other crap she thought might work herself into his bed.

He knew all about women like her, and while he had bought her a beer when she insisted, that was as far as he was willing to let things go with her. He knew what Carly was sniffing for, and he wasn't going to be the man to give it to her. After finishing his beer, he would send her over to the table of men who made it annoyingly clear what they had their eye on. And it wasn't the muted game playing on the television displayed on the wall above his head.

"Jake, why don't ya tell Carly here how good she looks tonight?" Tommy said with a lopsided grin.

Jake decided to play along, in hopes Carly would grow bored of him and Tommy and leave on her own. "Um, yeah."

She freed his arm and stepped back, showing him the body he guessed he'd failed to look at the first time she flaunted it. "Is that all you have to say, Jake?"

"Yeah, Jake, is that all you can say?" Tommy added.

"You look exceptionally good tonight, Carly," Jake answered.

Tommy tried to hold back the laugh bound to leak out any second.

Jake jabbed his elbow into his best friend's gut. "You're only making this situation worse."

"Hey, I'm an engaged man. Do you really want Em on your bad side?" Tommy shouted because of the alcohol he'd been consuming for the last hour.

"What in the hell are you talking about?" It was settled. Tommy was drunk and not hearing or thinking clearly.

Not too long after Jake had entered the bar tonight, Tommy had sauntered in as well. He ordered and then downed his first shot of whiskey before even acknowledging that Jake was seated beside him. One thought had entered Jake's mind—Em. The easygoing guy had troubles on the brain, and Jake was staying out of that boat unless his buddy strapped a life jacket on him and forced him in. Em was a strong-willed woman, and Tommy was just learning what he was going to be up against *'til death do us part*. Jake loved Em, considered her a sister. She was demanding and meddling, but she would go to the ends of the earth for the people she loved. Most people found her irresistible, but they didn't have to live with her.

Tommy had been expecting to hang out with Bradley, but since Bradley had already left for the night, he was the one Tommy was having drinks with. And it was also now Jake's job to take care of his friend.

After several shots, he had Minny switch Tommy over to beer. The guy would have a major hangover in the morning, but he looked as if he'd needed a night out, and Jake, for once, was watching out for his buddy. Bradley and Tommy had dragged him out of this hole at least a couple of times a week for a year. He was happy to return the favor.

Carly ran her fingers up and down his arm. "What's got you ignoring me tonight?"

He'd wanted to say something else entirely, but his mama taught him how to treat a lady. Even Carly Sanders deserved respect; after all, deep down she was just lonely. Much like the rest of the people in the world, he guessed.

Tommy must have seen the wheels going around in Jake's head because he spoke up first. "I can give you best-bud privileged information that Jake is never capable of ignoring you. You stop every man in his tracks, darlin'."

"O-kay, I think you've had enough, buddy." Jake removed the half-drunk beer in front of Tommy.

"Hey! What in the hell are you doin', man? I'm not done with that."

For a drunken guy, Tommy was quick. He almost grabbed the beer from Jake's hands, but Jake was quicker. He handed the bottle off to Minny.

"Why don't we head on home?" Jake suggested. The last thing he needed was for Tommy to go a little too far. He owed it to the man to keep him from tumbling over the edge and regretting his decisions tomorrow. "If you're not ready to go home, you can hang out at my place for a while."

"I'll pass. I want to stay right here and drink. I deserve a night to be a man."

"You can leave if you want." Sometime in the last couple of minutes, Carly had moved from Jake to now leaning against Tommy.

"Yeah, that's not going to happen," Jake said to Carly. He tried to pull Tommy off the barstool. "Come on. It's time to go."

"We can leave in a bit. Not yet, though," Tommy said.

Something past the glossiness in Tommy's eyes had Jake agreeing. "Okay, but I'm staying by your side."

"You scared he's going to have some fun for a change?" Carly spouted off. "That woman keeps him on such a tight leash it's a miracle he hasn't already wandered."

"No, I'm scared he'll make a stupid decision. One I can guarantee you he would greatly regret." With that Jake turned back to his beer. Thirty more minutes. That was all the time he was giving the guy.

A few moments later the door opened just as he looked up. And in walked Tommy's bride-to-be and Anna. Both ladies were forced to walk right past them, leaving a refreshing, new scent of perfume lingering in the room. It took a few minutes for his stupid friend to come up for air from his conversation with Carly to see Em and Anna sitting at a table in the back. Em was the one Tommy should be scared of, but Jake was slowly discovering he might be a little scared himself…just not of the same woman.

****

"I told you. Look at him over there," Em reminded Anna while a booming laugh was coming from Tommy's direction.

"I think he's a little drunk, Em." Anna tried to calm her wound-up-tight friend. During the drive over, Em had used every man-bashing name she could think of— everything from Anna's favorite, jackass, to doo-doo head.

"Don't make excuses for that bastard. If Carly is who he wants, then fine. He just better not come crawling to me when he gets herpes. He can let that slutty nurse take care of him."

Anna didn't condone what Tommy was doing, although what that actually was, she didn't know. The guy stared with a silly grin, nodding while the blonde stayed glued to his side. Anna now knew the woman was Carly, and according to Em, had many suitors. Em had a right to be beside herself with anger, but Tommy couldn't be a caged lion who resided only in Em's world. He was a man. A man who had his own thoughts and opinions. If Em wanted to keep the guy she loved, she was going to have to lighten up on the guy a little.

Carly was the one flirting. Every now and then Anna noticed the woman would cast a glance over her shoulder in Jake's direction. She'd even reached over and patted his thigh a couple of times. Carly obviously wanted Jake and was only trying to make him jealous by flirting with Tommy. A man like Jake probably was used to women staking their claims on him. At least Em could take a breather.

"I think she wants Jake. I really wouldn't be concerned about Tommy." Except *she* was concerned, which didn't make sense. Why should she care that an attractive woman wanted her blue-eyed future date? He was free to have any woman he wanted, and Carly was making it clear she was going to be that woman. Did it matter that they had just agreed to have dinner together the next night? She was a fool for ever agreeing.

Her body remembered their encounters. She could still feel his gentle touch burning through her skin. The thought warmed her in places she had no business being warm.

They had made eye contact briefly when she and Em entered the bar. As soon as she saw him, she tried pulling her gaze away but couldn't. He had changed from his tight, butt-hugging uniform pants and ripped T-shirt to clean jeans, a button-down western-style shirt with the sleeves rolled up to his elbows, and his cleats had been replaced with work boots. A baseball cap was pulled down low, once again shading his eyes. His features remained unreadable as he had glanced from his beer bottle to her standing in the doorway. She hated not being able to know what he was thinking.

"Earth to Anna, hello. Where are you in that head

of yours? Are you listening to me?" Em snapped her impatient fingers in front of Anna's face.

"I'm sorry. I'm here. What were you saying?"

"I said I don't care who she plans to go home with. My man is over there hanging on her every word."

"What can I get you two ladies?" a petite, spunky girl asked.

Because of the meds she'd taken earlier that night, alcohol was out of the question for Anna. "Only a soda for me." The girl turned to Em, who had both eyes glued on her soon-to-be-deceased future husband. "Just bring her a beer. If she doesn't like it, oh well."

"Sure thing."

Anna wished she could have something other than a soft drink. Her nerves were borderline shaky. She didn't want to be forced into staring at Jake and the woman she was beginning to strongly dislike. "I wanted to thank you for making me go to the softball game tonight," she said, trying to make conversation with Em. "It was actually a lot of fun." The distraction seemed to work for her and Em both.

"Wow, you liked something about Patience? We need to call the *Patience Gazette* and put out an announcement."

"Ha. Ha."

"Now back to my big problem. How can I marry someone who's so easily interested in another woman?"

Anna took her drink from the bartender and set it in front of her while Em did the same, apparently satisfied with the beer. "Don't be silly. There will be a wedding. Whatever is going on over there is nothing." She didn't know if that was entirely true, but Em had nothing to worry about. "In a few minutes, Tommy will walk over here and give you that smile that makes you melt, and you will both go home and make up."

As if on cue, the man in question left his barstool and wandered over to their table. He only staggered a bit, seeming to catch himself easily. "Now, what brings my beau-beautiful bride out?"

"You're drunk." Em had her arms crossed, as if she were searching for words. "You have fun?" She pointed her head toward Carly, who had turned her full attention to Jake.

"Actually, I did."

In a way, Anna felt sorry for the guy. She'd gotten to know Tommy a little bit in high school because of his friendship with Jake and knew he'd loved Em from afar through most of those years. His love was evident to everyone. Not until a few years after Anna left town had Em reciprocated those feelings. Em didn't seem like a woman who would be insanely jealous, but what a woman felt underneath all that armor sometimes went unnoticed by others. Anna could relate.

Em's eyes turned a shade that indicated a storm brewing. "So what did you and Ms. Slut of the U.S. of A. talk about?"

"Now why would you want to say something like that? Carly actually is a very nice person. She's a nurse."

Anna could see the sweat pouring off Tommy's forehead. Poor guy. He was already sweating out the alcohol he'd apparently drunk a lot of.

"Nice? You sure you want to go there?" Em asked.

Tommy grabbed a chair. He turned it around so he could straddle it.

Em reached for her purse. "Don't get comfortable.

I think it's time for you and me to leave."

"Now?"

"Yes, now. Get up."

He slowly got to his feet. He patted Anna on the head, meaning it as a friendly gesture, but he made Anna feel like some well-behaved animal.

"Can you get home okay, Anna?"

"Yes, Em. You go. Have fun making up." She winked and watched as they left the bar.

Thankfully, she had driven her own car. Otherwise, she would have to be stuck in the car with them all the way to the other side of town. Even though her two crazy friends fought hard, they made up just as hard. It was actually sweet. They did love each other, and that was all that mattered. For their sake, she hoped love did conquer all.

Suddenly, she felt lost, looking around at the group of people she didn't know, taking in the clinking of bottles, the couples shooting pool, and loud guys laughing and hollering over the ballgame. Everyone knew how to have fun. She couldn't stay there. What woman went to a bar by herself? Maybe a woman trying to pick up a guy, but she wasn't that kind of woman. She didn't need a guy, nor did she want one. Her life was complicated enough. She took another sip of her soft drink, and before she stood, a tall man loomed above.

"Leaving already?" His voice reminded her of velvet.

Swinging her gaze, she glared at the man interfering with her exit plan. Her heart jumped in response to him being so near. "I don't have much reason to stay."

"Ouch. You sure know how to put it to a guy." Jake cupped a hand over his heart.

"Didn't mean it as an insult. I was here for Em, and she just left with Tommy."

"Wanna dance?" A slow smile spread across his face.

"No."

"Why not?"

"I think we've already tried that, and it didn't work out too well for us."

"True, but we can always have a do-over. Make a new memory of our past."

How insightful. If only they could have do-overs in life. Her life would be different, and she didn't doubt his would too. But that wasn't the way life played out. Their only option was to learn how to deal.

Without asking, he took the seat Tommy had recently occupied, the seat closest to her. She needed to stay focused on the way-too-attractive male taking up residence at her table.

He examined her a little too closely for her liking. "You sure are attractive."

"I'm nothing compared to your lady friend."

"Who?"

"The one over there not taking it kindly that you're talking to another woman." Crap. She hadn't meant to say that aloud.

"Who? Carly? Never noticed."

"I find that hard to believe since her breasts are out to here." Anna cupped her hands out in front of her chest. "Just drop it. It's nothing. Forget it. You want to lose your date to someone else, so be it."

"Jealous?" he asked.

"Of course not," she responded.

"Good, because let me make it clear to you, if I wanted Carly, I would have her. She would be more than willing. Overall, she would be an easy lay, but I don't want *her*."

What did he mean by that? He said it as if there were another *her* he wanted. Was it possible he had another woman lined up...or worse, waiting for him back at home? Surely not. He could be a jerk, but he wasn't capable of just being cruel on purpose, and he had to know that would be downright wrong.

She took a sip of her watered-down soda to give herself a minute. Jake's intense stare brought her attention back to him.

His mood seemed lighter than it was when she'd seen him earlier. During the game he'd been too serious for a *fun* ballgame. Now his charming and cocky ways were back. She didn't know which she liked better. The charming Jake caused her to be off balance.

She found most men easily forgotten, but Jake was one she could never forget. "Was Tommy okay? Em was pretty upset."

"Why are you changing the subject?"

"I have no say in who you go to bed with, or anything else for that matter." It was always best to stick with the easy and straight-to-the-point answer.

"I want you."

Shock and anger bubbled in her gut. Shock won out. Her heart pounded, and her palms sweated. "I don't want to hear any more."

"What's wrong with talking about sex with me?" He tilted his head to one side.

"I just think we need to leave the past in the past. I

agreed to the three dates. Can we just leave it at that for now?"

"Fine, but sometimes the past comes back to a head, and you can't do anything about it, Anna."

Chapter Nine

Although this was only an arrangement for her to get back what was rightfully hers, Anna still wanted to look nice. Before leaving, she stopped in the apartment bathroom for the second or third time to get a look at herself in her favorite pair of jeans. Could be better, but not bad. Most objects did look terrible in those hotel-sized mirrors. She opted to keep it casual, so instead of wearing a too-hot tank top, she dressed in a three-quarter-length sleeve, teal-blue top with some simple beading around the collar. After all, she didn't want Jake to think she was anticipating their evening together—because she was not. She kept telling herself she was only doing what needed to be done.

She decided to not let the top down on her car. No need to mess up the hair she'd spent a good thirty minutes styling.

The drive over to her house was similar to the last, except last time she hadn't been expecting to find her ex-boyfriend standing on the front porch. The road still curved left first and then right, dipped in all the familiar spots, and ended at the same destination she had been all too eager to once leave. Funny how now she was willing to make a deal with the guy she swore she would never have anything to do with just to get back to this house on the curvy stretch of road.

Since it was summer and the days were longer, she

was able to see more of the outside of the house, parts she had been a little too preoccupied to give attention to before. The yard that had once shown abandonment now reflected hard work and pride. The fresh coat of paint that had been applied to the house covered the once-chipped front porch columns. With the addition of the black barnyard shutters that matched the new black-shingled roof, the windows stood out. Shrubs that had once grown up over the porch had been trimmed back, and daylilies lined the front of the flower bed, adding enough color to make the entire bed stand up and take notice, but not enough to take away from the house.

She walked up the steps to two welcoming rocking chairs framing the big picture window that looked into the living room. She tried to peer in, but the curtains were drawn shut. That didn't stop her from remembering the smoke-stained walls, puke-green carpet that matched the appliances, and the blue furniture. A chill ran down her spine. The outside of the house was easy, but the inside was going to be harder to deal with. She'd experienced a lot of pain and hurt between those walls, and a fresh coat of paint could not fix it.

But she had to continue with her plan to live in the house if she ever intended to put all that pain behind her once and for all. It was probably going to be the hardest thing she ever tried to do, but she needed to relive what went on in the house so she could have a normal life, a life where she wasn't tormented by nightmares. She had to come to terms with all she'd been through.

She sat in one of the chairs and stared out, proud of the scenery. Her mother would have been proud too. She would have gone in, but she heard music and soft singing from the side of the house. She took a minute to take a breath before standing and going to face Jake.

A new small porch had been added to the house. She'd always thought one should be there. It only made sense since the kitchen door that led outside was there. She hadn't seen it last Saturday. Apparently, Jake had been busy. Maybe she was taking advantage of him and all the money he was sinking into her house, but that was a ridiculous thought. It wasn't as if she were making him do this, so she shouldn't feel bad for what he did with his money.

A rock ballad streamed through the new screen door. Jake had his back to her but must have sensed she was around. "Hey, sweetness."

At first the newfound nickname had irritated her, but now, not so much. It seemed natural, and she liked the way it rolled off his tongue every time he said it.

"Back at ya, slugger." Was she flirting? It sounded like it. She hadn't been around an eligible man in a long time. She didn't even know what she was doing anymore. Even though she wasn't interested in Jake in that way, she could still enjoy herself a little, and if that involved flirting, then so be it. She could flirt with a man and leave it at that—she was sure of it.

"You keep calling me that, and we won't even make it to dinner." He still had his back to her, so she couldn't see his face. When she didn't say anything in return, he turned to peer at her over his shoulder. "Don't worry. That was just a joke. But I do like the nickname."

Her heart slowed back to normal rhythm, and she hoped it was from relief and nothing else. This degree of flirting was beginning to be acceptable, but it stopped right there. "The house looks great," she said.

"It's coming along. I've still got some work to do on the inside, but hopefully I can have a lot of that done before our three dates are over."

If he only knew how much work the inside needed. There were things he didn't know existed and would never be able to change. The inside required more work than just what stood out to the naked eye. She didn't know exactly what the rooms needed to cleanse them, but she was sure it was more than Jake had bargained for. He could never know the evil she had endured.

"My mother would have loved the daylilies out front. She had always wanted to plant more than bushes. She wanted it to be pretty."

"Do you like them?"

"Yes, of course. Why wouldn't I?"

"Just making sure. Ready to eat?"

She walked onto the new porch and braced herself for everything that came with entering her childhood home. All the memories and emotions flooded back, like a slideshow being played over and over in her mind.

"You all right?" Jake asked.

She hadn't noticed he was waiting on the other side of the screen door.

Anna put one foot in front of the other, opened the door, and let it slam behind her. The panic and anxiety she expected to wash over her never did. Her chest didn't constrict. Her lungs didn't close off her breath. She didn't feel light headed, and she didn't faint. At least not in the kitchen. It was strange to be back there again, but that was expected for anyone who had been away as long as she had.

The same ancient green stove and refrigerator stood at opposite walls, connected by stained white countertops and cabinets. The window over the sink looked out onto the backyard. A two-seat kitchen table situated in the middle of the room had a couple of plates, napkins, silverware, and one single burning candle sitting on it.

"You okay, baby? You lost a little color there for a minute."

"I'm fine. I just haven't been in the house in a long time. It looks the same."

"Shit. I'm sorry. I forgot that you haven't even been inside. You want to look around before we eat? Not much has changed in here, except maybe bits and pieces of the master bedroom. I've been working on it off and on, depending on the weather. I don't like to stay inside on a sunny day."

"No," she blurted out. "That's all right. I'm starved. Let's go ahead and eat while it's hot."

"Whatever you say. Tonight's about you."

That took her aback. "Me? Why me?"

"Because you're the one who agreed to these dates." He sported a wicked grin.

She was thankful for the lightness of the mood. "Real funny." She smiled back, and it felt good.

"Tell me why you stayed in Linden. I mean, what do you like about it?" Jake asked as they both sat at the rectangular table for dinner.

"My aunt lives there, for one. I also grew to like the people and town. It's simple."

He cut into his steak and took a bite. "It's not much bigger than Patience." He said it as if he knew it, so matter-of-factly.

"It's about the size of Patience…but different."

"How so?"

"I guess it's just the people are different. They don't know every part of my past. What they know is what I've told them, and that's peace of mind for me."

"What's wrong with your past? Why do you care what others think and know, for that matter?"

The aroma from her baked potato and steak warmed her insides. She took time dressing her potato, giving herself a minute to think about how to answer. She loaded hers with ranch dressing, butter, and shredded cheese. The cheese melted on contact. After taking a hefty bite, she answered. "I don't know. I guess parts of my past are painful."

Jake set down his fork and wiped his mouth with a napkin. "Anna, I think we need to talk about a few things. I—"

"No. Not tonight. There's more to my past than just you, Jake. I don't want to talk about it. Not right now, at least."

"Okay, but when you're ready, there are a few things I need to say to you," he said. "What do you do for work?"

If only he knew all of her past… Indeed, there was much more to it than his breaking her heart. There was a dark part. What would he think about that part of her life? Would he feel sorry for her? The prospect of being pitied was the main reason she kept her troubled childhood to herself. Would he think she was dirty in some way? She didn't know if she wanted to find out what his reaction would be.

"I work at a small insurance company. It's mostly data entry, but it's work, and I like my coworkers."

"You're not happy."

"What? With my job?"

"Yeah. When you talk, you sound unhappy."

"It's not what I want to be doing forever. I have other dreams, but for right now it pays the bills."

"And what do you really want to be doing?"

"I have plans of opening up my own coffee shop and bookstore. Nothing fancy, just a place people can go to escape their lives for a little bit."

"I can see you doing that."

"Really?"

"Yeah. When you talk about it, your eyes light up and you almost sound giddy. It's cute."

While finishing dinner, they talked about Jake's work with the house and how he had enjoyed the distraction. He spoke with so much pride in his voice. Anna was taken aback by his attention to details, considering home renovation was fairly new to him. After all these years, they still understood each other.

****

She was stuffed, but the steak and baked potato were excellent. Or maybe they weren't, but she had been living off frozen dinners, so shoe leather would have tasted good. Jake insisted she relax with her glass of wine while he cleared the table. She took the opportunity to have a look around the living room without an audience. The same dingy walls stood around her. Lots of pain was stuffed into the average-size room. Jake had replaced the old furniture with gently used pieces.

Gazing out over the front yard through the picture window, she sensed his presence behind her. The intensity in the room went up a notch or two, and she was sure he, too, could feel it. They remained silent for a moment, which was fine with her. The silence gave her time to think and mind her breathing, to slow it before she had an anxiety attack. She took a sip of wine, followed by a couple more—anything to keep her moving and not thinking. She let the last taste linger on her tongue.

"You're uncomfortable with my closeness." He finally broke the silence.

"What? No. I'm fine." She caught his gaze in the reflection in front of her.

"Then what's up with all the drinking?"

Damn, she needed to get it together.

When he twirled her around to face him, her body craved to be touched. His eyes took on a serious and dangerous look. She could have sworn she heard his heart beat just as rapidly as hers.

"I've had a problem for the last four or five days," he said.

"What's that?" she asked in a fragile voice.

"I've been starved for this one thing." He held up one finger. His drawn eyebrows warned her of the trouble she was in.

He removed the empty glass of wine from her trembling hand and placed it on the coffee table. "You are too serious most of the time, and you always seem to have something going on in that pretty head."

And then to her utter surprise, he kissed her, hard. His mouth sank over hers, forcing her to fall back until she rested on the window. There was no denying need and a burning passion filled the kiss. After the initial shock of his mouth running over hers, she could feel him deliberately slow the pace and allow her to catch up. She instinctively kissed him back, wrapping her arms around his neck, much as he'd made her do the first time they danced. His tongue snaked between her lips, and she matched it by using hers too. They shared a connection so strong it caused things to happen to her body that she'd never experienced. A moisture surged between her thighs, wetting her panties.

Good God, this man was known for being gifted at many things out on the baseball diamond, but this intense, mind-blowing kissing was his true talent.

What was she doing? Kissing Jake was not… Her brief thought of clarity was lost as he broke the kiss and turned her away from him so she was again facing the window and her backside was pressed firmly against his front. He leaned into her body, not allowing all his weight to rest on her, but enough of it so she could feel the hardness between his thighs. She should have stopped her stupidity right then, but her need for him outweighed her reasons. She was lost in the moment and couldn't will her body to stop what felt so damned good.

Her body hummed with passion and her own needs. She wanted this man, but… "Jake, stop." She pushed him back. "I can't do this."

"I know." His breath was ragged. He didn't push off her body just yet. "I didn't ask you over so we could have sex. I want you to know that."

"I never thought that."

"Good."

He placed a kiss in the hollow of her neck. He followed it by gently tracing a line down to the middle of her breasts. A shock zapped her into a different reality. Her nipples reacted to his touch, but she didn't much care. He left her chest and moved down her stomach, circling her belly button. With both hands plastered to the window glass and head down, she sucked in a breath. Though he only touched her shirt, his fingers burned a line through her skin. When he moved lower, she bit her bottom lip to stop the moan wanting to escape. Allowing this to continue was wrong on so many levels, but she wanted this. No, she needed this.

"I know we can't have sex, but I want to take care of you. I want to make you quit thinking so much and just feel what is happening right now. Can you do that, Anna?"

She hadn't been with a man in years, and while her experience had been okay, she had wanted more. She wanted to feel what other women talked endlessly about. She wanted to be a normal woman who could allow a man to meet her needs every now and then. So she nodded her acquiescence.

With no urgency at all and both of his arms wrapped around her waist, he unbuttoned her jeans and pulled down her zipper. Before moving any further, he stopped, as if asking if she was completely comfortable with what was about to happen next. She couldn't protest even if she had wanted to. She was past the point of no return. Her heart beat through her chest, her vision blurred his reflection, and her ears hummed— blocking out all other noises. She was completely lost to Jake. And it was a glorious place to be.

Her breath caught as he slipped one hand inside her jeans, inside her panties. Oh. My. Lord! Caught up in the stroking of his fingers, she heard him say, "That's right, sweetness, just feel. No thinking."

That was not an issue. She couldn't think of anything beyond his skilled fingers gliding across her sex. In tune with her body and what it craved, she shut her eyes. Jake took extra care with that special part that drove a woman out of her mind. She was hot and on the edge of a mind-blowing orgasm. It was intense—and simply wonderful. She moved against his hand and shook uncontrollably. The rhythm became fast and urgent. Mind clear of everything else going on in her life, she drank in the moment. As if knowing it was time, he leaned in, pressing his hard body against hers, and kissed her softly on the shoulder—and that time she couldn't stop her moan as the sensation rippled through her. *Wow.*

****

Jake was kissing her milky skin as she cried out. He had become hard with the first thought of kissing her soft mouth. The moment she came he thought he, too, would explode. He needed this woman, but he was telling her the truth when he said he wasn't out to just have sex with her. If she had asked for more, he would've had his pants down in a heartbeat and sheathed himself inside her warmth. She wasn't ready for that, though, so he was content to give her what she didn't know she needed, an orgasm she would never forget. He took pleasure and brought himself more pain at knowing he was the one to give it to her.

It was all right that he was faint and limp. Being swallowed up by something other than himself caused his body to come alive again.

"Thank you." She still sounded spent.

"Anything for you, sweetness."

****

140

She woke to a creak in the floor. She opened one eye to peek at what was causing the floor to settle, but deep down she already knew. It was the devil. He hadn't visited her in a little over a week, so it was just a matter of time before he would come. He stood over her, and she slammed her eyes shut and tried to slow her breathing to a normal pace so he wouldn't know she was really awake. When he reached under her nightgown, she forced her mind to take her someplace else. She had always wanted to go to Disney World—that's where she would go tonight. A ride on the teacups with her mother.

Anna woke, sat up, and instantly reached to turn on her bedside lamp. Her gaze searched the apartment, checking for anything out of place. "It was just a dream, Anna. Nobody is here." She got up and poured herself a glass of water. After taking a long gulp, she felt calm enough to crawl back between the sheets. She laid her head on the pillow and left the light burning beside her. She might be an adult now, but every now and then, even an adult needed a nightlight.

****

Anna arrived an hour before Em's bachelorette party started. Seeing only a black SUV in the drive, she knew Em was the only one home. She cracked the door open. "Em, it's me." She let herself in, figuring Em wouldn't hear the knock because of the loud music being played. Em had a thing for the old stuff, but Anna only hoped they didn't have to listen to "I'm Every Woman" and "Respect" all night. But she wasn't holding her breath.

She couldn't help but smile at the excessively suggestive decorations. Everywhere she turned, a male body part stared her in the face. There were balloons, streamers, a tablecloth with matching centerpiece, and any and everything penis related. No wonder Em had insisted on decorating for her own party. Her friend knew there was no way in hell Anna was capable of choosing such provocative things.

She was thankful Em took the responsibility away. Since she was the maid of honor, it technically had been Anna's obligation to the bride. She was going to have to make it up to Em. If it had been up to Anna, the party would have consisted of balloons with the word *Bride* printed on them and solid pink plates and napkins. While she would have never dreamed of throwing this kind of party, she admired Em's bravery and sense of fun. She only hoped to have the same kind of free spirit. Maybe for tonight she could forget about all things Jake related, have a good time, and be the woman who could throw a penis-themed party.

"What do you think? Does it need more balloons?" Em came from the kitchen carrying a meat-and-cheese platter into the living room. She looked vibrant in her hot pink dress. It was cut low in the neck and exposed cleavage every boy in the surrounding two counties had admired back when they were teenagers. The dress was tight fitting, showing off her curvy body, and stopped above the knee. Was she really wearing zebra-print stilettos? *Only Em.* On anyone else her outfit would have seemed like something worn on Hooker Street, but it came across as stunning on Em. Her hair and makeup looked as it did any other day—perfect. She made Anna look plain and boring in a pair of jeans, camisole, and matching cardigan with black strappy sandals.

"No, I think you're good on the balloons, but you

might need some more of everything else," Anna teased.

"Seriously? Damn. I knew I needed more streamers." After stomping her foot, Em headed back to the kitchen.

The countertops were covered in every type of platter. Anna hadn't seen that much food since Em and Tommy's bride-and-groom party. There were chips with guacamole dip, desserts, a chocolate fountain, strawberries she assumed went with the fountain, more meats and cheeses, bite-size sandwiches, and a cake still enclosed in a box. She only hoped the cake wasn't in the shape of a penis too.

"No, Em, everything looks great. A little suggestive, but you did a good job. There's only one thing."

"What?"

"Please don't tell me the cake is shaped like a penis too. I don't think I can eat a male body part with a straight face."

Em had one hand on her hip and swiped a cheese cube with the other. "Not even Jake's?"

Stunned was Anna's only reaction. "Em."

"Just saying. The way I hear it, you two have seen each other several times *alone* since you've been back, and a woman can't resist a man who looks that good for long."

"I've only seen Jake once alone, and all of those other times, it was unexpected—and might I add that I wouldn't have seen him at all if someone had warned me he was living at my place?" She eyed Em.

"We've already discussed my reasons for hiding that information. You'll thank me later when he has you spread out on your bed, pleasuring you to the point where all you can do is moan his name."

"Good grief, Em, you're about to get married. You shouldn't even be thinking about Jake in bed."

"I might be getting married, but I am a woman, and any woman—even you—can appreciate a man like Jake Lawrence. Now that we've got that settled, let's finish setting up. The girls will be here soon."

Em would've probably had the entire town informed before sunrise if she knew Jake had given Anna one mind-blowing orgasm last night with his gentle touch. That was not something Anna needed at the moment. She didn't know what to think or how to feel. Of course she had been pleasured, but what was she to think about Jake touching her, making her feel those things *there*? Did she want it to happen again? That was the big question.

There was no mistaking he wanted her. The bulge behind his zipper drove that home. Did she want him back in that way? Plain, logical, carefully planning Anna couldn't justify being with Jake, but the wanton, carefree, wild, nonthinking Anna wanted crazy sex with him. At least, if she was actually having or thinking about having an affair, it would be with someone she knew, and even though she couldn't trust him with her heart, she would be safe with him physically.

"Anna, help me hang this streamer above the door," Em hollered over the music.

****

Fifteen minutes later, people started arriving one after the other. Anna didn't realize Em had so many friends, but she hadn't exactly been around to know much about Em's life. They talked every week, and she heard about most of these women in one conversation or another, but she hadn't known how close Em was to them and how far apart she and Em really were. She didn't think life had stopped in Patience when she suddenly departed. She just hadn't thought about the people, especially Em, and how their lives had changed whether she was physically there or not.

Em had come to see her once or twice, but other than that, their friendship had been maintained by phone calls. And Em never asked her to visit. She knew Anna hadn't been strong enough to face Patience yet.

For the next hour Anna busied herself in the kitchen. She threw away empty plates and cups, refilled the chip bowl, and made small talk when it was required. Most of the girls knew her because of Em, but she didn't have much in common with them. They were people Em worked with, a couple of cousins, and the others were family on Tommy's side. Em was an only child and came from a small family, so she only had her mom there, which Anna thought to be embarrassing. She'd never dreamed of seeing Mrs. Bradshaw and penises in the same room.

Mrs. Bradshaw was the spitting image of Em, or rather, Em was a spitting image of her. She looked as if she were in her late forties when in fact she was close to sixty years old. As a teenager, Anna had once asked her what her secret was to looking so young, and she'd said a stress-free life and a popular face lotion sold at most drugstores. Ever since then, Anna had made it a habit to use the same lotion every night.

It didn't matter what she did or who she talked to; she couldn't stop thinking about Jake. Her feelings for him were becoming an issue. The closeness and kissing were becoming too much for her. There were two dates left, and then he would be gone, out of her house and life. She had hated making the deal, but what other choice did she have? One of the reasons she'd come back was to live in that house and come to terms with her past. How could she do that if Jake was there? The house and Jake were more than she could handle at one time. Her meds kept her sane and out of a dark pit, but they didn't do miracles.

When she was stressed, she ate, and when she ate, she gained twenty pounds, but it was that or give in to Jake's advances—so she chose the food because it was safer. She snatched a miniature chocolate chip cookie off a plate and sighed in complete bliss as the sweetness covered her tongue. God, how she loved chocolate. If she didn't quit doing this, her bridesmaid dress would not only be snug, but she wouldn't even be able to zip it. She ate one more cookie and left the kitchen.

"Why, Anna, where have you been hiding? I was hoping to see you tonight. We didn't get to talk at the bride-and-groom party. It's so nice of you to come home for Emilee's wedding. I know she's thrilled." Em's mom gave her a tight hug.

Mrs. Bradshaw was like a second mother, always offering guidance when her own mother couldn't. "Oh, Mrs. Bradshaw, I have missed you. I see you are still using the same face lotion."

"Oh quit, child. You're being silly. I'm actually looking my age. It's damn depressing. Emilee started stressing me out about this darn wedding. It's all her fault. Today she had me out all day looking for this green dip she's fallen in love with."

She smiled at the woman for remembering their

conversation all those years ago. Em and her mother were going to have to visit Linden. Maybe they could have a girls' day of shopping and catching up.

Mrs. Bradshaw pointed a finger at Anna. "I want you to come by the house this week for lunch. Mr. Bradshaw will love to see you. He was always fond of you." Holding up her hands to shield her lips, she whispered, "Unlike some of these girls who run around wearing childlike dress-up clothes and all but sleep with every guy who walks into Ollie's."

"I will. I'll call you in a few days, and we can set it up."

"Sounds good. Now I've got to go, honey. This party isn't appropriate for a lady of my age. I could take Emilee over my knee and whip her heinie for throwing such a disgusting party. How Tommy puts up with her I will never know."

"He's a great guy."

"Yes, he is," Mrs. Bradshaw agreed.

The woman left, giving Emilee a kiss on the cheek before walking out the door. The fond gesture only made Anna feel more alone while in a crowd of people. She'd felt much like this at the last party she'd attended in Patience. How she wished her mother were still here. But she couldn't think of that right now. Tonight was about Em. Maybe it was time for her to let go. Just for one night, the world would keep revolving.

"What's up?" Em had taken a break from dancing. She had long ago kicked her shoes off and was clearly in a good mood.

"Nothing. I was talking to your mother. We're having lunch this week."

"Please tell me you've done more than arrange

food in the kitchen and make lunch plans with my parents."

"What? I love your mother. It's nice to see her. And you threw the party. The least I could do is refill the chip bowl." Em wasn't buying the explanation, but Anna couldn't tell her the real reason she was so distracted and removed from the party. She would only ask a million questions and probably tell Tommy, which would mean Jake knowing she had liked last night more than she was willing to say.

"For one, I don't want you to refill any bowls. You are here to have a not-like-Anna good time. If someone wants chips, they can find the damn bags in the pantry. Second, I know you love my mother. I love her too, but please talk to someone your own age. You are twenty-nine. Act like it. You don't always have to be the safe, designated driver, Anna. Promise me you will let go and have fun. If you need to, you can sleep on my couch. Okay?"

Em knew her all too well. She said everything Anna already acknowledged, but it was nice to have a friend tell her it was all right. "I promise."

Chapter Ten

"What do you think the women are doin' right now?" Tommy asked as he threw a line in the water.

"Probably watching some romantic comedy or singing along with the oldie station into their hair brushes."

"How is it you know more about my future wife than I do, Brad?"

"You'll have to ask her about that. I don't kiss and tell."

Tommy punched Bradley in the arm. Jake, along with Tommy, knew Bradley was just shitting him.

Jake took three beers out of the cooler, popped the tops, and handed one to each guy before he set his own between his legs. He had already drunk one and needed to slow down. After two beers, he never drove, and he wasn't about to ask these two jackasses to take him home. Plus, he was a changed man and tried to stick to his two-beer limit. After this little bachelor party, all he wanted to do was go home and sleep for days. He hadn't gotten much sleep the past few nights, and he could feel it in his body. He was too old for this stuff.

"Thanks." Bradley and Tommy both spoke at the same time, still keeping a close eye on their floaters bobbing in the water.

"No prob."

He usually liked fishing, especially on a humid

night when the beer tasted good and he was in good company. Tonight was about Tommy, but Jake couldn't get his mind off Anna. He hoped he hadn't scared her after his greediness. What a jackass move. She wasn't ready for that. She was a woman who thought things out, planned, thought some more, and then followed through with her plans. He needed to respect that.

What the hell—she honestly didn't want him. The only reason she was going on these dates with him was because she wanted him out of her life, not because she wanted him in it. Maybe he should just give in and let her have the house, move back home with Bradley, and continue with his love 'em and leave 'em lifestyle. Women flocked to him down at Ollie's, women who were willing to make him forget all about his troubles. The only problem with that logic was that when the sun came up, he would still be in the same predicament— wanting Anna.

"Hey, bro. Are you here?" Bradley waved his straw cowboy hat in front of Jake's face.

"What?" He wasn't ready to leave his thoughts just yet.

"Wanted to know if you're going to do some fishing or just sit here looking lost."

Jake realized he hadn't even thrown his line in. For some reason he was ticked that Bradley called him out on it. "You just stay over on your side of the boat and not worry about me fishing. I'll do what I damn well please, and if I want to sit here drinking a beer or two and listen to you jackasses talk only about women, I will."

"So-rry. What's your deal? This is a bachelor party, not a self-pity party for Jake. Get over screwing up with Anna and start fishing."

Bradley was way off his game. Little shit never knew when to keep his mouth shut.

"You'd better watch yourself. I'm in no mood for your insight on my love life."

"Well, maybe you should listen to someone because all you've done is mope around since her little ass got back into town. I mean, at the softball game you bit my head off every chance you could."

Jake stood, careful not to spill his beer or rock the boat. He and Bradley hadn't been in a throw-down, kick-your-ass type of fight since…well, the last time, but he was about to make his little brother relive his last ass-kicking. Which, now that Jake thought about it, wasn't that long ago.

"What are you going to do? Kick my ass because I'm telling the truth? Go ahead. I'm not a kid anymore, and if you remember from a few days ago, my punches hurt just as much as yours, so be prepared. I won't be holding back." Bradley turned away from Jake and went back to staring at the water.

"Whoa, guys, there's no need for anyone to kick anyone's ass. If anything, I should kick both your asses for throwin' me a worthless bachelor party."

With his fists clenched at his sides, Jake sat down and took a hard pull on his beer. He leaned back and propped his boots up on the cooler. This was stupid. Was he really going to have another drag-out fight with his brother when in all honesty the guy was speaking the truth? He pulled his ball cap down over his eyes. And he tried blocking everything out. He was terrible to Anna, a bad friend, and now he was a bad brother. He totally sucked.

The ringing of a cell phone interrupted the quiet. Probably Em or a woman who kept Bradley's number on speed dial. He knew it wasn't his. He didn't have a woman keeping tabs on him, and he was fine with that. He answered to nobody.

"Hey, Em, what's up?"

He was right. It was Em calling Tommy. She was probably making sure they were really fishing and not at a strip club putting hard-earned dollars down some woman named Candy's panties. He should've done something like that. At least then he would stay distracted, but Em would kick his butt, and he already had one woman mad, or was it happy, now? He couldn't keep up, but he couldn't handle another angry woman. Corny as it might sound, Em was a firecracker waiting to explode on the Fourth of July, and he didn't want any part of that.

He could tell something was wrong when Tommy reeled in his line. Only two things made the man stop fishing—being out of beer and Em. "We'll be right there. Love you too." Tommy hung up the phone. "Reel 'em in, boys. The women have a little situation on their hands."

"We leave those women alone for one night, and what do they do? Get in a heap of trouble that they need a man to get them out of." Bradley still had his line in the water, clearly not wanting to leave yet. He probably didn't have a woman lined up for the night.

"What's going on?" Jake was already sitting upright, ready to take charge.

"Not completely sure. All I know is it's about Anna and Cara."

Shit. This was not going be good.

****

"Anna, I think you need to slow down on the down-home punch. You're not used to drinking."

Anna could sense Em wasn't worried yet, but she would be there soon if Anna didn't get it together. "I'm f-fine. I'm just havin' a hard time walkin' at the moment." Funny how when she was drunk, her southern accent became more clear. "Just give me a minute." She held a pink cup in one hand and gripped the side of a chair with the other. It was the only thing helping her sit up at the moment.

"Here, why don't you eat this, get something in your stomach? It might help soak up some of the alcohol." Em held out a cracker, but Anna protested.

"I'm already fat. Why are you tryin' to make me fatter?"

"You're not fat." Em grabbed the cup out of Anna's hands. "Now eat this damn cracker and stop being difficult. You see Alice over there? She grew up with five brothers. She can take you down to the floor and force this damn cracker down your throat. Which way do you want to play it?"

Anna took the cracker. She'd met Alice earlier and immediately knew she was not someone to mess with.

"Okay, I ate it. Can I get up now? I want to dance." As soon as her feet hit the floor and she rose out of the chair, the room started turning. She held herself still for a minute before testing out her wobbly legs. When she only wobbled slightly, she considered herself able to walk. Anna had seen Jessie earlier and knew she was the type of woman who could hold her liquor and have a good time.

Tonight she was dressed in holey jeans, a plain

white tee, and her ponytail was pulled through a trucker ball cap. Jessie stood by a large, toy-bin-looking bucket full of some concoction Anna had never seen. Any other time, she would've passed on the fruity-looking drink, but tonight she wasn't Do-Good Anna. She was a let-go, throw-caution-to-the-wind kind of woman.

"*Heyyyyy*, Jessie," Anna said, slurring her words.

"How's drunk feel, girl? You want some of my homemade punch?"

"That's why I'm over here."

"All right, then." Jessie filled a cup to the rim. "Here you go. Now the thing is, you have to drink all of it. Understand?"

"Completely. Wanna dance? I've never actually danced before with a woman. I mean, I danced with Jake the other night, but he isn't a woman, if you know what I mean." Anna giggled.

"You know I'm straight, don't you? Your eyes aren't playing tricks on you, are they?"

"No. I mean, yes, I know you're not in love with me. I just thought you could teach me how to dance."

"Well, if you want to dance, we are going have to change this damn music. Em is completely impossible when it comes to the radio.

"Em, can we please listen to something besides 'Respect'?" Jessie's voice carried over the classic song. "How about a good women-take-control kind of song."

Em pointed a stern finger in Jessie's direction. "Hey, this is real music. You're just too young to appreciate a good woman song."

"Em, you're only two years older than me. You need to update your music collection. Soul music is fine and all, but you need some country and western. Please.

My ears are bleeding."

When the first country song blasted through the speakers, Anna was already on the coffee table, throwing her head around and splashing half her drink on Em's new zebra-print rug. Her hair had escaped from its tight ponytail and now hung loosely in her face. She thought it was by a current female singer, but whatever the song, she was ready to get down to it.

Em shouted to Jessie. "Why did you give her another cup? It took all I had to pry the other one out of her death grip."

"She looked as if she needed it. Look at her." Jessie took a break from drinking her own punch long enough to point at Anna, who gave her a thumbs-up. "She's having a good time."

"I can see that, but you see my rug. It took weeks to talk your brother into that, and now it's stained with your punch. Hope you don't have plans tomorrow."

"Well, no. Why?"

" 'Cause you will be here scrubbing it up."

"Why me? Your friend there is the one who spilled her drink on it."

"Who gave her the drink?" Em patted Jessie on the butt and hurried off. "I need reinforcements."

Anna should feel guilty for ruining the bachelorette party. But to her credit, Em had told her to have a non-Anna time, and that's exactly what she was doing.

"I got it," Anna said to the ringing doorbell. After jumping off the table and stumbling her way to the front door, she swung the door open and barely missed her face.

The woman on the threshold held out a six-pack of beer. "Sorry I'm la—you're not Em."

"Hey, everybody, look. Cara is sorry she's late." Anna hadn't planned on screaming across the room, but since having her first drink, her voice had come out louder than usual. The music went silent, and she could hear her own heart beating. "Cara, come on in. You should try some of Jessie's lunch."

"You mean punch, honey. She should try some of my punch."

"Shut up, Jessie," another girl mumbled from the opposite side of the room.

Anna turned her head around and bowed to Jessie. "Sorry, I mean punch."

"What's going on in here?" Em came in the room with a cell phone to her ear. "Shit."

"No, it's okay, Em." Anna put her arm around Cara and dragged her in the house. "I'll take one of those, if you don't mind? You don't mind sharing, do ya? Oh, what am I sayin'? You love sharing, don't ya, Car?"

Cara glanced from Em and back to Anna. "Sure, go…go ahead."

Anna pulled out one of the beers, popped the top, and turned it up. "I've not drank beer in, oh, I guess since Jake and I… Oh crap, was I supposed to say that? Cara, you know Jake, don't ya? That's right. You and Jake know each other real well."

Cara's face turned deep red. She didn't move away from the front door.

"Cara, why look so scared? You didn't look so scared eleven years ago when you were screwing my boyfriend." Anna was up in Cara's face, pulling the rest of her hair down from its loosened ponytail. Her shoes were off. Now what? Oh, her earrings. She was supposed to pull her earrings out. At least that's what she saw in the movies when the girlfriend confronted her cheating ex's lover.

"It wasn't like that, Anna."

"I'm sorry. I know I've had a little too much to drink, but did I just hear that come out of your mouth?"

"I can explain."

"I don't want explanations, you little redheaded bitch. You couldn't keep your own boyfriend, so you thought mine would do just fine, huh?" Anna tossed back the beer before she hauled back and spit a mouthful of it in Cara's face. "That's what I think about your explanations."

Em hung up the phone and ran to the door, tripping on several pairs of shoes in the process. "Okay, Anna, you've had a lot to drink. Let's go sit down in the kitchen, and I will put some coffee on. Sound good?"

Anna pulled out of her grip and lunged toward Cara at the same time.

"Can I have some help please?" Em called out. "Alice, put the cup down and make yourself useful over here."

She didn't stand a chance with the built woman in the corner, so she let Em walk her to the kitchen. "Em, you should let me go. I deserve this. After all these years, I should get to shove her down on her ass. Please let me have her."

"Anna, you're drunk. I'm not going to let you get in a fight. You would regret it tomorrow."

She pouted her way over to the barstool. This was just great. All week she'd been putting Jake off when he tried talking about what went wrong between them. And now, when she thought she was strong enough to face the problem head-on, no one would let her do anything about it. These people sucked. What was the point of having fun when you couldn't do things you normally wouldn't do?

Her night wasn't over, and she wasn't going to let this go just yet.

****

"Shit," Jake muttered to no one in particular. Putting Anna and Cara in the same room together wasn't going to go over well. Everybody knew that. He doubted they had seen each other in the past eleven years, and if Em called Tommy for help, it only meant the little reunion wasn't a happy one.

"Maybe it's not that bad," Bradley said from the back seat. He'd had a few too many beers and wasn't thinking clearly. That was probably why he couldn't remember the reason those two women in the same room was a very bad idea.

Tommy whipped the truck into the drive, almost taking out his mailbox and a few cars parked along the side of the road. Jake jumped out of the truck before Tommy came to a complete stop. He needed to get in there—now.

"Good grief, Jake, you'd think something bad was going on." Bradley had somehow made it out of the truck without stumbling and was on Jake's heels.

"Bradley, why don't you just shut the fuck up?"

"Fine."

Jake flung the door open. The only way one would notice it was a bachelorette party was by the amount of penis decorations. Except for the whispers, he didn't hear any other sounds. All heads looked up as he entered, followed by Bradley and Tommy.

"Now, this is a party. I should've just hung out

with the ladies. Why didn't we do something like this?" Of course Bradley would be amused with all the penis decorations.

The absence of loud music and men-bashing let him know everything he needed to know. Anna had done something. Cara regretted what she and he had done long ago, so his only guess was that Anna was drunk and confronted her. This was his fault. Things were out of hand because of the mistakes he'd made. The Cara thing was an overdue conversation. And eventually Anna was going to have to listen to him.

"Where is she?" he asked the first woman he encountered. She didn't say a word, just pointed him toward the kitchen.

He could hear someone crying and another woman trying to soothe her. He saw her and came to a halt. She looked a mess. Her head was lying on Em's shoulder, and her hair looked like bees had made a permanent home in it. He didn't know what to do. Should he run to her? The only thing he knew he couldn't do was leave her. That was not an option.

Anna raised her head, as if sensing someone else had entered the room. He couldn't tell from her blank stare if she was relieved to see him. It didn't matter. Whether she liked it or not, he was going to be there for her.

"Jake, thank God you're here." Em let out a long breath.

She might have called Tommy, but Jake knew she had really wanted him. The concern in her voice had to mean the situation was much worse than he might have originally thought. "Is she okay?" His voice dropped a few octaves and gave away the worry he was trying to hide.

"Will you two stop talking about me like I'm not in the room? Oh, and Jake, I can see the worry all over your face. You can take it and shove it. You don't get to feel anything when it comes to me. Leave and take that redheaded bitch with you."

"She's been like this for twenty minutes. One minute she's crying, saying she's fat and sucks, and the next she is using language I've never heard coming from her mouth. It's like she doesn't know what kind of drunk to be. Please help. Nobody out there knows her well enough to know what to do and help me, and Jessie is just disappointed there wasn't a slap-fest. I hated to interrupt the fishing trip, but I didn't know what else to do."

"It's fine, Em. I'm glad you called. Can you give us a minute?"

"Sure, let me know if you need me. I've been trying to make her eat crackers, but I'm not promising there won't be hurling." She hugged Anna and patted him on the shoulder before leaving them alone.

Someone turned the music back up. Em was obviously trying to give them some privacy. She was a good friend. Tommy was getting a good woman.

Anna had her head on the counter, staring at the floor. She was either attempting to avoid him, or it hurt too much to pick it up. She wasn't going to make this easy for him, and he knew that. He just hoped he got her out of there without too much of a scene.

"Sweetness, will you look at me, please?"

Her hair shielded her face from his view. It also put him at a disadvantage when it came to being able to read what she would do next. He wanted to be prepared in case she decided to be a mean drunk and haul off and slap him in the face. He'd let her do it because he'd deserved it, but that didn't mean he didn't want to know it was coming.

He tucked a piece of hair behind her ear. Her mascara was running down her cheeks, and her face was splotchy. She tilted her head toward him, letting him see her tear-filled eyes. He could handle a spitting-mad Anna, but this Anna was a different story. A crying woman did him in, especially when that woman was one he cared deeply about.

Jake rubbed her back, making his body respond immediately. What was wrong with him? This was not the time, but he couldn't help it. Every time he touched her, he wanted to only touch her more. He needed to get it together.

"Can I get you out of here?"

A booming voice entered the room. "There any food in here? My party didn't come with food." Bradley either didn't know they were in there, or he didn't care—probably both.

"What the fuck! Can't you see we're in the middle of something here? Get out."

"*Whoaaaa*, what's wrong, baby?" Bradley knocked Jake out of the way so he could get to Anna. He leaned in and murmured. Jake could hardly make out the words, but if he knew his brother, and he did, they were not just words of encouragement. They were come-on lines he used on every woman around town. Any other woman, he couldn't care less—it was better that Bradley take care of them than him—but not Anna. There was no way he was letting his drunken brother anywhere near an intoxicated and vulnerable Anna.

"Bradley, if you don't get out of here right now, I'll pick up from that fight earlier and knock your ass out, got it?"

Bradley never turned his focus off Anna, and she didn't take her eyes off him. This was going to turn into bloodshed if his brother didn't leave that instant.

"I'm just being the man you never could be." Bradley jumped away from Anna, throwing both hands in front of his face. The guy never backed down from any fight, but he looked frightened. "Sorry, bro, that was out of line. I'm drunk...and well, you know how I get. I didn't mean it."

"No, you're *rrr...right*," Anna cried. "Bradley, he never was a man. He knows it. That's why he's so threatened right now. He knows he's a jackass."

Blood rushed to his face, and he could feel the heat radiating from his body. So he was dealing with two drunks—one who didn't know when to shut up and the other who turned out to not be the nice drunk he was hoping for. Crap.

"Bradley, I'm going to let you slide on that little remark, but you'd better get out of here. Have Jessie drive you home."

"No. I don't want you to go, Bradley. You're the only one here besides Em who cares about my feelings and what I want. Can you take me home? No, wait... Do you have a bathtub?"

"Yeah, baby. Might even have some bath salts too. Why?"

"Because I haven't been able to take a hot bath since I've gotten to Patience, and I really want to. My apartment didn't come with the privilege of having a tub. Why don't I just sleep at your house?"

No fucking way! He figured she was trying to get a reaction out of him, and it was working. "No. I can't let you two do that. I'll drive you home, Anna."

"You heard the woman." Bradley was feeling brave again. "She wants me. I do have a tub and all. Didn't you rip hers out of the house?"

"You took out my bathtub?" Anna asked in a voice he was sure had the potential of breaking glass.

Jake ignored her altogether, because he had other concerns—his asshole of a brother.

"I've let you stand upright long enough, more times than you deserve, so I would advise you to catch a ride with Jessie and get the hell outta here. Now."

"Fine. Anna, I better go. I've had a little too much to drink, and if something was to happen to your pretty little face 'cause of me, I would never forgive myself." After tipping his straw hat, he gave her that southern-boy wink. But he turned around one last time before leaving the room. "Oh, and, Anna, you come by any night and use my tub…or anything else you need."

"Bradley. Now." Jake was relieved his brother had left before punches were thrown. He didn't want to fight him, but he would have if needed be.

"You didn't have to threaten him, you know. He was just being nice, and I wanted him here."

"He's had too much to drink. I didn't want him taking advantage of you."

"Why? Because that's your job, right? Don't think I don't know about your track record. I hear things—all the women are eager to share the details of their wild nights with ex-ballplayer Jake Lawrence."

"I've never taken advantage of you, Anna. You know that."

"No, never sexually, but you have taken advantage of me. The woman in the living room is evidence of that. You do remember Cara, don't you, or have you had so many redheads since then that she doesn't even rate a memory in your pea-sized brain?"

She rose from the barstool for the first time since he'd arrived. He imagined she was gripping the counter to keep herself from swaying. When he rushed to her side, she stopped him by putting up a shaky hand.

"Don't touch me."

What patience he had was just about gone. His head hurt, and his body ached. She might not have wanted his help, but he had been called here, and she was by damn going to get it. "Anna, I'm going to have to touch you. You won't make it to the truck."

"Truck? You think I'm going anywhere with you?"

"You'll either walk out this door with me, or I'll carry you over my shoulder. Which way do you want it?"

"What's up with everyone threatening me tonight? First Alice, and now you. I'm tired of it. Nobody will be carrying me anywhere. So you can just go home."

He vaguely remembered seeing a woman who looked to have the same strength as a bodybuilder drinking a beer when he'd come in the door. That had to be Alice. He could see why Anna listened to the woman. If only he had the same effect on her. If she wasn't willing to leave with him of her own free will, then he had no other choice but to carry her out.

He swept her up, threw her over his shoulder in a fireman's hold, and headed toward the front door.

"Hey," she protested, putting up a good fight, kicking and screaming.

"Stop it, Anna. You're only making it harder on yourself."

Tommy ran in front of him, threw him his truck keys, and quickly opened the front door.

"Thanks, man. I'll bring it back to you tomorrow."

"Just don't let her hurl in it."

He tossed her in the front seat and cursed Tommy for putting the lift kit on his truck. After making sure there weren't any limbs hanging out, he shut her door and ran to the other side before she tried to bolt.

She was staying only a few minutes away from Em and Tommy's place, but he didn't want to take her there. He wanted her with him. And considering the state she was in right then, he knew she would have only protested if he asked, so he turned in the opposite direction from Garrett's rental and headed out of town to Anna's, his home at the moment.

"Jake, you take me home right now."

"That's what I'm doing."

"No, you take me to Garrett's. I will not be staying with you."

"Well, you see, honey, I'm the one driving, so I get to choose where you go now, don't I?"

"Uhhhh, you're impossible." She threw her hands in the air. She also mumbled a few other choice words, but he couldn't make them out above the dual exhaust.

She stared out the passenger window the rest of the drive. That was fine with him. It wasn't as if she would remember their conversation anyway. He drove slower than usual, not ready to face her yet. She was pissed at him, and when she got pissed, there was no telling what was going to come out. Add being drunk on top of that, and he was in a hell of a lot of trouble.

When Jake put the truck in park, she fumbled with the door handle. "Stay right where you are. I'll come around."

"I'm about to puke." She covered her mouth.

He jumped out of the truck, barely slamming the door shut behind him. Opening hers, he could tell she was trying desperately not to hurl. She didn't succeed. As soon as he turned her toward him, she puked all over his button-down shirt.

"Fuck."

She looked at him with tear-filled eyes.

"Hey, hey, don't cry. It's going be all right."

"No, it's not. I've made a mess out of everything tonight. I'll be surprised if Em ever talks to me again."

Jake took his shirt off, threw it on the ground, and picked her up. After wrapping both arms around his neck, she started sobbing on his chest. Was it possible she could hear his heart beating wildly? He didn't want her mad at him, but he could handle that better than this. He didn't trust himself with her when she was vulnerable and touching him. His body instantly reacted to the simple contact.

With her still wrapped in his arms, he bent low enough to open the door and turn the light switch on. He held her so close to his chest it hurt. After laying her on the couch, he placed a pillow under her head and covered her with the blanket he kept on the back of the couch. A flashback entered his mind—the last time they had both been in that same room. If he wasn't hard already, that simple thought would've made him.

"Stay here. I'll be right back."

"I've been told it isn't good to break the seal," she informed him.

What in the hell was a seal, and why shouldn't he break it? "A what?"

"To pee. At Em's party, someone told me not to break the seal to go pee."

"Uh…okay." That still didn't tell him anything. Maybe it was a woman thing, and he was best off not knowing. Hell, she probably didn't know what she was talking about.

When she fisted the blanket but didn't try to move, he figured he had enough time to clean up and put on a pot of coffee. This was going to be another long night, and he was going to need as much caffeine as his maker could pour out. He only turned on the lights required for him to see, not wanting to bother her in case she was falling asleep.

After starting the coffee, he stopped by the bathroom to wipe off his chest before going to the small bedroom to pull on a clean T-shirt. When he smelled the strong aroma coming from his coffee maker, he headed back up the hall to check on Anna. He stopped in his tracks. She wasn't on the couch. The blanket was tossed on the floor. He ran to the window and looked out to the drive. Thank God the truck was still there. She couldn't have gone far.

"I'm in here," he heard her fragile voice say.

He turned to the kitchen, and there she sat at the small table, bringing a cup to her pale lips. Another woman had never looked so beautiful to him.

"I would've brought you a cup to the couch."

"It's fine. Sorry I threw up on you."

"No harm done. I probably deserved it."

"Yeah, probably," she said honestly. The hurt was evident in her trembling voice, her slight movement, the dullness in her usually sparkling green eyes.

God, those eyes. They had such a strong hold on him and about brought him to his knees.

Jake grabbed a cup from the cabinet above the coffee maker and poured himself a cup. This was going to be the first of many for the night. He took a seat across the table, forcing her to look him in the eyes. Whatever she had been through that night—the good and bad—he wanted to see it all. "What happened tonight, Anna?"

"I'm boring and could never throw a penis party. I wouldn't expect you to understand."

"Do I even want to know what that means?"

"Just an Em thing."

"Then I don't want to know." He took another sip of coffee. "You're way off, you know. The world can't handle another Em. They want the real Anna."

"Did you see the party Em threw?"

"Penises. Hard to miss, but I said I don't want to know any more."

"Well, she didn't even trust me to throw that kind of party. She was right, but still I want to be the kind of woman who could."

"First of all, there are few people who have the balls to throw that kind of party. Em is in a league all her own. You're amazing, Anna. Don't you realize that?"

Tears streaked down both sides of her face again. He wasn't helping the situation. It had been selfish of him to bring her there. After moving to her side, he knelt in front of her, grabbed both hands, and brought them to his lips. He placed a gentle kiss on them while looking up into a set of eyes that wrecked him from the inside out.

"You don't have to do that," she said in between sobs.

"I know I don't, but I want to. Let me take care of you tonight."

"Like the other night?"

"In a way, yeah."

"Okay."

Jake brought her to her feet and wrapped two arms around her waist before he buried his face in her hair. It smelled of the same fruity, intoxicating fragrance he was becoming familiar with. The gentle kiss she placed on his neck brought him back to life and made him think about things no man had a right thinking with a drunken woman in his arms. He'd done a lot of things with a woman, but that was not one of them. His dad would be cursing him from above for just the thought of it.

"Can I use your shower?"

"Yeah, go ahead. I don't have a tub, you know."

"Don't remind me. I'm still going to kill you for that."

Chapter Eleven

Anna walked back into the living room fifteen minutes later. His head was hung low, over his third cup of coffee. He snapped upright as soon as he heard her patter her way into the room.

"Hey, what the hell?"

She stood there in front of him buck naked with her damp hair brushed back. He could see her beautiful features now that her face was rid of tears and mascara. Her breasts were erect, making him become the same. After he took a ragged breath, he let his gaze go lower. She was curvier than he remembered, but the curves made her look like a normal woman—just the way he liked them.

Anna wrapped her arms around her midsection and dipped her chin toward the floor. Jake instinctively grabbed the blanket and hurried to his feet. He wrapped the fabric around her.

"I'm-m n-not," she stammered, "what you're used to?"

"No, you're not." And that was the God's honest truth. She was in every way not what he was used to. She had a magnificent body.

"How dare you?" She wiped a few tears from her cheek. "How humiliating. You sure know how to let a girl down easy." She spun away from him.

He caught her by the shoulder and twisted her

around. He needed to look her in the eye. "Anna, I didn't mean that in a bad way. You were right when you said you're not what I'm used to. You are more. You're beautiful."

"Why aren't you excited to see me, then? I thought this is what you wanted?"

"Honey, I am more than excited to see you. Just look down." He gestured, and her face flushed. "That's what you do to me every time I see or touch you. Hell, I get hard just thinking about you. This"—he motioned between him and her—"is not what I wanted for us. At least not tonight. I want to take care of you. Not take you to bed."

"Oh. I just thought—" He cut her off by giving her a soft kiss on the lips. It was over before it started but had the same effect as if he'd thrown her down on the floor and explored every part of her mouth.

"That is the most I had planned for us tonight. When we do more, it won't be because you're drunk, feeling brave, and trying to be someone you're not. It will be because you want me as much as I want you. Got it?"

"Got it."

"Why don't you go grab some jogging pants and a T-shirt out of my second drawer, and then we can find something on the television to watch? I'm staying in your old bedroom."

****

Her childhood bedroom. He was sleeping in there? She didn't know if she should feel turned on at the thought of him sleeping between the same walls she'd once stayed in or disgusted at the thought of him being exposed to such filth. Of course, he didn't know what had gone on behind that door, but in some strange way, his being able to stay in that room and not be able to feel what she had been through seemed like a betrayal.

Anna entered the bedroom with a sense of dread and shame hanging over her. They were emotions she'd been trying to bury for most of her life.

So much for not being affected by this house.

Of course she didn't feel comfortable in her old room. Her stomach did a free fall, causing her to feel sick, and this time it wasn't because of the alcohol. She needed to get a grip. That little girl no longer existed. She had more control over her life now.

The room was closing in on her. The bed was in the same place, in the center of the room, with a small nightstand to the right. A dresser sat on the opposite wall by the door with a tube-style television placed on top of it. The walls were painted the same light shade of purple she and her mother had picked out together, only now they were faded and stained from age. Picturing Jake sleeping in such a girly room amused her. Her room would have appeared exactly the same if it wasn't for the ball caps hanging on the bedposts and the navy-blue comforter covering the bed. It didn't look like a room a ballplayer would stay in.

She needed to get out of there. She pulled open the second drawer, jerked out the first shirt and jogging pants she saw, and slipped them on. The pants were big, so she tied them as tightly as she could and hoped they wouldn't fall to her ankles. She had already shown him way too much for the night.

She made her way back to the living room with a plastered smile on her face. He didn't need to see the pain her/his room caused. He patted the spot on the couch next to him. She sat down but made sure not to sit too close. Jake pulled her closer and put his arm around her shoulders. It was as if he knew just what she needed.

He switched the television on to an older show they had kept up with as teenagers. Without speaking, they watched the dysfunctional family play out their lives. The show always made her feel as if life could be worse. That her life was what she made of it. As a child, she hadn't gotten a choice when it came to her life, but she did now, and she refused to make nothing of it. She wouldn't allow her own dysfunctional family to ruin things for her.

As a teenager, she'd wished she had Jake's family. Growing up, he had a mother, a father who taught him to play baseball, and a brother to fight with. She'd had her mother, and she loved her more than anything. Her mother made life bearable, and Anna wished she were there now, able to see the woman she was trying to become. Now she was alone in the world, and she was the only one who was going to see what she accomplished and how unattainable those dreams had once been.

She couldn't fully concentrate on the sitcom because of her thoughts of the past, but was mostly distracted because of her closeness to Jake. He was warm and safe. With him there, her childhood home felt somewhat safe. She really did trust him. It was a nice feeling to have for once.

He switched off the television. "I don't know about you, but it's been a long day. You ready to get some sleep?"

"Yeah. Sleep sounds good." She sat up and

stretched out her arms, pretending the thought of sleep was overtaking her as well. Even though sleep was going to be impossible. Her insomnia and need for sleeping meds were something very few knew about, and she planned to keep it that way.

"I don't know what you want to do. You want to sleep in my bed with me—nothing more, I promise—or I can sleep in here and you take the bed? Whichever you feel comfortable with is fine with me."

"I'll sleep on the couch."

"What? No. You take my bed. It's fine. I promise."

She couldn't sleep in that room. It just wasn't going to happen. Even after the three dates, when she moved back in, she had no plans of sleeping in her old bedroom. Nothing good could possibly come from it. She carried those awful memories with her every day and didn't see the need to put herself through that kind of pain voluntarily. "Jake, I don't want to be another woman who is in your bed," she said instead of telling him the truth. "I'll sleep on the couch, okay?"

"Come on, Anna. Can we just table that conversation tonight?"

"I'm not trying to bring anything up. I want to sleep out here. I constantly toss and turn, and I'll keep you up all night anyway."

"I can't let you do that. I've passed out on it several times and can tell you it's not exactly sleeping material. Stop being stubborn and take my bed."

"I can't, Jake. Please just go to bed." Her voice was more of a plea than anything.

He kissed her forehead and stood. "Goodnight, Anna." He walked to the kitchen, probably to shut off the coffeepot. He returned to the living room and gave her one last look before he started for the hallway.

"Jake."

"Yeah?"

"Thanks for tonight."

"It was nothing. See ya in the morning." With that he walked away, leaving her in the glow of a lamp by the couch.

"Now what am I going to do?" The clock above the television read two thirty. Sunrise wouldn't come for a while. She didn't have anything to take for sleep. She waited about thirty minutes, making sure Jake was asleep before tiptoeing to the kitchen. She turned on the light and went to the cabinet that was used as a medicine cabinet when she lived there. Hard liquor was on the top shelf, but she'd had enough of that for a lifetime. Just below that shelf sat what she needed. She took two with water.

Anna padded back to the couch and lay there staring at the ceiling. What a night. It had all started with her filling the chip bowl and ended with her naked in front of her ex. Tomorrow she was going to feel the humiliation of her actions, but for now, she needed to concentrate on sleep. She was going to need her strength to face Jake, Em, Jessie, and Bradley.

Crap. Did she really hit on Bradley? She could vaguely remember their conversation, but she knew it was not going to be one of her finest moments. How was she going to face him? He was Jake's brother, for God's sake. Tomorrow was going to be bad. She wasn't a good, fun drunk—she was just plain embarrassing. And she'd forgotten about what had gotten this thing started—Cara.

She'd been caught off guard by the sight of the

woman who had been quick to give Jake something Anna never had. She'd felt good, and the words had just spilled out, literally. In the past she'd never gotten the chance to defend herself, and it was overdue. She wasn't embarrassed about that. No, she felt liberated, strong. She felt like the type of woman who could throw a penis-themed party.

Maybe.

She wished she hadn't all but threatened to cause bodily harm to Cara. Mature, grown women didn't go around punching and spitting on other people. She was better than that. She didn't know when, but there was going to come a time when she would need to apologize to Cara for tonight. Lord, could this trip get any stranger?

An hour later, she rolled over on her side, holding tightly to the blanket, and fell asleep.

****

Anna was going to be sick. The smell of frying bacon overtook her senses, and she couldn't control the substance rising from her stomach to her mouth. She left her makeshift bed on Jake's couch and stumbled her way down the hall to the bathroom, thankfully not stubbing a big toe in the process.

Way to be positive.

The need for air was essential if she didn't want Jake to see her hurl for a second time. She shut the door, washed her hands, and splashed cold water on her face, all without looking at her reflection in the mirror. The need to vomit subsided when the cooling sensation hit her clammy skin. Leaving the bathroom, she headed for the kitchen. What time was it? How could anybody be up this early cooking? The thought was inconceivable.

"What are you doing?" Anna walked in the kitchen, holding her stomach and knowing she resembled death, or at least close to it.

"Making breakfast. Want some coffee?"

"Yes, please. Have any creamer?"

"Don't have creamer, but I do have milk."

Jake sounded way too perky for her liking. She hoped he didn't expect good company. If so, he wasn't getting it. She wanted to sit in silence, drinking her coffee. After two cups she might be up for talking, but even that was kind of iffy.

"That'll do." He poured her a cup and turned back to frying bacon. "How'd you sleep? It probably sucked, huh?"

The morning routine she'd adopted many years ago was obviously not going to happen. "It was fine."

"I thought with all that tossing and turning you do, I might've found you on the floor this morning." Even though his back was to her, she could see him grinning at that very moment.

"I wasn't on the floor, was I?"

"You're not much on talking, huh?"

"Not a morning person," she said in irritation. "If you don't mind, I would prefer silence."

He finally got the point and shut up. Anna drank her coffee, loving the taste going down her throat, coating her stomach.

He put a plate of bacon and eggs in front of her. "Eat this. It will help with the hangover."

The silence with her coffee didn't last long. "What part of *no talking* don't you understand?"

"Why don't you start being a little nicer to me and

eat the damn food?"

"Fine." She picked up her fork and took a small bite of eggs. It was more to get some peace and quiet than really wanting the protein. But to her disappointment—and Jake's satisfaction—they actually weren't half bad. She ate more and more until they were gone.

"See. I told you they would make you feel better."

"You must've had a lot of hangovers to know the secret to getting over them."

"I've had a few."

"Well, this will be my last one. I don't see why people drink, knowing this is how they will feel the next morning."

"You don't always feel this way. You just don't know how to handle yourself."

"I guess," she admitted.

They sat in silence for the next minutes, eating and drinking their coffee. It was kind of nice to sit at a table with someone, have breakfast, and argue over hangovers, with one telling the other to shut up. Would this have been her life if things hadn't gone horribly wrong?

No, she wasn't going to think of that. She would just enjoy the day and the moment.

Part of the night had been okay, and the morning wasn't too bad, but after she left, she wouldn't have moments like this with Jake again. She couldn't risk her heart, not ever again. She had two dates and Em's wedding to get through, and then she would be gone.

Anna heard her cell phone ringing from the bathroom. It was still in her pants' pocket from the night before. She was in no mood to talk, so she let it go to voicemail, but then it started ringing again. Who would be calling her this early? Everybody knew she was not a morning person. Everyone except Jake.

"I don't think they're going to give up. I'll get it and tell them you're asleep."

Ahhh…he was figuring her out. She had to admit it didn't take him long. It was probably no one important, a wrong number or something.

Whoever it was, they weren't talking to her this early in the morning.

****

Jake walked to the bathroom to answer Anna's phone. She was like a hornet in the morning, and he didn't want the person on the other side of the phone to get their ass handed to them on a platter. Nobody deserved her wrath when she was awakened this early. Finding the phone in the second pocket he looked in, he answered it before the caller gave up.

"Hel—" Before he could finish, a high-strung female was hitting all kinds of notes he didn't think existed. "Hello. Who is this?" he asked when he found a break in her yapping.

"Who is this? Where's Anna?"

"Anna's barely awake. She's drinking her coffee."

"Well, who are you?"

"Jake Lawrence, ma'am." He tried giving her the Lawrence charm his brother was always reminding him about, but it didn't seem to be working in this particular situation.

"What have you done to Anna? I know good and well she wouldn't be with you if her life was in jeopardy and you were the only person alive who was capable of saving her." Her voice was so high pitched that the only way to keep from losing all his hearing was to hold the phone several inches away from his ear.

So the woman knew about his history with Anna. She sounded a little over the top to be Anna's friend, but what did he know? Em had been her best friend since grade school. "Who is this again? I forgot."

"I didn't tell you my name, you worthless bastard."

All right. He'd thought he was pretty good with women, but this one was a force to be reckoned with.

"I don't know who you are, but I can tell you that I've done nothing to Anna. She came home with me on her own...well, sorta. Anyway, she is here by choice. You should be thanking me. I took care of her last night."

"I'm sure you did," she said. And Jake could almost see her rolling her eyes at him through the phone.

The woman irritated him to no end. What did she really know? "Okay, you're really too much for me to handle this early in the morning. Can she call you back later in the day? Thank you. Oh, and ma'am, have a nice day."

Before she could get another word in, he hit End, muted the phone, and slipped it back in Anna's jeans. What a psycho. He hoped to God he never had to come face-to-face with her.

"You know she's just looking out for me." Anna stood in the doorway, clearly having heard the whole conversation with the crazy woman.

"How long have you been standing there?"

"Long enough to know you just got an earful from Liza."

"You sure do have some opinionated friends. I

thought Em was bad, but oh no, this woman is a piece of work. Is she single?"

"No. Why?"

"Just thinking she would be perfect for Bradley. He needs a woman like that to keep him in line."

"I like Bradley too much to let him endure Liza."

"Yeah, I figured out *how much* you like Bradley last night."

Anna looked sexy as hell in his clothes, holding a cup of coffee, leaning against the doorjamb. She turned him on by just looking at him through sleepy eyes, but he couldn't let her get away with the whole Bradley thing. That was pretty low, even if she had been drunk. That hurt.

Her gaze fell to her coffee cup. "I walked right into that. I don't remember much about what happened after I had my first couple of drinks. Sorry."

"Well, just don't proposition my little brother again."

She winced. "I did no such thing."

"Honey, you were so wasted you don't know what you did. I'm glad I was there. Otherwise, you would be waking up in Bradley's bed instead of on my couch."

"Was it really that bad?"

"Not going to lie—yes, it was that bad."

Jake walked the few steps to her and leaned down to lay a kiss on her cheek. When she didn't pull away, he went a little further. She was sober now, and whatever she allowed him to do, he would do in a heartbeat. Tilting her chin up with his pointer finger allowed him to stare into her eyes. If he'd asked if he could kiss her, she might've told him to go fuck himself, so he didn't. Just going for it and accepting that she might slap him, he bent down and touched his lips to hers.

The nipples jutting from the white T-shirt she wore were proof she was responding to the simple touch of affection. Sliding his tongue across her soft lips, he wet them to prepare her for what he would do next. A soft sigh escaped from her lips, and a sexy breath wrapped around his cock. He braced both his arms on either side of her and pinned her to the doorframe. He couldn't let her go before at least getting a small taste of her. Her lips parted, and his tongue slipped inside.

A kiss had never done this to him before. He had seen some beautiful women, but he hadn't wanted one as much as he wanted Anna.

"God, I want you so bad right now." He groaned while pushing up against her body, making her feel what she was doing to him.

"Jake." Her voice came out as a whimper against his mouth.

"Yes, baby."

She put her hands up to his chest to push him back a step. It took him a minute to figure out what she was doing. If he hadn't gotten the point by her pushing him away, he got it when he looked at her face.

"What's wrong? Did I go too fast? We can slow down if you want."

"No, you did nothing wrong. I can't do this. Last night was a mistake. I'm sorry for leading you on. I shouldn't have come out to your living room naked." She shook her head. "I'm sorry."

"Don't ever be sorry for that. If you hadn't been drunk, I would have hauled you to my bed in a heartbeat. You know that, don't you?"

"It's not that. I'm glad you didn't. It would only make things harder right now. I can't be with you…ever. I was drunk and not thinking straight. You did us both a favor when you turned me down."

"I don't see how I did us any favors. You're making me regret my decision."

"Me sleeping with you last night would almost be as bad as me going home with Bradley drunk."

"You're fucking kidding me right now, aren't you? You're telling me I mean as much to you as my brother does. Well, isn't that just dandy? I try doing the honorable thing for a change, and I get shit on."

"I didn't mean it like that, Jake."

"I don't let you leave with my drunk brother, who would've been down your pants before you made it out of Em's drive. I bring you here to watch over you, you come in my living room buck naked, and even then I turn you down, being the good guy I'm usually not. And now you're telling me you should've just gone home with Bradley. That's fucked up, and you know it."

Was he really hearing her right? What the hell kind of remark was that? He left her standing in the bathroom and headed to kitchen. When she walked in the room a couple of minutes later, he had his back to her. He was dumping food down the disposal, throwing dishes around in the process, because it was the only way to let out the anger burning a hole in his gut. What he needed was to be in the batting cage. In his baseball days he wasn't known as a homerun hitter, but right about now he could put on a show at a homerun derby.

"Jake, look at me."

His head snapped around to face her. The anger he

knew all too well rose in his chest, and it was just a matter of time before he did something he wouldn't be able to take back. A plate went smashing into the wall across the room before he could control himself. It was nowhere near Anna, but the sound echoed through the room, and she jumped back anyway.

"This is fucked up. You want my brother, go get him. I'm sure he'll pencil you in sometime this week."

Jake was still ranting when she slid to the floor, gripping her knees.

****

Anna couldn't hear his voice or see his face anymore. Her ears rang, and little black spots danced in her line of vision. Once again she was a young girl stuck and unable to do anything. The darkness was coming, and if she didn't do something, she would only be giving in to those feelings. No matter how much she inwardly screamed at herself to get off the floor, she physically couldn't move. Her heart beat wildly, and sweat drenched her skin.

Not now—get up, Anna. Do something. You have to do something, anything.

She could see it all over again. Her mother had sat in this same spot after her stepdad slammed her against the wall. Her mother's face had been pale and blank. As a child, Anna had been terrified for her mother but was unable to do anything to help her. She endured her own hell at night and wasn't strong enough to face the same hell during the day.

"Anna? Anna, you okay, baby? I'm so sorry. I didn't mean to startle you. Can you stand?" Jake pulled her toward him.

"Don't touch me!" It crossed her mind to just give

up, crawl into a ball, and block it all out. But she couldn't do that. Not this time. She needed to get up and face the demons that scared her. "Don't touch me, you bastard." Her voice came out weak, but it held the same intensity as if she had spat it in his face.

He stared at her for a long, quiet moment before speaking. "I'm sorry, Anna. I didn't mean to scare you. When I get mad, I lose my temper sometimes. I'm just so sorry." He rubbed both hands over his stubbled face.

She was thankful when he backed away from her and the wall she leaned against. He planted himself in a kitchen chair and stared at the floor. She could tell he was mad at himself, and she would have felt sorry for him if she wasn't so pissed.

She continued sitting on the kitchen floor, not yet trusting her legs. She didn't need him rushing to her side if she just happened to do a face-plant on the linoleum. Instead, she sat in place until her breathing slowed and her eyesight cleared again.

"Jake, I'm going to get up now. If I lose my balance and start falling, let me." She looked him in the eye to emphasize her request. He wouldn't just let her fall, but she wanted to make it clear that she didn't want him near her. He nodded, so she inched her way up the wall until she stood straight. He watched her carefully, but he didn't make any movements in her direction.

She left him sitting and steadily made her way to the bathroom so she could be alone. She splashed cool water on her cheeks, staring at the face that glared back at her. Her saddened eyes resembled those of her mother's all those years ago. "What am I doing here, Mom?" She turned her attention upward, as if her mother could see and give her the answer she needed.

She stripped out of Jake's clothes and slipped back into her pants and tank top. The smell of Jessie's homemade punch, still embedded in her clothes, brought back a night she just wanted to forget. She took out her cell, seeing five missed calls—all from Liza. Being reminded that Jake was trouble and that she needed to stay a county away from him was not what Anna wanted to hear. Instead, she punched in Em's number.

"Hey, Em, can you come pick me up at my old house? Yes, everything is fine. Tommy's truck is okay. See you in a bit." She closed the phone and pulled herself up on the counter to wait on Em. When she heard the SUV pulling in the driveway, she headed out of the bathroom, past the kitchen. Jake still sat in the chair. He gave her one last look, a look that told her he was desperately sorry but didn't know what to do except let her walk out the door.

She was glad he didn't try to stop her. Not even giving the house one last glance, she left him.

Chapter Twelve

"So what happened? Why couldn't Jake drive you to my house? He has to bring Tommy's truck back anyway."

"Oh, he was still asleep. I didn't want to wake him." Anna didn't dare look at her friend. Instead, she stared out the passenger window. She never could lie. Em would see straight through her story.

"Anna, Sober Jake doesn't sleep past seven. What's really going on?"

"It's nothing, really. We stayed up late watching television. He must have been tired." She was partly telling the truth, so that couldn't exactly be telling a lie.

"Don't tell me you two stayed up watching some old sitcom and not getting it on."

"I didn't come here to *get it on* with anyone. Please drop it, all right?" She needed to change the subject, quickly. "What do we need to do for your wedding this week?"

Em left the subject of her and Jake alone to talk about her wedding, which was coming up in less than a week. For the next short minutes back to Em's house, they talked about flowers, the cake, getting with the photographer, and tons of other last-minute details Anna couldn't really focus on at the moment. She loved her friend and was thrilled for the happiness she'd found with Tommy, but she wasn't up for wedding talk.

When they arrived at Em's, she took her purse and shoes Em had remembered to bring with her. She hugged her friend and promised to call that afternoon to discuss their plans for the week.

Alone at last.

Garrett wasn't in the office, so she didn't have to worry about him pestering her for information about where she'd been last night and why she was just now getting home. He was a nice enough guy, but she didn't want him to start being nosy.

She walked into the studio apartment and flopped on the bed. What a night…what a day. And it wasn't even nine yet. All she wanted was a bath, but she settled on a shower. She couldn't wait to go back home and soak for an hour in her tub. The thought made her want to pack up and leave right then, and she might have if it wasn't for the wedding and her responsibility to her friend. She had to stay for the wedding, and then she was out of Patience for good. She jumped in the shower long enough to wash up. After putting on panties and a tank top, she crawled under the covers. Sleep, that was what she needed. And it just so happened that she had no problems sleeping during the day.

****

"Why did I let you talk me into this? This is ridiculous. You're about to get married, Em. Why do you want to be here, again?" Anna didn't like the idea of being at her old high school—at a bachelor auction at that.

She wasn't interested in having a bachelor. Anna had only agreed to come out tonight because she'd missed out on some girl time over the past couple of

188

days.

She and Jake hadn't talked since their fight about something she couldn't understand. It had to be about more than just Bradley. While she'd sat on the kitchen floor, he'd sent her mind back to a series of events where cigarette smoke filled the air, people screamed, and deodorant cans, dishes, or vases were hurled across the room. She needed to concentrate on getting Jake out of her house, mind, and dreams so her healing process could begin. He was making things impossible by dragging the damn dates out and not letting her get the intense, hot, tempting moments out of the way.

"I told you, you need to get out and have some fun. Plus, if you win us a bachelor, you might get out of helping finish the bridesmaids' bouquets."

"Wait—you never said I have to bid."

"Well, you can't expect me to, can ya? I'm getting married in a few days. Hell, Anna, that will just give the old women at the hair shop something juicy to talk about."

They made their way through the crowded room of single women, all ready with wads of cash and checkbooks, wanting to get the hottest male they could afford. Apparently, Em wanted to get in the front row. They pushed and shoved through the collection of fragrances until Em was satisfied with the perfect spot. The women ranged from their early twenties to her sixty-year-old next-door neighbor, Ms. Edna. Anna wasn't even going to bring it up. It was mind boggling to think of Ms. Edna bidding along with others half her age.

That didn't stop Em, though. "Is that Edna? We need to watch out for her. I've seen the tips she's been getting. We can't let her outbid us."

"What? Let's get back to the part where I have to bid so you can get help for your wedding. Do you actually trust a man—a single man at that—to make your bouquets?"

"I trust a single man more than a married one. A single man has more experience at using his hands. I bet they are better than Mrs. Lena at the Flower and Gift Shop...cheaper too."

"Yuck, does Tommy know who he's marrying? All you talk about is sex, sex, and more sex."

Em scanned the crowd, pointing out the competition, ignoring the little comment. She was serious about this? She gestured to her left. "There's Carly. Don't let her get any of the good ones. I refuse to lose to her. Anybody else is okay, but not her. I'm tired of her hitting on Tommy, along with any other unavailable male, and I will take her down."

Anna laughed. "Whoa, killer."

How could she forget the five-foot, seven-inches tall busty blonde at Ollie's the other night? Every woman and man for that matter could tell that Carly had her sights on Jake, and she looked like a woman who was used to getting what she wanted. She agreed with Em—Carly was not outbidding them.

Talking to her best friend was not going to get her out of this stupid idea, one that would result in embarrassment, or something worse. Not that she had anything better to do. She just wished to be anywhere but there. If she wanted to think of hot single men, she would just pick up her current read, which provided as much excitement as she needed. But she had been a lousy friend lately with the whole party incident and being MIA the past couple of days. What the hell.

"Fine. I'll do the bidding, but you will do the buying. Deal?"

They shook hands and agreed on their game plan. They decided Jessie would be bidding on Bradley, for what Em said were obvious reasons, and a few women who Em worked with would be going for sexy firemen or cops. They had to worry about Carly, Ms. Edna for some crazy reason, and Georgia. Who would the bubbly woman bid on?

Em gave her three hundred dollars and an extra two hundred in case they needed to outdo Carly.

"How much was Mrs. Lena charging for the bouquets, anyway?"

"Eight hundred big ones. Crazy, huh? I've known the batty woman all my life, and she can't cut me a break. We went with her for the bride-and-groom party, so you would think she'd give me a discount. Oh no… Well, she lost my business. I will do it myself or get a hot guy to do it before I pay her that much. It's the principle of the thing, you know?"

Anna had known some woman back in Linden who paid over a thousand but decided against bringing that up. Em had a heated opinion, and Anna wasn't going to worsen the situation. She would just be the type of friend who would bid on a hot guy for her. Tommy was a good man to deal with Em on a daily basis. She had a way of keeping life interesting, but at times that full force personality could be exhausting too.

"Okay, it's starting. Get ready to find me a guy."

The lights dimmed, women squealed, and the song "I'm Too Sexy" blasted through the speakers on both sides of the stage. Just then a dark-haired fireman came out and ripped off his thin shirt, leaving him in only jeans and flip-flops. Was it just her, or were fireman supposed to come out wearing only uniform pants held up by red suspenders? Maybe that was just a stereotype or something you only saw in calendars. He was extremely attractive, but he just didn't do it for her.

Baseball players were more her thing, and eleven years ago she had been burned by one, so now she was left with nothing that made her hot inside.

The casually dressed firefighter went for two hundred dollars, while a few more men came out and were auctioned off for one hundred a piece. Two of them were a little potbellied but would have made good helpers. The other guy looked terrified. Anna was thankful Em passed, because if the guy was scared of all these screaming women, he definitely would have wanted to run from Em.

Oh, wait—not all women were coming for just help around the house. They expected a night of full-blown pleasure. The thought made her mind jump to Jake, but before it could linger, the next guy strutted his way out on the stage.

"…and this one runs a successful business here in town. Garrett's a catch, ladies. Get those checkbooks ready. Let's start the bidding at fifty dollars." The principal was really trying to sell the men. It was apparent the woman wanted money for the athletics department, and she was willing to say anything good about each guy to get the most money for them. "Do I hear a hundred?"

"Bid two hundred. Garrett is perfect." Em yanked Anna's hand up, eager to win the businessman who had caused Anna so much trouble.

"We, I mean, I bid two hundred," Anna yelled out.

Garrett grinned like a possum. Great. He was clearly going to take this the wrong way. God, why did she let Em get her into the worst situations? It was as if she were back in high school again and Em was dragging her on a double date with a pimple-faced boy just so she could go out with the hot older brother. This is where her strong backbone would come in handy.

"Two fifty," some woman in the back shouted, but Anna couldn't make out her face through the sea of people. Garrett was going for some serious dough.

"...sold to the woman in the back. Come claim your man." The principal, who was having too much fun, hit the podium with her bare hand.

"Oh. My. God. Is that Georgia?" Anna hadn't expected that. "Why would Georgia want Garrett? She sees him every day."

"Maybe there's a little office romance going on there." Em elbowed her in the ribs, making her double over.

"Calm down. Jeez, you've probably just bruised my insides."

"Quit being a baby and concentrate. We've lost our first guy. We need to stay focused."

"There have already been six or more men who have strutted their stuff. Why haven't you let me bid more?"

"I've got one other man in mind. I'll let you know when I see him. I've heard he is *extra* good with his hands, if you know what I mean. Now shush. Here comes Bradley. Let's see how much Jessie is willing to throw down."

"How can you be so sure Jessie will spend her

hard-earned money on a guy who's never had a relationship longer than a week?" To Anna, Jessie came across as a stern woman who wouldn't allow any man to run over her. Not that Bradley wasn't handsome and even more charming than his brother. It just didn't seem likely that Jessie would waste her time on a guy who was so dead set on never settling down. At least that was the way Jake made him sound.

"Just watch. Believe me—I know these things. She doesn't think I notice, but she's had a longing for him for years."

Em was right. Jessie was up to six hundred dollars on the man looking comfortable in tight pants, work boots, and button-down shirt revealing half his chest. Damn Lawrence boys. He tipped his straw hat when he saw her and Em, flirting in his own way. Flirting was probably just what he did to all women, young and old.

"…eight hundred…nine hundred." A young woman up front yelling out above the crowd prompted Jessie to up her bidding price. Jessie wasn't the only one who couldn't resist the Lawrence charm. This girl looked not even twenty, probably didn't have the money. Mouth open wide, she appeared to be in a trance or something. "Nine hundred and fifty dollars."

The principal hit her podium with the palm of her hand again. "…sold to the woman up front. Have fun!"

Anna and Em simultaneously turned back to the spot where Jessie had been standing at the beginning of the auction. She was gone. The hardheaded woman was probably spitting mad at the thought of losing to some young girl who had spent her life savings on a one-night stand that would result in Bradley forgetting the girl's name by sunrise. Her heart went out to Jessie.

Even though Bradley maybe didn't know he was breaking her heart, his never-ending interest in other women had to hurt all the same. But Anna doubted Bradley was innocent when it came to Jessie.

"Shit. Jessie is going to be pissed. She doesn't like to lose, particularly not to another woman—and especially when it comes to Bradley, whether she wants to admit it or not."

"Jessie knows Bradley takes a new woman home every other night. Why would this be any different?"

"There's a big difference. Usually Jessie is flirting and rubbing a little too close to other guys in front of Bradley, showing him what he will never get. Tonight she put herself out there, alone, and she just got her pride stomped on. We might not wanna get in her way for a while. It could get ugly."

"You're planning a wedding to her brother. We can't exactly ignore her."

"Right. Well, that sucks for us."

"Now, ladies, we saved the most beloved and heart-breaking bachelor in Patience for last. Let's start the bidding at two hundred."

A man wearing a faded gray T-shirt, jeans that were neither tight nor loose—just fitting in the area that mattered to most of the women in the room—and the usual ball cap shading his dangerous eyes waltzed on the stage. Jake just got better and better looking each time she saw him.

Her mouth went completely dry.

The women in the crowd started hollering as if he were some rock star, but duh, he used to be a major leaguer, and women liked that. He also was easy on the eyes.

"Anna, get it together here." Em snapped her fingers, bringing her back from the same trance the young woman had with Bradley.

"What?"

"Start bidding. It's already up to three hundred. Bid four."

"You're joking, right? I can't bid on Jake. How's he going to help you with a wedding?"

"We've already discussed this. He's the best with using his hands." Em placed her hands on her hips and practically rolled her eyes. "Now start shouting out numbers."

"No. If you want him, then you start handing out the money."

"We had a deal, Anna. It's my wedding, and I deserve to have whomever I want. Please do this for me. You don't want me to be the center of town gossip, do you? Because that's what will happen if I do the bidding."

This was going to be worse than Jessie losing her guy to that googly-eyed girl.

What the hell—she just needed to get it over with. It's not like she had to take him home. He would be helping Em, and that was it.

"Five hundred," she yelled a bit too loudly before she could talk herself out of it.

"Come on. Say six. Carly is eyeing him and is willing to pay a small fortune for the talented baseball player."

As if the woman in question could read Em's lips, Carly hollered over all the groaning single women who couldn't afford the high amount. "Nine hundred thirty-dollars and sixty-two cents."

"Wow—did she just spend her last cent?" Em asked.

"I think she did." Even Anna was astonished. The idea of losing like Jessie was too much. The thought of him going home to another woman would only cause her to toss and turn all night. As hard as it was to admit, she couldn't stand thinking about him and other women. He might be an overly cocky bastard most of the time, but as Em said, they couldn't lose to Carly.

"Sold!" the auctioneer called out. All the women parted ways, some complaining, others congratulating one another.

What just happened? She glanced around the room, looking for something that made sense. It couldn't have been over. She wasn't done yet.

A tap on the shoulder had Anna turning around a tad too quickly to face the problem she didn't even know she had—Carly. Her tight black dress allowed little room for anything else underneath.

"Hope there's no hard feelings. I didn't know you still had a thing for Jake, honestly. We made plans to go out sometime, so I just picked the time. Pretty good strategy, huh?"

Was this bimbo serious? Okay, Anna didn't know if Carly really was a bimbo, but at the moment she didn't care about accuracy. For one, she didn't have a thing for Jake. And two, he was the one making her go out with him, and it must not be just her because he had apparently made plans with Barbie here. She couldn't speak. The room fell silent, even though she could see mouths moving.

Finally, Em saw she was having trouble. "Oh, it's no problem. Anna was getting Jake for me."

"You?" Carly held a hand up to cover her mouth. "Are you and Jake...you know?"

"Now, Carly, do you think I would really tell you something like that?"

"Right. Anyway, have a nice night. Too bad you didn't land a guy, Anna."

The sly remark pissed Anna off and must have made Em even hotter because before Carly could stroll away to claim her prize, Em hollered out above the women near them, "Just so you know, if Anna really wanted Jake, he wouldn't be leaving with you right now."

A sense of dread washed over Anna. She had embarrassed herself more than Jessie had, and to make matters worse, Em was announcing to a crowd of gossipy women that Anna probably wanted a reunion with Jake.

Em didn't notice the effect losing Jake had. If she did, she knew better than to bring it up. Goodbye hugs were given. Em left to help her mother with more wedding preparations. Anna had parked her car in the back gravel lot she'd used when she was a teenager. It was a surreal feeling to be walking out of the same doors to the same parking spot. The only difference was that now she was an independent woman who got to call the shots when it came to her life.

She put the top down on her car and soaked up the cool night breeze. Speeding out of the lot, she longed to be the woman who ended up with Jake tonight. He'd only given her a taste of what he was capable of, and that hadn't satisfied her. This kind of passionate desire wasn't going to go away by just spending a few hours curled up with her nighttime reading material.

She bet Jake was an amazing lover, and as Em loved to point out, he was amazing with his hands. God, she just needed to shove these feelings down to the point where they could never resurface. What she needed was to do something un-Anna-like, and she knew exactly where to go to do it.

****

After a quick drive through town, Anna sat at an oversize table facing the only television in the bar. Except for a glass of wine before coming back to Patience, she had rarely drunk alcohol. Now she could be a bartender. Tonight she wanted something different. She didn't want anything to make her plastered and embarrass her any more than she had earlier in the night, but something that coated her insides and made her forget about her life for just a few hours.

She didn't want to think about Jake and the woman he was taking back to her house. He was more than a little angry over her being drunk and hitting on Bradley, but he could take a woman home and nothing would be said about it. Men were jackasses. The thought of him and Carly together made her sick, but she pushed it aside and concentrated on the thing she could control—herself.

The nightmares from the last couple of nights had rattled her more than she liked to admit, and she needed a distraction, something other than Jake. Maybe being out with strangers and having a few drinks would help take the pressure off. If others could have a drink or two to help them unwind, then she could too.

Alan Jackson blaring on the jukebox, balls cracking at the pool tables, and laughter were the only sounds she could hear. The scents of greasy foods and cheap cologne filling the air forced her to remember what she was doing. She'd never been to a bar alone, but for once she didn't feel as if she needed someone around to make her comfortable.

A round, balding man taking her order suggested the perfect drink for her. She ordered two with a large helping of chicken wings. Because she didn't want to draw attention to herself, she kept her gaze locked on the flat screen, which of course was playing an Atlanta baseball game. She picked up a handful of peanuts and tossed them in her mouth. Sitting there watching the franchise Jake had once played for was complete torture. Not to mention her team was playing just a station away.

Ollie, the owner, brought her order with a little wink. It wouldn't hurt to ask. "Hey, Ollie, you know it would mean a lot to me if I could watch the Sparks game."

Patience was a diehard baseball town, and she didn't know what more Ollie would want when it came to changing the channel. Her simple white tank was cut low and snug. When she bent over just a bit to retrieve her drink, his gaze dropped to her chest. His cheeks instantly turned rosy red. That was a mistake, but it got the job done. Score one for the girls! She should feel dirty, ashamed, something, but instead she didn't care if the old man got a look-see.

"Uh, sure thing, honey. Now if a riot breaks out, I'll have to change it back, ya see?"

"I understand. You've just made my night."

Now, this was going to be a good night. The first sip of her amaretto sour made her nose turn up a little, but after the next couple of swallows, her mood lightened, and she began enjoying the game, food, and drinks. After she pulled her hair back in a tie, she grabbed a wing and gave the television her complete attention.

"Good God, ump, do you not see that ball was way off the plate? Damn it!" Her man, Jax Dalton, was at the plate, and the damn ump had just called strike three. Her team was down by two, which wasn't a big deal seeing that it was only the sixth inning. The New York Sparks were known to do their best work in the ninth.

Only a few murmurs were spoken after her little umpire-bashing rant, but other than that, no one cared about the New York game being on. Good thing, because she would have fought any man in the place.

One day she was going to be in those stands cheering on her team.

"Is this chair taken?"

She was so wrapped up in the double play she didn't even look up to see the man standing beside her. She kicked the seat out, never allowing her focus to leave the screen.

"Do you always come to bars alone? It's not safe for a woman like you to be alone in a place like this."

Chapter Thirteen

Jake knew it was going to be an interesting night when he walked into Ollie's to see Anna slouched back in a chair, drinking some girly drink and forcing chicken wings down her throat. She'd even talked Ollie into changing the channel. The girl was good, because nobody had ever accomplished that before. But then again, nobody in Patience would dream of watching a team other than the Rockets.

She looked exceptionally hot in her plain, fitted top, jeans that were cut at the knees, and flip-flops revealing red-painted toenails. No wonder Ollie gave in so easily.

He took a seat at the dark far side of the bar. He was in a foul mood after the auction. Nothing made sense.

"What can I get you, Jake?" Minny asked.

"Just a beer."

"How'd the auction go? Heard someone say you went for some major cash," she said nonchalantly while pulling the cap off his beer and placing the bottle on a napkin in front of him.

This was not what he wanted to talk about. "I guess you can say that, but it was a mix-up. Now I'm here drinking a beer with you and watching a damn Sparks game."

"I know. The locals haven't complained yet. A lot

of the men like Anna, if you know what I mean." She winked and scooted off to her next customer.

Yeah, he knew what she meant, and he didn't like it one bit. A lot of guys were eyeing her, but luckily no one had made a move.

Why would Anna bid on him? And why in hell did she bid on Garrett? There was no doubt in his mind that she felt something, but for her to openly express that in public was hard to wrap his mind around. It took balls to do what she'd done. He'd hurt her the other day. Well, he'd done more than that. He'd fucked up. Anger had gotten the best of him. So he couldn't blame her for leaving.

Walking out onto the stage, he'd seen her, and at that moment, being in front of a hundred screaming women didn't appeal to him. He only wanted one woman, and he couldn't have her. She seemed to be struggling with the idea of bidding on him, but in the end she had, and she had lost.

Fuck.

Why did Carly have to be there and ruin his night? It was for charity, and he was willing to be bought by Edna in exchange for yard work, but he was not some sex slave. He could see that was exactly what Carly had in mind, and he wasn't a cheater. And whether Anna wanted to believe it or not, they were dating.

"What the fuck?" Jake muttered behind clenched teeth when a man strode over to Anna and took a seat next to her, a little too close at that. So some bastard had decided to make a move on his woman.

Tex had been interested in Anna since the bride-and-groom party. The guy had a "love them and leave them" reputation.

He gripped his beer bottle to the point his knuckles turned white. Tex was a good buddy to play softball or go out fishing with, but Jake was not going to sit there and watch him take advantage of Anna. "Minny, I'll take another."

"You sure?"

"Yes. I'm not drunk, damn it."

The spunky girl ran off to fetch another beer he really didn't need, but if he didn't have something in his hand, he was liable to go over and punch Tex right in the face.

He had thought excessive drinking and fighting every asshole he ran into was a thing of the past, but now with Anna back in town, that's all he could think about. When he couldn't be with her, he drank, and if any guy touched her, he wanted to beat the living shit out of them. If he wasn't careful, he would be going back to his old ways, and it wouldn't have anything to do with his injury or loss of his mother.

Tex gripped Anna's hand and started twirling her around. Jake didn't like that another man had his hands on her. It wasn't out of jealousy. It was that they were technically dating for the next week or so. God, he was thinking like a woman. *Get a grip, dude.*

New York was winning, and Anna was clearly in a good mood. It was the bottom of the ninth, and it looked as if the blue and white were going to take this one. He would let her enjoy the win, but after that, he was getting her away from Tex.

When the last ball was thrown and New York won, giving them the best record in baseball, Jake decided it was time to interrupt the little celebration going on.

But the craziest thing happened. Tex looked up to

see Jake coming. He then turned and gave Anna a light kiss on the mouth and walked toward the exit.

How dare the little fuck kiss her right in front of my face and then run away like a coward. No need to start anything. Those days were in the past. He was a better man. Tex was gone, and Anna would not be going home with the son of a bitch.

****

"I see your pansy team won again. You must feel pretty damn good."

Anna recognized the male voice coming from behind her without having to turn around. She could feel his breath on her neck and smell the cologne that had become familiar to her. Just the sound of his deep, manly voice sent a chill through her entire body, making her stomach do funny things. She didn't want to turn around to look into those deep blue eyes, most likely shaded with a ball cap, and wonder what he had just done with Carly.

Quit feeling sorry for yourself and turn your ass around.

"You can't call them a pansy team when they have the best record in baseball right now."

The space separating them buzzed with an electric current. She couldn't move. The only thing she could do was stand there and torture herself by looking at a man she would never have.

"You have a good night with Tex?" he asked.

He said it in a way that told her a couple of things—one, he'd been watching her for some time if he saw Tex, and two, he hadn't spent any time with Carly. If he had, he wasn't as good as everyone said, and she highly doubted that. The thoughts made her feel giddy, or maybe the two drinks had.

"Actually, I did. It was fun to have someone to watch the game with."

"You know he was only interested in getting down your pants? He couldn't care less about your precious ball team."

"Jealous, Jake?" She gave her head a playful tilt.

"I'm not jealous of that asshole," he retorted with little conviction. "I just wouldn't let any woman who had been drinking walk out the door with him."

"I wasn't leaving with him. I was simply watching a baseball game with the guy. Plus, I thought you two were friends?"

"We are. How do you think I know all this?"

Both fists were clenched at his sides. He looked as if he could take down a semi. What was the deal? She hadn't expected this. After all, he was the one who had left with some Barbie doll tonight. He was the one who accused her of wanting his brother. And he was the one who had smashed a plate against the kitchen wall. When she took a minute to let all three of those things sink in, she was mad all over again.

"Well, thanks for—"

"Why the Sparks?" Jake interrupted.

Baseball was a safer topic of conversation. Hearts couldn't be broken unless the World Series was involved. "Their team is always stacked with the best players, which always keeps things interesting. They have more championships than any other sports franchise in history. And let's not forget about Jax Dalton."

"No, I'm not talking about stats. I mean, why do you follow that team instead of the one you were raised on? Why did you quit watching Patience's team? My team."

Okay, turned out baseball could not be a trusted topic. At least not between them. "Because I didn't think of you when I watched them." After dropping that truth-bomb, she grabbed her purse and made her way past him, but not before brushing up against his side. Everything in her body became aware of the feelings she'd been having for the past week. She tingled in places he hadn't even touched, and the feeling only intensified when he reached out and grabbed her arm before she could step away.

She was forced to look up at his face with her body pressed hard against his. He made no move to release her. She wasn't sure how long she looked into his eyes, trying to read his thoughts.

"It seems you're thinking about me now, even after watching a New York game. And as far as Tex goes, the guy is a jerk when it comes to women. I was only looking out for you. Why can't you understand that?" His voice was more tender but stern. He eased his grip, but not enough that she could pull her arm out. Did she want him to let her go?

"I do understand that, but I'm a big girl. I know when a guy is only interested in what's under my panties," she said with a shaky voice.

His gaze fell to said panties. Well, actually, he could only see her jeans, but the intensity in his stare made her aware of what he was actually envisioning. She kept her gaze on his face, because she wanted to appear strong and not rattled by their closeness. With his hands on her, she couldn't think logically.

"Will you let me drive you home?" His voice was

low, just above a whisper that blew through her ear. It was sexy and intoxicating. She could have melted in a puddle right there at his feet.

"W-why?" Did he really have plans to take her home and see what was under her panties? Did she want him to?

"You've been drinking. It's been made clear you can't handle your liquor."

He did have a point. She'd proven that at the bachelorette party. However, she didn't want to put herself in the same position again. While she knew he wouldn't hurt her, the memories from that night were still fresh in her mind. She wasn't drunk now and didn't need rescuing.

"I'm not drunk, Jake."

He pulled her closer, causing her to let out a startled cry, and allowing her to feel every part of him, even the bulge pushed against his zipper. She fixed her stare on the place they touched and noticed she was rubbing against him. It was the only natural thing to do.

What was happening here? They were in a public place, for God's sake.

She could barely croak out "Ja-ke."

"You feel that?" he asked. "Answer me, damn it. Do you feel what you do to me?"

And if her brain hadn't been made of mush, she might've jerked out of his hold, demanding he never speak to her that way again. But because she was having trouble thinking and speaking at the same time, she gave him a pass. And because, after all, this was her Jake, a man she'd loved so much at one time that he'd had the ability to hurt her badly.

All she could muster up was a slight headshake.

This was too much for her.

He was too much for her.

"This is what you do to me every time I think of you, whether you're in the room or not. So can I please drive you home?"

"Yes."

****

Jake stole a kiss before shutting the truck door and hurried over to his side, almost sliding across the hood of his truck. He couldn't leave Ollie's parking lot fast enough. He stirred up a little gravel and headed in the direction to either one of their places to finally have his way with Ms. Anna Kelly. Hearing her simple *yes* was music to his ears.

"Your place or mine?" he rasped.

"Mine." Good. It was closer. He didn't know how much longer he was going to be able to hold out as his cock throbbed against the front of his jeans.

He'd never wanted, or desperately needed, a woman as he did Anna at this moment. Usually, he didn't feel so drawn to the opposite sex to the point that it was a matter of life or death. This was different. This was a hunger only she could appease. He had to get to their destination, quickly.

Somehow he made it to her apartment before having to pull over to the side of the road and take her right there for anyone to see. He came to a full stop only inches from the apartment door. After leaping from his monster of a truck, he jogged over to the passenger side before Anna had a chance to open her door and maneuver her way down. He lifted her with ease and then brought her to the ground.

Because the door was unlocked, all she had to do

was turn the knob.

He switched on the lamp nearest the door and brought the room to a soft glow. His back was only turned from her for half a second, but apparently that was too long. Without skipping a beat, she was on him.

She wrapped both hands around his neck and kissed him as he had planned to do to her. In response, he kissed her back with equal fervor. This was "the light a fire under your ass" Anna he had seen that day in his driveway.

This side of her was so hot and unexpected. The girl he'd known back in high school would never have latched onto him like this. That seventeen-year-old girl could kiss with passion, bring him to his knees with just a look, and was beyond the prettiest girl he'd wanted to sleep with, but she had not been the type who took the initiative in the back seat of his mom's car. That was his doing. And back then, he had been a teenage boy who couldn't keep his hands off his beautiful girlfriend, but a few times he wondered what it would be like if she came on strong.

It had taken eleven years, but he was finally getting his damn wish.

He pulled away long enough to lift the shirt over her head, showing just enough cleavage and revealing a simple white bra. Her perky breasts were what a man would refer to as a handful.

"Good God, woman, you're killing me here," he growled. The night she'd walked out of his bathroom beautifully naked, he'd wanted her, but the timing was wrong. That night had also been different. But this was perfect. This was desire, passion, and need all rolled up in one. That night had been all about his taking care of a woman he would always want to protect. Sure, he'd been tempted by her nakedness, but he liked to consider himself a gentleman. And no matter how hard it had been for him to turn her down, he knew sex was not something she'd needed right then.

"Take this off." Anna grasped his shirt as if it were the only thing to save her.

"My pleasure, sweetness." He slowed down from a wildcat's pace to something that she would remember.

He unbuttoned each button, slowly, letting her see all of him, little…by…little. He wanted her to crave him to the point she was in so much sexual pain that she begged him to relieve her. Not that he doubted her, but he needed to make sure she wanted him as badly as he longed for her, the way he had desired her since that first day she'd stomped up his driveway.

"Come on, Jake. Off with it."

While he was tempted to fulfill her request, he intended to savor this moment with her—the way she tasted and felt beneath him. He wanted to take in the beauty of her green eyes as she gazed up at him with desire when he sank deep inside her.

She fumbled to unbutton his jeans, but he stopped her before she pulled them and his boxers down at the same time. "Not so fast, baby. No need to rush." He gripped both her hands in his. "We have all night."

"I want to have sex with you." Her bold statement almost made him throw her on the bed and claim her as his right then.

Instead he kissed her hard, letting his actions speak louder than any words he could muster. With his mouth still planted on hers, he walked her backward to the queen-sized bed. When the back of her legs hit the bed, he gently pushed her on it.

"Scoot back onto the pillows."

She did, and he crawled inch by inch up her body. Starting with the point between her belly button and jeans, he kissed his way to her perfect breasts. He loved the way her stomach quivered at his touch. It brought him complete satisfaction.

"Rise up on your elbows so I can undo you." The change in control made him happy. While he did love her take-charge attitude, the man in him liked being able to run the show.

He reached behind her and flicked the hook that was holding in the part of her he wanted out and free. After tossing the bra to the side, he cupped both breasts and marveled at how perfect they looked in his hands. While pressing her back to the bed, he pinched one pert nipple and rolled it between his fingers. He loved the way she responded to him.

He ran his tongue over it as she expelled a ragged breath. Meeting her eyes, as if telling her his next move, he suckled one breast and caressed the other with his hand.

She ran her delicate fingers down his spine, and a tingling sensation rippled to his core.

"Woman, I'm the one supposed to be doing the pleasuring right now. I'm dying just from you touching me like that."

A smile broke out on her face. "Just doing my part."

He unbuttoned her jeans, and with her cooperation, they both pulled them down until they resided on the floor. She wore flaming-red panties, reminding him of the high heels she'd had on the night they danced at the bride-and-groom party.

Damn.

Red was for damn sure his new favorite color. His breath caught, and he had to force himself to take another…another…and another breath after that one.

"If I'm going to lie here so exposed, can you at least take yours off as well?"

"Honey, if I didn't love those red-hot panties right now, you would be a lot more exposed."

He complied with her request and removed his jeans. And just to make her feel more comfortable, he shucked his boxers too, plopping free his erection.

She gasped and then bit her bottom lip. Which was the reaction he wanted her to have.

He lay back on top of her, nibbling at her neck, enveloping himself in her feminine scent. He used his hands to explore her body and stopped them on top of her panties. When that didn't satisfy him, he slipped his hand under them, deep into her. She was already ready for him. Not able to stand it anymore, he yanked down the panties he loved and returned to her heat.

Yes.

Her head sank deep into the pillow, and she cried out. "Ohhh…"

She moved against his hand, causing the perfect friction. Every expression displayed desire. Her eyes slammed shut as she moved in a rhythm that suited her. Pleasure overwhelmed him.

"That's right, baby. Go with it."

Her body tensed, and he knew she was about to come. "God, Jake…" Goose bumps broke out all over her skin. Her groans wrapped around his erection, making it hard for him to hold on himself. He had to have her, now.

"How was that, sweetness?"

****

A sexy cloud surrounded her. Her vision was unclear, and her heartbeat fast and unsteady. In only one week she'd had two orgasms from the touch of Jake's hand. If she'd had any doubt about his skills before now, all that was washed away. Now she understood why he'd won a Gold Glove while playing third base—he was skilled at everything he did. And if she didn't know just how talented a baseball player he was, she would've sworn to anyone that giving orgasms was his specialty.

She wanted him inside her, but she wasn't expecting any more pleasure for herself. She longed for the feeling of intimacy with him. Sex could be good, intense, primal even, but when it was with *the* right person, it was so much more than that. That kind of sexual passion was not something she was familiar with, but she had to believe it existed. Otherwise, why did people plan lives together and get married? If sex was just about human instincts, then why stick around for the long haul? Why not just get in and out?

When she had been with her one and only lover, Chris, she'd had one orgasm and knew from listening to other women that it was almost impossible to have two. The guy had to be really good. And while she didn't doubt Jake was talented, she didn't think of herself as a person who would be good in bed and capable of having multiple orgasms. Em had two. Liza had two. Not her.

Chris was a "one night see if you can" type of experience. So she didn't know how she would actually be in the bedroom. Her body had wanted more, but her mind held her back from the pleasure she craved from a man. A man like Jake.

"Amazing," she finally replied. She couldn't wrap her head around what she felt and how open she was with him. Had she really cried out his name? God…yes, she had. Who'd have thunk it? Anna Kelly, a wild woman in Patience.

She liked that he shed his jeans and boxers when she asked. When she moved at a faster pace, Jake slowed things down and put her at ease. He was a considerate lover.

Her breath came out shaky at the sight of his masculine body. With her only having been with one guy in her lifetime—and even then she'd dimmed the lights—she didn't know what to expect. But no matter how many times she'd thought about being with Jake, her idea of his physique still didn't come close to how his body actually looked.

His mouth sank over hers, and all her thoughts were put on hold. The fragrance from the gardenia bushes planted next to the apartment drifted through the open window and filled her head. That and his manly smell wrapped her up in the moment. She needed him tonight. Unable to resist, she pulled him close to her, wanting to feel all of him. They explored each other's mouths until her lips were sore and on the verge of going numb. She wanted Jake inside more than just her mouth. She was desperate to have him deep inside her. Her palms ran over his broad shoulders, through his unruly hair, and down his biceps. She marked his stubbled cheek and strong jaw with her kisses. After all these years, they were finally going to be together.

And what was even better was that she had no fears.

He left her side long enough to go to his jeans and pull out a small square piece of foil. After ripping it open, he quickly rolled the condom over his erection. She was about to feel all of him. The thought of finally getting to be with the man whom at one time she had loved with everything she had made her giddy. She resisted thinking about all the reasons why this was a bad idea and focused on the thoughts that reminded her she was a grown woman who could have big-girl sex with whomever she chose.

"Open up, baby." He came back on top of her, settling between her thighs. "That's right. Now get ready, because your night is just getting started." Brazen desire entered his stare, and she knew she was in for a ride.

Anna leaned up to kiss him while so gently moving against him. Her breasts tingled as they never had, and heat oozed through her veins. She drank in every part of Jake as he sank on top of her. She surrounded herself with his sexiness, while melting against his warmth. She kissed him again, hard, making sure she planted this memory in his mind forever.

He entered her slowly, as if trying not to push too hard. "So tight, baby." Inch by inch he filled her. Completely. She took all of him in, accepting everything he had to give her. As he rocked into her, she matched each thrust. It was simply instinct to move with him.

With the soft light of the moon coming through the window and the glow of the lamp he had switched on, she could see every expression written on his face. He couldn't hide anything if he tried. The desire shining in his eyes had her trembling. Being with Jake was something she'd fantasized about since they were teenagers. But while she knew his feelings for her had been strong back then, right now he showed he wanted her on a much deeper level. Her heart almost exploded in her chest just thinking about it.

She felt sexy tonight because of him.

"Wrap your legs around me," he said.

When she did, he sank even deeper into her. If that was even possible. How was she taking all of him in? She hadn't had sex in several years. He was too big.

He lit a fire inside her as he kissed his way from her mouth down to her neck. *Not the neck.* His kissing and nibbling on her neck left her weak. Just like the first day in the front yard, she tilted it to the side to make it more accessible to him. A soft moan leaked out between her lips. The feeling of his now-hard thrusts and his soft kisses was too much for her system.

His head fell forward as he pumped inside her faster and faster. She met each one, giving him all she had. "So good…so good."

"You too." She was on the verge of another release, and that shocked her. How was this possible? This was a welcome surprise. "Jake?"

"Yes, baby." His breath came out ragged.

"I'm about to…have another one."

"That's not a bad thing. Can't hold back."

With one more thrust she left her body and went somewhere else for a minute or two.

"Just ride it out."

Jake's curses were covered by her own cries as her second orgasm rippled through her body.

"You okay, sweetness?" He rolled them to their sides, wrapping his arms around her body, locking them together in a strong embrace.

"Yeah, just…"

"Faint," he said with an overconfident smile.

"Yeah. Something like that." She'd never felt so exhilarated in all her life. In one night she had revealed her feelings by bidding for her ex-boyfriend in a bachelor auction, gone to a bar alone, accidently showed cleavage just to watch a New York ballgame in Patience of all places, and then come full circle by sleeping with the ex-boyfriend. She really was wild in Patience.

But that still didn't erase all the things that were wrong between her and Jake. He was living in her house. And they'd just had a huge fight, which had resulted in his breaking a dish against the wall. The argument had brought up memories she wanted to bury.

When her stomach settled, she said, "Jake, about the other day—"

"No, not right now. Let's not ruin this. I know we need to talk about that. And I will say that I am more than sorry and could kick myself for the way I frightened you, but for now I would just like to lie here with you if that's all right."

She agreed. Bringing up something that could turn this perfect night into another bad memory wasn't worth it. She had enough of them already, and for once she wanted to have something good, something she could look back on and say *now that was one heck of a night*.

She nodded. "Yeah, we can do that. Jake?"

"Ummm."

"Will you just hold me?"

"No need to worry about that. I was planning to hold you all night, sweetness."

With that they both drifted off, and Anna slept peacefully for the first time in a long time. She didn't require a little blue pill to settle her mind and force her to drift off. And better yet, she slept without any bad dreams. It was a good night and would be a good memory.

Chapter Fourteen

Anna stretched, and every muscle screamed out in delight. She embraced the early morning light that streamed through the trees in the open window across from her bed. In all her adult life, she'd never wakened so rested. So this was how she was supposed to feel.

Wait…what is that? All kinds of alarm bells went off.

A stroking sensation jolted her half-awake body into high alert. Her heart thumped rapidly. Her breath came out in spurts with every stroke against her bare thigh.

"About time you woke up, sweetness."

Jake! Thank God. Jake was whom she was pressed up against in her bed. He was the one who had held her the entire night, as she had asked, and he was the one rubbing his callused hand up and down her bare leg. For a few seconds he'd taken her back to a place in her mind she didn't want to ever think about in his presence. She would not taint what they had with *those* memories.

"Why are you touching me?" she asked, unable to mask the tremble in her voice.

"I was trying to wake you. I didn't mean to startle you. Sorry, babe."

She rolled over to face him, sleep still in her eyes. "It's early, slugger," she said with surprising ease.

Letting something that had seemed so terrifying just seconds ago roll off her back was a major accomplishment.

"Slugger, huh? I've never been too keen on nicknames, but I have to say that one has grown on me."

"Well, slugger, what time is it?" She was only in a slightly foul mood with it being morning.

"Eight. What's up with you and mornings anyway?"

"Just can't seem to like them. After a couple of cups of coffee, I usually am fine, but not till then."

A wicked, confident smile spread across his face, showing his perfect white teeth. "I think I can find a substitute for your coffee addiction." He pulled her closer and kissed her.

Parting her lips, she gave him all of her to explore and take as his own. And he did. He prodded, taking over her mouth and mind. "I think I can get used to that." She didn't regret her wording because she was past the point of worrying about every one of her actions. But she hoped he took it lightheartedly and not as an indication that she thought they were going to be waking up like this forever.

"I could get used to giving it to you."

"Jake?"

"Let me guess. You still need your coffee?"

"Yes. Sorry, but I can't function without it. I know I sound like some junkie, but I need it."

"And here I thought I was the one who could satisfy every one of your cravings."

"Believe me, you did last night."

"Oh yeah, I still got it," he said with a dorky fist

pump.

What did that mean? Had he been without sex for a long time? Surely not. She'd seen the way Carly looked at him. And she imagined all women looked at him with that same lust. No, she wouldn't go there. It didn't matter how many women he had been with, nor did it matter how long he had been going without holding a woman as he had her last night.

He left the bed, and she instantly missed his closeness and warmth. She could see his backside clear as day. And it was a perfect butt, not that she had seen any man's bare butt before, but nothing could be any better than Jake's body. Her cheeks flushed as he found his boxers and pulled them up his long, athletic legs.

"Where are you going?" She wanted him back in the bed with her.

"I worked up an appetite last night. A man's got to eat, and you need coffee."

He was making her coffee? Had she ever had a guy make her coffee before? Duh, no. She had never even had a man sleep over before last night. "You don't have to do that. I can make it." She sat upright and searched the bed for her shirt.

"No, you keep your cute little ass right there, because I will be next to you as soon as I find something to fill my belly and get you your cup of joe." He rummaged through her almost-bare cabinets until he found a box of cherry pastries and her can of coffee. After grabbing his breakfast and making them both a cup of coffee, hers with creamer, he handed her a cup while he planted a kiss on her lips.

"Be right back." He went into the bathroom and shut the door.

She took her first sip of coffee and allowed herself to enjoy her memories of the night before. Had she really had sex with Jake last night? Yes, she had, and it was amazing. More than amazing. Amazing didn't even cut it when it came to sex and the pleasure he brought her body.

"What are these, Anna?" Jake came out of the bathroom, holding up a medicine bottle.

His question took a minute for her to process because of her brief daze about last night. He held a bottle of her antidepressants. How had he found those? Why did he have her medication?

"Anna?"

"Where did you find those?" She didn't want her voice to sound panicked, but she was. He wasn't supposed to know about her problems. It was bad enough that Em and Liza knew.

"They were sitting on the bathroom counter. I saw them when I was washing my hands. Why do you have them?" He shook the bottle.

She leaped off the bed, forgetting she was naked. When Jake's gaze fell to her breasts, she once again rifled around the bed until she found her shirt. She pulled it on, not caring it was inside out. "What were you doing going through my things?"

"First of all, I wasn't going through your things. I was washing my hands and saw them on the counter. I picked the bottle up. Why do you sound so upset about this?"

"I'm upset because you were snooping through my bathroom. You had no right to pick the bottle up. Did you—"

"Did I read the label? Yes, I did. Why didn't you

tell me you take antidepressants?"

Oh God. Her stomach dropped. Jake knew about her issues. There was no way or reason to deny it. Her name was written in bold letters on the bottle. He knew they were hers, and what was worse was that he knew what the pills were used for.

She snatched the bottle from his hands. "They're nothing."

"I'm not stupid, Anna. They are something. They are antidepression pills. Please, baby, tell me what's going on with you."

"Don't give me that pity talk, Jake. I don't want to hear how sorry you feel for me. Can we just drop it? I want to go take a shower."

"No. You are not walking away from me. I do not feel sorry for you. How could you think that? I just would like to know you better, and apparently there is a lot I don't know. I want to be there for you."

If she wasn't so mad, she would have been touched by his need to be supportive. But he was a little too late for that—a decade late. "You're a little late on the being there part, Jake. You really want to know what's wrong with me… Well, be prepared, because my life isn't pretty. I take medicine for depression. It's not that big of a deal. A lot of people have to…doctors and lawyers even."

"I never said it was a big deal. I know people suffer from depression and have to be treated. I just didn't know you did. That's all. I'm not judging you or anything. I wasn't snooping. I saw the bottle sitting there, and not thinking, I picked it up. You never mentioned anything about it, so I was curious. I'm sorry if I did something wrong. The last thing I want is for you to be mad at me."

Anna stood there a minute to check her emotions. She didn't want to say something she would regret, and the way her temper was ready to boil over, that was a very real possibility. They had shared an amazing night together. She didn't want to tarnish the memory with her issues. Even though she didn't want him to be, he was now a part of the ugliness in her life. At least in some way. He didn't seem weirded out by it. Instead, he acted as if it were no big deal.

"Can I ask you how long you have been taking them?" he said when she continued her silence. His voice was soft and sounded so caring.

She gave up. Having a mental illness was a part of her life, and now he knew. Who cared? If he had a problem with it and thought she was some unstable person, he could just walk out the door.

"I started taking them about a year after I left Patience. I was feeling really down more days than not. I became uninterested in my own life and didn't seem to find joy in anything. I knew I needed help but was too ashamed to admit it. I guess I felt like a failure. Anyway, I finally went to the doctor, and I was diagnosed with depression. I only take a small dose, and it helps. I won't feel bad about it."

"Oh, honey, you shouldn't feel bad about it. You have no control over it. I hate that you had to go through those dark times before you figured out what was going on. I'm glad you went to the doctor and allowed them to help you. That's brave." He tried to touch her, but she held up a hand.

"I mean what I said. I will not feel bad about my problem. It is a part of my life that I have to deal with, and some days it's not easy. I used to care what people thought, and I guess in some way I still do because I didn't want you or anyone else in Patience to know, but I'm trying to not be that person. I can't change my life for anybody, so if you have a problem with this, I need you to tell me now."

He had moved closer to her, but he didn't touch her. "Anna, I mean what I say too, and I want you to hear me when I say this—I could give a flying fuck about some medicine that you have to take. And I say fuck those who do have a problem with it, but I have a feeling it's more you feeling ashamed by it. Others probably couldn't care less. This is a part of who you are, and I wouldn't change you for anything."

Jake welcomed her into his arms. That wasn't the reaction she expected. Who was this man? Wrapping her arms around him, she buried her face in his chest and breathed him in. He accepted her, and she never wanted to forget how that felt.

She pulled back enough so she could see his face. "How are you okay with this?"

"Why wouldn't I be? You are still you. You are still the sexy woman who blows me away every time she enters a room. You are the same Anna Kelly."

"I know, but I just didn't expect you to look at it as no big deal. You are only one of three people who actually know."

"You are not the only person who has had to take depression medicine. I had a Triple-A teammate who suffered from depression and had to take medication. He hid it from most people too, but we became really close. I mean, it was hard not to because we saw each other every day. I don't know how we even got onto the subject, but he told me he had to take some medication. I began to understand a lot about it through him. He was a great friend to me, and I never thought anything less of him because of it. We all have *something*." He shrugged. And she realized she didn't even care that he knew.

"Jake?"

"Yeah, sweetness?" He kissed her on the forehead, making her feel almost childlike.

"I also have to taking a sleeping pill at night. Otherwise, I will never fall asleep."

"Did you take one last night?"

She shook her head. "Surprisingly, I was able to fall asleep in your arms. It was the best night's sleep I think I've ever had."

"Like I said, Anna, it doesn't matter to me. But maybe I just found a way to stay in your bed."

She laughed. "You think we can crawl back in bed for a bit longer right now?"

"Only if you lose that shirt." He was already pulling her shirt over her head. Any other time she would have been self-conscious about standing completely nude in front of a man. But now, with Jake, she felt so free, and it was exhilarating.

After their lovemaking, Anna curled into Jake's side and drifted back to sleep. She was exactly where she wanted to be.

****

"Where have you been? I've been sitting here waiting for almost thirty minutes," Em yelled when Anna entered CC's Diner. Her friend was seated at a booth, spitting-nails mad.

"Sorry. I overslept."

"It's one in the afternoon. Who sleeps that long? Seriously, Anna, you need to go see a sleep doctor."

A couple of years ago she had considered the same thing but decided there was no doctor who could cure what she was experiencing. She had to put her past behind her, which was her only way of overcoming her demon, the one that visited late at night in her dreams. One way to put her past firmly in the past was to stop thinking so much and actually be a person who lived. She wanted to be a person who could have sex the night before and act perfectly normal about it the next day.

"This time was a little different." Anna could feel a revelation coming, and she relented, not really wanting to hold back about her night with Jake. She needed to talk about it. And although she was concerned about Em's ability to keep a secret, she had no one else she would share such private information with.

"I slept with Jake last night." She couldn't stop from blurting out the words.

Em's eyebrows shot up behind the soft drink she'd just raised to her lips. "You did what? I know I have to be going deaf because there is no way in hell I heard you say what I thought you said."

Okay, that was a mouthful, even for Em.

"You heard right. It happened last night after the bachelor auction."

"I can't believe this. I need details. Don't leave anything out."

Em was probably going to be the only one who would be happy about this development, because Liza was going to kill her. Anna didn't see Liza forgiving Jake anytime in the near future.

Liza was one of the friendliest people Anna

knew—unless that person happened to be Jake. It didn't matter that her friend had never met him. It also didn't matter that what happened between Anna and Jake was eleven years ago. Time did not heal all wounds, according to Liza. She played hardball when it came to men. One of her favorite activities was making a man grovel. Anna didn't know how in the hell her friend was one of the best therapists in Linden. Or how she had kept a boyfriend.

"Details, Em? I don't know." She scanned the hometown diner. "This isn't the safest place to talk about things like this."

"Oh, come on. The only two people in here can't hear without the help of a hearing aid. Mr. Johnson and Old Man Mannard couldn't care less about your sex life. Get to it." Em shook the laminated menu in Anna's face.

No getting out of this. She'd been the one to bring it up. What was wrong with her? Could she be a woman she had never been—one who had a sex life? One who was wild? Yes, she could.

"Okay, but you'd better keep your mouth shut, no letting tidbits slip while you're coloring some teenage girl's hair."

They did their promise handshake.

"After the auction I was bummed. I didn't know I wanted to win Jake until I lost him. After you and I separated in the school parking lot, I went to Ollie's to—"

"Sorry, but you did what?" Em asked, clearly not sorry for her interruption. "Why did you go to a bar alone?"

"What's wrong with that?" How could going to

Ollie's alone be the more shocking news than the mention of Jake? "I wanted to have a drink and accomplish something on my own for a change."

"You should have told me. I would've gone with you."

"I needed to do it by myself. I know it seems silly, but I had something I needed to prove to myself." And she'd proven it. She went to a bar—alone—showed cleavage and all. She'd even been kissed by the handsomest men—if she counted the peck from Tex. It had been a good night for her.

"So at the bar Ollie changed the channel to the Sparks game."

"He did what?" Em asked, shocked again.

"Em, do you want to know what happened or what?"

"Yes. Sorry. Go ahead." She pretended she was zipping her lips closed, which they both knew was impossible for her.

"So I watched the game with Tex, and don't even say anything," Anna added before Em could interrupt again. According to Jake, Tex was still the same kind of ladies' man he had been back in high school, and she needed to stay clear. "After the game, Tex left"—no need adding the peck-on-the-mouth part—"and Jake walked up to me. He apparently had been watching me from his seat at the bar. We started talking about how I root for a pansy team, just the usual, and one thing led to him driving us back to my place."

"So how was it? I mean, the sex. How was the sex?"

"Really good," Anna admitted, unable to hold back a grin. She couldn't lie, nor did she want to. The sex was more than good. It was terrific. When she'd been eager to rush through it, he'd slowed down the pace, forcing her to experience every incredible kiss and touch. And to top it all, he'd made sure she came first, that she was once again taken care of before his needs were met.

She loved that he took special care with her body. Her body was not in shape like an athlete's, but he seemed to love her curves. When he suckled her breasts, weighing them in his hands, she could have gone over the edge without him touching any other part of her body. She'd never had a man look at her as if he were about to feast on her, and she wouldn't have minded that a bit. And even though she was the one who'd asked him to stay, he'd said he had intended to do that very same thing. The whole night was magical. Even when he'd found out about her depression secret, he was okay with it, and it didn't seem to change anything. Damn. She was giddy again.

"So was this a onetime thing, or are you two starting up a fling?"

Funny how Anna hadn't really thought that far ahead, something she was prone to do with all aspects of her life. Thinking and planning were what kept her in line and sane. Apparently not this time, because she hadn't thought about much more than the great sex. Now that Em had brought it to her attention, she had to think about it. Would they have sex again?

Em must have read Anna's face and knew the wheels were turning. "You know I am a J-Ann fan. I really am, but I just don't want to see you hurt and feel the need to stay away again. I've liked having you around, and I sure as hell will not let Jake keep you away from me again. I know it was my idea for you to mess with Jake a little bit, but maybe that wasn't the safest thing."

Anna had forgotten that her actions had affected more than just her. They had affected Em, Ms. Edna, and maybe even Jake. "I make my own decisions. I wanted to sleep with Jake, and so I did. And you know I had other reasons, too, for leaving Patience. It was not all because of Jake."

"I know. I just don't like thinking about the other, so I blame everything on Jake. He doesn't deserve it, but life isn't fair, and he was an ass."

They rarely talked about that part of her life. The memories were too overwhelming for Anna, and Em had recognized early on that it was best to be a silent supporter.

Leaving the painful subject better known as her childhood, she returned to the question Em had asked. What was she expecting out of this thing with Jake? They still had lots to discuss, but even if they didn't, she couldn't have a fling with him. It was only a night filled with great sex, something she had needed. She'd needed it more than she would have ever thought.

"No, it's not a fling. It was just a one-night thing, nothing more. I came here for your wedding and to sell my house. Not to get swallowed up in some reckless relationship. But I did agree to see him again tonight."

"Reckless?"

"Do you not remember how the guy was on the ball field or the way he now drives? Yes, he is definitely reckless, and I don't need that in my life."

"Well, anyway"—Em swirled her straw around in her glass—"whatever you decide is your choice. But you need some reckless, if you ask me. You are too uptight, and I'd rather you have hot sex than consume alcohol. Whatever you want, you better hurry up and decide, especially if you're seeing him again."

She and Em hadn't talked about what had happened the night of the bachelorette party. Em had been busy with work and the wedding, and Anna had not wanted to talk about it. Em had known that and kept their talk away from the whole Cara lashing.

"I'm really sorry about your party, Em. I was never a good drinker, and when I saw her, I turned into a jealous high schooler. I'm so embarrassed."

Em waved her off. "Don't be silly. I would've reacted the same way if it was Tommy. I keep putting you in situations where you are thrown for a loop, and I am the one who needs to be apologizing. I can't believe I failed to mention Tommy and Cara are distant cousins. I think on his mom's side. I messed up."

"It's fine now."

"I'd say so. When I picked you up at Jake's the morning after the party, I thought y'all had had some big falling out, but just look at you two. I'm the one about to get married, and you're the one off having crazy, wild sex."

****

Streaks of purple and orange stretched across the twilight sky. It was vast and open, a perfect night for baseball or softball.

Kids snatched up their bats, gloves, and balls. They were ready to play. A young girl, probably around the age of five, was learning how to play catch with her dad. Both child and dad beamed with every catch. Watching the two brought back the memory of his parents and how they each had, in different ways, supported his love for the game.

Being drafted out of high school gave him the headlining story in the *Patience Gazette*. His mother stayed on the phone most of that next day, receiving congratulations for her older son's accomplishment, while he'd spent most of that same day staring at the diamond that started it all. The place he'd played his first T-ball game. He wanted to live up to that little boy's expectations again. That little boy was innocent and had looked at baseball as being simple. Win or lose, he loved the game. But he had to admit winning was so much sweeter.

He was reluctant to leave town because of his mother and Bradley. But his mom refused to let him give up his dream. She was the pure example of strength and courage. After all, it had taken those two things and more to overcome the death of a husband and raise two rambunctious boys.

God, how she would have been saddened at the man he was today. Of course, she had offered him comfort with daily phone calls after his injury, not that he appreciated her attempts nearly enough, but if she could now, she would've slapped him silly for going out every night, getting plastered, and not remembering the girl or even the night before, after her death. That's what he'd needed: a good slap in the face. But everyone around him was too afraid. They wanted to give him time. He didn't need time. He needed his mother back.

Losing her was worse than the night he'd touched home plate for the last time in his major-league career. While it was his dad who had introduced him to the game of baseball, it was his mother who'd nurtured his love of it, supported him, made sure he was at every game and practice. She had convinced him not to settle for anything less than what he dreamed of. And he'd wanted to play baseball for the Atlanta Rockets since his dad took him and Bradley to their first big league game.

Like any other seven-year-old, he was in awe at the size of the field. He didn't want popcorn, cotton candy, or even a souvenir he could take home and brag to all his friends that he'd gotten to see a real game. All he wanted was the game. He didn't think he said a single word the three hours it took for San Francisco to beat Atlanta by two runs. From that day on, he'd planned to play shortstop for Atlanta. He never played shortstop, but he played third base for the same franchise that included most of his idols. And just like them, he'd thought he was living out his glory days.

Nothing could have been further from the truth. He had been cocky enough to think some kid in the cheap seats would see him—number twenty-five—and beg for that number to be on the back of his baseball jersey.

Using his good leg, he pushed his body off the concrete building housing the concession stand. He didn't have time to ride the road back down memory lane. He had a much-anticipated date with his lover. Wow, did it feel good to finally be able to say that.

"Whatcha doing, sweetness?" he asked as he walked up beside her.

She stopped midstride. "Where'd you come from?"

"Concessions. Ms. Rachel Bell makes some damn fine burgers. You ready?" he asked after a rush of kids passed.

"For what?"

He only smiled.

"Kids? We're going to watch a Little League game? That's what you really want to do for our second date?"

"Don't let these five-year-olds fool you. They can pound the ball just as good as a ten-year-old. The only thing with this age group is their attention spans. One minute they're making a good throw to first base, and the next they're throwing dirt above their heads while sitting on the base."

"I bet they're so cute."

"They drive their coaches crazy is what they do, but yes, they are cute."

That was why he didn't coach little kids. He helped the ones who took baseball seriously and let the patient men handle the ones who were only there because of their parents. Sadly, many parents pushed their kids because they had never gotten the chance to play and actually be any good at it. He'd seen it when he was a Little Leaguer, and now that he was back, things hadn't changed much.

With his hand on the small of Anna's back, he guided her through the crowd to the field in back of the park. He expected her to pull away from him, but when she instead slightly turned to him and smiled, he thought maybe she now looked forward to their dates.

Hoping he wasn't pushing his luck, he grabbed her hand as they climbed the bleachers to the top.

"Do you come here often?" she asked.

"What? Come watch the youngsters play?"

"Yeah?"

"I try to catch a game here and there. I usually come when I start to think of my career and how it started on this same field when I was five years old."

"Have you been thinking about it lately?"

"Yeah. I mean, I always think of baseball. It's hard not to, but some days it hits me more."

She placed her hand on his knee. "You miss it."

He placed his hand on top of hers, and their gazes collided. "I would be lying if I said I didn't, but I'm learning to cope with the loss."

"I get it. And I'm really sorry, Jake."

"I know," he said, even though he didn't understand what she *got* when it came to coping with loss. Maybe she was referring to the death of her mom, which made complete sense. "Why don't we table all this talk about the past and watch these future Hall of Famers show their stuff out here on the diamond?"

It was bottom of the first with the home team batting. Jared, a young first-year Rockets player, was up to bat. He had the attention span of a gnat, but he always got a hit. The coach had to pick the kid up so he was actually facing the plate, then arrange his legs, and put his elbow in the correct position. He had two strikes, and on the third pitch, he hit the ball as hard as he could. It didn't go far, but the crowd cheered.

"Go, Jared, run. Ruuun, baby. That's my boy," the mother screamed. She had the same response every time her son tapped the ball. Jared was tagged out before he reached first base, but he didn't care. Judging by the priceless look on his face, just tapping that ball was enough to keep him coming back year after year to play.

Lance was the next player to the plate. Unlike Jared, Lance had been playing a couple of years. He already knew how to position himself, just the way Jake

237

had taught him. After hitting the plate a few times, he pulled back his elbow and zeroed in on the baseball. On the first pitch, he fired the ball clear to the fence. Most of the opposing team's outfielders were young and inexperienced and had no chance of throwing out the speedy boy now rounding second.

"That kid's really going to be good. How old is he?" Anna asked.

"That there is Lance, and he's six. He's a good kid. I worked with him a little before the season started."

Anna eyed him. "Do you do that with a lot of the players?"

"Just the ones who ask. For your information, I don't have this big ego where I think I can teach everyone to be a ballplayer."

"That's not what I meant. I just wondered if you gave lessons to lots of the kids. You do know what you're doing and all." She turned back to face the field, but he could see her watching him from the corner of her eye. "I mean, you're no Jax Dalton, but I guess—"

"Watch it, Kelly. Don't be talking that *crap*." He looked at the people sitting around them. If there hadn't been so many kids nearby, he would've used some much harsher words.

She laughed.

Damn it. She knew he loathed New York. "It's not funny."

She bit her bottom lip, trying to hold in another giggle but failing. "I'm sorry," she said when she finally collected herself. "That was wrong."

"Ya think?" He scooted away, putting a couple of inches between them.

"Jake"—she playfully tugged on his arm—"you

know you can't stay mad at me all night." She inched closer to him, while he only kept moving farther away from her. He didn't stop until he was almost sitting right on top of the older man next to him, who gave him the stink eye. "What are you going to do now?"

She was right, but he still held his ground by staying silent.

"What if I made it up to you?"

Now she was talking. He could think of a few things she could do to make it up to him. "I'm listening."

"What if I kissed you?"

He turned to face her. "I think I'll forgive you for a kiss."

She leaned in and gave him a kiss on his cheek. "How's that?"

"Not what I was thinking, but it'll be enough for now."

He explained that just like with his softball team, the Little League games only went for six innings. After the last out, the home team walked away with a fourteen-to-ten win. The crowd cheered as the two teams lined up to give high fives to one another.

Just as he did every other time he'd come to watch a game, he gave each kid a fist bump and congratulated them on their good game. A few hellos were given to both him and Anna, and after chasing a few of the kids around the bases, he and Anna were left alone.

He leaned his back against the chain-link fence. "Are we going to talk about last night?"

A rosy color crept up her neck. "What do you mean?"

"Sweetness, have I brought up a pleasurable

moment you would love to hit rewind on?"

"Jake Lawrence."

If she could tease him, he could do the same. "What? It was pleasurable, wasn't it?"

"There are kids around. You should be ashamed."

"The closest kid is two fields away. You wouldn't be trying to avoid this subject, would you?"

For a second he thought she was going to slap him. Thankfully, that wasn't the case. "Maybe I feel it's wrong to talk about sex at a park when any kid can approach. You are pretty famous around here, and anyone can just walk up."

He chuckled. "If that's what you say. You want to know what I think? I think you enjoyed it so much that you're a little embarrassed. You did, after all, do a lot of moaning and 'oh, Jakes,' but that's nothing to be embarrassed about. I tend to have that effect on women."

"You are so full of yourself, you know that? Maybe all that moaning was just a way for me to not hurt your ego. *Maybe* sex with you wasn't as good as you think. You ever think of that?"

"Now I know you're lying."

"Um…can we talk about something else right now?"

"Sure. How about we discuss you coming back to my place and enjoy round two of our lovemaking, or would it be round three if you count this morning?"

"I'm sorry about your mom, Jake."

"Wow, where did that come from?" That was out of the blue. And not what he wanted to be talking about. He turned to position himself on the fence, facing the field.

"Just something I should've said a long time ago."

Just thinking about all he and Bradley had lost caused his chest to ache. He stared down at the cleat-indented clay. "It was hard, and I wish I would've handled it better, but I didn't, and that is something I am going to have to live with. It was a storm of emotions I wasn't prepared to face and feel. I pretty much gave up on my life and dug myself into this hole nobody could get me out of. I was saturated with grief. I don't even remember much of what happened or what I was doing."

For this reason he'd needed something to keep his mind busy. Anna's house had rescued him.

"You had a right to be beside yourself with grief. It's natural, Jake. You can't keep beating yourself up about it."

He wished everyone would stop giving him a pass. He didn't deserve it. "I gave up, sweetness. On everything that mattered to me. I left baseball, my friends, and my brother, for God's sake. Bradley was hurting too, and what did I do? I became a drunk he had to go pick up after last call every night. I am the eldest. I should've been a better brother to him. I should've taken care of him instead of the other way around." And him being a disappointment was not the only problem. While he was at it, he might as well admit the rest. "Did you know I possibly could've returned back to the game that next season? I hurt my knee pretty bad, but if I would've finished my treatment and rehab, I could've maybe made a comeback. I could still be playing this game." He gestured to the small field they were standing on. "I was going to, in the beginning, but then my mom died, and I was just lost."

"No, I didn't know. You want to tell me about it?" she asked.

And when others had asked him that very question, he, in a nice way, said *hell no*, but it wasn't like that with Anna. In that moment she wasn't just his lover. She was that teenage girl he considered his best friend. He took a much-needed breath. "My team was ahead by one in the bottom of the sixth. Jonsey hit a bullet to centerfield, and there was no way I was settling on third base when I knew I could make it home."

"You always were one of those annoying players who thought they were God's gift to baseball. You know fans cuss you through the television, don't you?"

He smiled. "Yeah. But they sure do cheer when we players come through for them in the end."

"Did you know when you were running around the bases how bad your knee was injured?"

"Even above the noise of thirty thousand fans, I could hear the pop. I immediately knew I'd blown out my knee. A knee doesn't just snap for any reason. I remember the pain being excruciating. How I kept running I don't know. The trainers told me I should've dropped to the ground instantly, but I guess I was too stubborn to give up and allow a pinch runner to run for me. So even though it meant a collision at the plate, I knew my team needed the assurance run."

"You sacrificed your body and career for the game. I know that's the kind of teammate you are, but you do know how stupid that was, don't you?"

"It's part of the game, sweetness."

"But do you not understand you scared the living daylights out of me? I sat there, watching your life change in between bases, and wasn't able to stop it."

That took him aback. "Were you there?"

"Not in the stands, but I watched from my living room. And that made it worse, because if I had been there, I could at least have made sure you were okay. At home, I was forced to listen to the commentaries and your manager downplay it. I know they didn't want to say too much before tests were run, but damn it, I was sick about it, Jake."

"Oh, honey." He stroked the side of her cheek. "I'm sorry you had to witness that. I didn't think you watched me play."

She offered him a shy smile. "It's a guilty pleasure."

That sounded pretty damned good to him. All those years she'd secretly watched him from afar. He couldn't wrap his mind around it.

"My mom loved watching you play too."

He turned his back to her and slumped his shoulders over the fence. "I should've called you when she passed."

"It's all right. I knew you were going through a lot." She draped her arms over the fence, beside him.

"No, it's not. I had just gotten injured, and I was a selfish bastard. When Tommy told me, I knew I should've gotten over my stubborn pride and called you, but I didn't. And then my mom died…and well, I wasn't any help to anyone after that. I will always be sorry for that."

Jake found comfort in the silence that fell between them after his apology. The only sounds were the cheers from the field above them. Words didn't have to be said. In that moment, through their grief, he understood Anna in a way he never had in the past.

"I miss her a lot, and I think about her every day. I'm glad we were together when she died."

"That's right. She'd moved from here to Linden to be with you."

"She wanted to be near what family she had, so she decided to stay with me and my aunt Lidia. I will always be thankful for the time we otherwise wouldn't have had if she hadn't made the move."

"If you don't mind me asking, why didn't you move back here?"

Anna wrapped her hands around the top of the fence and leaned back to stare at the sky. "I don't know. I guess it was because I was already settled with a job, and my aunt was there. My mom decided she could use the change. Between the three of us, it was like having a slumber party every night. We watched reality television while eating bowls of ice cream. As you can tell, that last part wasn't the smartest idea." She waved a hand across her body, as if she were showing him her flaws. He, of course, wasn't seeing them. "I mean, I should've known that eating cartons of ice cream wasn't the smartest slumber party activity."

He let his gaze fall to her body. "Sweetness, I don't know what you see, but what I see is a smoking-hot body with some sexy-ass curves."

"Oh God, I wasn't fishing for a compliment or anything."

"I'm just stating the obvious. You have an hourglass figure that drives me absolutely crazy. You want to know what I'm thinking right now?" He gave her a second to process that. "I want to take you back to your place, strip you naked, lay your sexy body out on the bed, and pleasure you until the sun comes up tomorrow."

He wished she didn't have to mull over the prospect of them being together again. For him it was an easy yes. It would always be yes when she was involved. But Anna never did anything without putting thought into it. But then again, maybe she was still a little pissed at him for moving into her house without her knowing about it.

"Do you really always just say what comes to mind?"

That made him smile. "No. If that was the case, I would've told you I wanted you the first day I saw you again."

"You pretty much did."

"Oh, right. Well then, yes, I do say or act on anything that comes to mind. Now what about showing me just how sorry you are about making that ridiculous Sparks comment?" He pushed off the fence and placed both his hands on either side of her hips. "I hope you don't think that measly little kiss on the cheek is going to be enough to satisfy a man like me."

Chapter Fifteen

Jake walked into his dark house, flipped on a light, and threw his keys down on the side table. A shower was calling his name. He turned on the water and stripped out of his clothes. After washing up, he dressed again.

He thought about going out, but where was there to go? Ollie's would be slow since it was a work night, but did he really want to go there? A cold beer along with some fried cheese sticks sounded good. Minny would be good company, and maybe a Rockets game would be on. Any other time that would be where he would end up. Eating peanuts, drinking a couple of beers, and hollering at the umps over a bad call. Now, thinking about spending his nights on a barstool kind of made him seem like a loser. What twenty-nine-year-old sat at a bar on a Thursday night? Maybe Jake the drunk, but he was no longer that guy. He liked to think he'd grown up and was dealing with his life a lot better.

Usually, Thursday nights were for playing softball, but there wasn't a game this week.

He knew where he wanted to be, but he didn't want to pressure her. Anna wasn't ready for him and what he had in mind, but the question was what to do about it? He had so many plans for them, but he would scare her if she knew what he wanted to do to her body.

And no matter what reason she gave herself, she'd

enjoyed the past two days on a deeper level than just two ordinary dates. Her face had lit up when they watched the game. He saw the pain in her eyes when they talked about her mother and when he mentioned his self-destructive ways. She was a mixture of emotions, and he loved every one of them. He couldn't even hide his love for the ass-kicking side. That was his personal favorite.

He snatched up his keys and headed to the only place he wanted to be, a place where he was starting to feel at home. It was a place he didn't want to leave.

****

Sure, Anna would have rather been with Jake, but she needed time to think. Tonight had been nice. Watching the small kids play a game she'd come to love brought her joy. In a way she envied them because she wished she could have gotten to play like that when she was a kid. Maybe she wouldn't just love to watch baseball but also to play it. No sense living in the past. Her mother had done the best she could, and Anna was thankful for that. No matter whether she played the game or not, she loved everything about it.

Freshly cut grass would always be one of her favorite smells. She loved the sound when the ball met the bat and skyrocketed across the field. And looking at tanned men displaying their athletic abilities while wearing tight uniform pants wasn't bad either.

When Jake had insisted they go get dinner at the diner, she'd declined and come back to the apartment.

Her mind was on overdrive, and she needed a minute to process everything that was happening. Her feelings for Jake were moving too fast. Was she even mad at him anymore? What about the whole Cara thing? Was she over that? He'd broken her heart. No matter how bad it would hurt to open that wound, they needed to clear the air. If she had learned anything about her life, it was that locking away her emotions was not the route to go.

Jake needed to hear all the things she'd wanted to say to him for the past decade. He needed to hear about her heartbreak. He needed to apologize and give her an explanation for why he'd slept with Cara so soon after they broke up. She'd come to Patience to find peace, and now she understood she needed peace with Jake too. They had come a long way since that first day she pulled up on Python, parked in her driveway, and had seen him standing on her porch. That day she could've happily smothered him in his sleep. Now she wanted to fall asleep in his arms.

Last night left her speechless. She was by no means the type of woman who went around having sex with hot men. Hell, she'd only had sex with one other man. But when Jake had sauntered up to her table at the bar, she knew she wouldn't need much convincing. Her Sparks had won and therefore would stay in their division's first place, and Jake looked jealous and sexy. She guessed she could thank Tex for the jealous part, but the sexy part was all thanks to the Lawrence brothers' good genes.

When he'd pushed her up on the bed and unbuttoned her jeans, her heart raced. Her breath caught in her chest when he laid eyes on her sexiest pair of panties. God, she was glad she had opted for them instead of her usual plain, back-of-the-drawer cotton ones.

She'd never felt so desirable and sexy. He made

her feel sensual and like the woman she had always wanted to be, a woman who could have wild, passionate sex.

She wasn't even embarrassed by her moaning and calling out his name. For once, she didn't stop to think. She just acted, and at that moment she'd felt wild. She wanted to yell, so she yelled. She wanted to moan out his name, so she did. It was empowering to be the type of woman she had always wanted to be. Strong. Sexy. Desirable.

Liza had tried calling her a couple of times over the past two days, and since it was so late, Anna decided it might be best if she emailed. Plus, she really didn't want to hear Liza's reaction to her sleeping with Jake. She fired up her computer.

Liza,

I feel like I'm saying I'm sorry a lot lately. But I'm sorry for missing your calls. Patience has actually been good. I'm still not staying at my house, but I'm not that upset by it anymore. I heard you gave Jake an earful the other morning. To tell you the truth, I think you scared him a little. I know you're looking out for me, but I'm okay...really. Don't worry!

I've agreed to go on a couple of dates with him. It's been surprisingly fun. I've been enjoying myself—a little confused, but that's only because I slept with him. You like how I slipped that in? Don't freak out—Jake and I had sex, and it was a-mazing. I kind of want to do it again. Is that wrong? Of course it's wrong. I'm angry at him, right? Hell, I don't know what I feel anymore.

You're my friend, and I need you to tell me what to do, even though I have a pretty good idea of what you will say. I know you're not a big fan of Jake, but he's been kind of great lately, if you take away the part where he's holding my house hostage.

The wedding is coming up, and I will be home not too long after that. I hope to be in my house by the end of this weekend. After I do some little repairs, I should be back in Linden. Thanks for looking after my aunt. I know she can be a handful, so thank you, thank you. I'll try calling you soon. Thanks for listening to me ramble.

Love you.

Anna

Anna closed her laptop and stripped out of her clothes. Since she was feeling sexy lately, she chose to wear her navy-blue Dalton tee with only her navy-blue panties. She wasn't normally one who tried to match clothing when she was only going to bed, but she was feeling more confident lately. She also sprayed a little perfume on her thighs and neck. Wanting to feel good about herself, she decided not to worry about her extra weight. Who cared if she didn't look like she had back when she graduated from high school and if her thighs rubbed together when she stood up straight? She never claimed to be one of those supermodel types. Besides, she was starting to feel good about her body. And it was great.

She threw the pink pillows to the floor and crawled between crisp sheets, propped two other pillows behind her head, took a drink of water to wash down the little blue pill, and picked up her romance read. The book opened to the dog-eared page. From the first word she read, she began forgetting all about her problems and confusion. There would be time tomorrow to worry about Jake and the feelings sneaking up on her.

The thing she loved about a book was it could

make her leave the world that existed for her, take her to another time and someone else's set of problems. Reading was her escape, and sometimes the only thing that got her through her troubles. She knew that at the end of a hard, emotional day, she could pick up a book and in an instant be sitting on the beach in Hawaii, hiking in the mountains, or having wild sex on a stormy night.

A warm breeze filtered through an open window, carrying the sounds of crickets chirping and the scents of summer she'd always associated with Patience. All seemed well outside, and Anna hoped it would be a good night for sleep. She'd only had a few nightmares since being back, but that was to be expected. Being back in Patience had to be what Liza would call a trigger.

When she couldn't read another word, she tucked her book away, switched off her lamp, and pulled the blankets up tightly around her neck.

****

She had a feeling tonight he would come. The devil and her mother had gotten into a yelling match. Well, he did most of the yelling, while her mother cried. Her mother slipped off to bed a little early, leaving Anna to do the same. But Anna wouldn't sleep—at least not yet. She needed to stay awake, because she had a feeling he would come to her room when he thought she'd fallen asleep.

She lay there, counting her own breaths and dreading the moment the door creaked open. She needed to be brave, but what did that mean? What was she supposed to do?

He left the door cracked open, allowing a little bit

of light to seep in. Ordinarily, the door was never left open. She opened her eyes to see him walking heavily over to her small bed. He pushed her baby dolls out of his path. Nothing was quiet about this night. Anna knew he was mad. He got down on his knees and knelt by her side. Clinching her body, she tried making herself as small as she could. Tiny tears leaked behind her eyelids. She wanted to scream. She needed to scream.

****

"Anna, baby, shhh…I'm here. It's okay." Anna lay curled in a ball, gripping her blankets up tight around her neck. She looked helpless and terrified. And that didn't sit well with him. Whatever dream she was having had her screaming and trembling in his arms.

After slipping off his shoes and pulling back the covers, he crawled into bed with her. With his back resting against the bedframe, he drew her close and hugged her tightly in his arms. It was all he knew to do. No words were murmured. He rubbed the small of her back, doing nothing but being there for her.

"You okay, baby?" he asked when her tears had finally come to an end.

She peered up at him, and he was a goner. So much pain resided in her eyes. He used the pads of his thumbs to wipe away the dampness from her cheeks and wished he could wipe away everything bad in her life. If only it were that easy.

She nodded and snuggled back close to his chest. "Yeah."

"You want to talk about it?"

"Not really."

"I think you should. It might make you feel better."

"It was nothing."

"Anna, come on. You were screaming when I walked in. I wouldn't call that nothing." He also wanted to tell her it wasn't safe to go to sleep with the door unlocked. But that was a conversation for another time. Right now she needed him for comfort, much like she had after the bachelorette party.

And what did she mean—nothing? She had scared the shit of him.

When he was about to knock on the door, he'd heard a scream, followed by the sound of crying out in pain. With no hesitation, he rushed through the door to find her using her blankets as a shield. A shield to ward off whatever she was dreaming about. What terrified her?

When she said nothing, he cursed himself for pressuring her. He was such an ass when it came to things that mattered.

Her gaze met his. "Jake," she whispered between breaths.

He leaned down close to her face. "Yeah, baby?"

She kissed him. He didn't know if it was wrong to kiss a woman who had just been terrified of whatever haunted her at night, but it seemed they both needed the connection. His tongue slipped between her wet lips and explored her mouth. Climbing onto his lap, she straddled him and wrapped both arms around his neck. She continued to kiss him urgently, as if it were the kiss that was going to save her. He lowered his hands to her ass and pressed her core against his erection. She let out a soft moan.

Only a thin pair of panties separated him from her moisture. Even though he wanted to be inside her, this was not about him. He was going to let her run this show and do as she pleased.

Pulling back, she lifted her shirt over her head. Hell yeah. He didn't know if he was more excited to see the damn Sparks shirt she always seemed to wear gone, or because he was going to see all of her. Probably a little of both. Her hair fell down to her shoulders. He swept it back with his hand and nibbled at her neck.

She dropped her head to the side in pleasure. "Ohhh," she purred, and he ran kisses from her neck to the swell of her breasts.

He dipped down to take one rosy nipple between his teeth, bringing it to a peak, and her breath became irregular. "Mmm…Jake, that feels…so…good."

God, he needed this woman. This was the only woman he'd ever wanted. If it was up to him, she would be the last woman he would ever have. In his mind, she was already his.

She reached under his shirt, laying trembling hands across his chest. Her eyes never left his. He explored those sparkling green orbs. Desire, passion, and maybe a little hope shone through.

He loved this woman. He really loved her.

He kissed her more softly this time, but she wasn't having it. She seemed to want it hard and fast. He matched her step for step, not letting up. Her fingers eagerly explored under his shirt.

"Damn, woman," he cursed in between kisses.

She pulled his shirt over his head and threw it to the floor.

He tried rolling her to her back, but she stopped him. Pinning his back to the bed, she ran light, feathery kisses down his chest. She circled one nipple with her tongue while she continued to run her figures across his stomach.

With his palm, he rubbed her inner thigh. As she moaned inside his mouth, he caught the sound, and that was all the reassurance he needed. When he moved his hand slightly upward to the thin piece of cotton, she raised up enough to give him the access he needed. Skimming his fingers over the outside of her panties, already damp with her arousal, he let out a hot groan that echoed from his chest. Just touching her turned him on. If this kept up, he wasn't going to be able to hold on much longer. And God, he wanted to hold on. He wanted to feel everything there was to feel about this woman. His woman.

Making her wait for her pleasure was his first thought, but he decided against it. Call him selfish, but he needed this just as badly as she.

He pulled aside the fabric and found what he'd been seeking. Heat.

She moved against his fingers and cried out, "Awww…Jake…please don't stop touching me. Not ever."

"Not a chance in hell, baby."

He'd never witnessed anything hotter than Anna with her back arched and head thrown to the side. Her firm breasts bobbled up and down, faster and faster, the closer she got to orgasm. A little sexy moan escaped from her lips just before she came.

"I need you out of these." She reached down to his jeans. After she unbuttoned them, his erection sprang free into her hands. She stared, waited a moment, and then started to massage him. *Yes*. He positioned her the way he wanted her, but she took control and put a hand on his chest, as if to signal for him not to move. She kept stroking up until his hips rose from the mattress.

"Anna, you'd better stop, or this is going to be over way too quickly."

"We can't have that now, can we?" She removed her hand and locked her gaze on him.

He studied every perfect line on her face. When she was in deep thought, one line ran across her forehead, but at that moment no line appeared. Passion ran deep in her eyes. She was the pure example of love.

"Anna, I want to taste you. I want to bury my face between your sexy thighs and feast on you. I wanted to last night, but things seemed to move too fast."

Every part of her body went rigid. When she only stared at him in response, confusion set in. Had she ever had a man pleasure her that way? He didn't want to think about any man being there, but it was a possibility. But then again, the way her body reacted at the mention of it, he doubted she'd ever allowed another man the privilege.

"I want you inside me," she said.

"I want that too. But I also want to do other things to you."

"Please, Jake."

He wanted her "please, Jake" to mean she wanted him to have her in every way possible. But that wasn't what she meant. There was more to the story, but he couldn't go into it right then. He needed her any way he could have her at the moment. His burying himself between her legs would come later.

He helped draw her panties down and positioned her on top of his cock, pressing her hips firmly downward. Even though it might not be smart, he didn't bother with using a condom this time. And judging by her soft expression, she wasn't too worried about it either. It was pure pleasure to be sheathed by her warm moisture. This was where he wanted to be. He wanted to be this way with her forever, or for as long as she allowed him to be.

And he prayed it would be forever.

He had been with her not that long ago. But it seemed a hell of a lot longer.

He pounded his hips upward until he filled her completely. Slowly at first, but when she met his every thrust, he knew she was okay. She kissed him deeper, and he pressed his tongue into her mouth.

She rose up to peer into his eyes, and he couldn't think of a more beautiful sight. They moved together as if they'd been doing this for years. Both seemed to know each other's bodies well. He admired her perfect, round breasts and molded his hands to them, teasing one taut nipple until she cried out.

"God, Jake. I need this. I need you."

"I need you too."

He rolled them over, and with no objection, lay on top of her, still buried deep in her warmth. He pulled back just enough so their pelvises still connected. But he wanted to see her. All of her. He wanted to take pleasure in the way she closed her eyes and accepted each one of his thrusts.

So much needed to be said and cleared up. He needed to tell her how everything had gone down eleven years ago. He needed to say that he loved her and had *always* loved her. When he'd said those words back when they were stupid teenagers, he'd meant them. He was reckless, sometimes a jackass, and a man who had been lost for the past two years, but he loved her. That he was sure of. He just hoped she felt the same way and that she would take him the way he was, and with the mistakes he had made.

He was no prize catch, probably never was, and he didn't deserve her. But hell, he hoped she wanted him.

"Oh God…" she whimpered. "Ahhh…Jake."

A few seconds later he was right there with her. "I'm about to come, sweetness."

Another stream of curses escaped his lips while he was on the edge of pure bliss. He pounded as slowly as he could will himself to until he exploded. Then he plunged deep inside her and took pride in the fact that he left a part of himself with her. He became a little light headed and spent.

Wrapping both arms around his neck, Anna held him close.

****

"Georgia, I'm so glad I ran into you. We still on for tomorrow?"

The bubbly woman sat behind her desk typing on her computer. Today she wore a pink sundress paired with—what Anna only guessed, because she couldn't see them—slip-on shoes. Her sleek blond hair hung just above her shoulders.

"Of course. Unless you have another date?"

"No. Why do you ask?"

"Don't be silly. Everyone knows how you and Jake Lawrence have been seeing a lot of each other. Not to mention I see his truck parked there every morning when I get to work. I can only guess it was left there from the night before."

Crap. She hadn't even thought about Georgia and

Garrett being able to see Jake's truck. What was the entire town saying about them? She guessed it fell into the juicy column. Before too long they would be on the cover of the *Patience Gazette*. The headline would read *Two Lovers Reunited*. "I guess you noticed that?"

"Girl, everyone has noticed. Personally, I think it's romantic. Obviously, I wasn't around back when you two were in love, but it makes for a good story. Two lovers who have found their way back to each other."

"We're not back together," Anna said, speaking a little too quickly.

"So it's just sex?"

"No." She didn't exactly know what it was.

"I apologize. I guess I'm being just a lot nosy. Sometimes you have to tell me to shut up."

Anna liked Georgia. She was sweet and had an unbiased outlook on the world. She saw things as they were and didn't try to hide what she was feeling. It was refreshing.

"You're fine. I just don't know what's going on right now. Men are confusing, if you know what I mean."

Did Georgia have a man? She had seen her bid on and win Garrett, but she didn't know, or was too preoccupied lately, to give it much thought, if anything had come of it. She wasn't sure whether she should ask, so she decided against it. While Georgia didn't mind asking the hard questions, Anna didn't want to be nosy. But she didn't mind listening to Georgia if the time ever came that she needed someone to talk to.

"Yes, I do. If you ask me, I think they like toying with us women."

"I've thought the same thing," Anna said, speaking

the truth. "So about the wedding—if you want, you can meet me here around four. The wedding isn't until six, but as maid of honor, I need to get there early."

"That sounds good. Besides, I've been looking forward to riding in your car."

"You can drive it, if you want," Anna said, not sure why she was offering.

"Are you sure?" Georgia's voice rose several octaves.

Anna wished she had the same innocence so that the simplest things brought such joy into her life. "I wouldn't say you could if I wasn't."

"Why have you been so nice to me? You don't even know me."

"I like you, and you're refreshing to be around. I might not know much about you, but I would love to know more. Everyone needs a *Georgia* in their lives. Maybe before I go back to Linden, we could go have a drink at Ollie's."

Georgia's eyes got a little glossy. But the woman held back a tear and smiled sweetly. "You go there?"

"Yep. I've gotten to know the owner pretty well. Why don't we make that our second date? We'll have the whole town in an uproar before I leave."

After receiving a hug, Anna left Georgia to her work and headed back to the apartment. The rehearsal dinner would be in a few hours, and she wanted to have plenty of time to get ready. And that had nothing to do with the fact that she was going with Jake.

Noticing Garrett next door to her apartment at a vacant house, she walked over. She hadn't seen anyone coming or going from the place, which probably explained why he was putting up a For Sale sign.

"Hey, stranger."

He turned from his task of pushing the sign into the soft ground to pivot in her direction. He wore black dress slacks and a white polo shirt. How could he work with a woman like Georgia and still not have any color in his wardrobe? There was no way the two of them were dating. But then why would Georgia bid on him at the auction? That would hopefully be a topic discussed at Ollie's.

"Hi, Anna," he said.

"I've been meaning to stop in and talk to you."

"You've been busy."

"I guess you could say that. What's up with this place?"

"The owners left town a couple months back. It used to be a children's consignment shop, but the couple decided to move back to their hometown before their young son started school."

"Well, that's more business for you. But what a shame for the house. It's lovely."

And it was. The two-story house was a deep blue with white trim and white shutters. There were two porches, one on the upper story and the other on the bottom, that ran the length of the house. Colorful flowers lined the paved driveway.

"What about your house? Has Jake given it back yet?" His gaze dropped to the ground.

She could tell he'd been beating himself up over the whole deal and the part he'd played in it. "I'm working on it. I think I have one date left."

"Look, Anna, I'm really sorry about that. I shouldn't have listened to Jake. I should've asked you first."

"It's fine, Garrett. I won't lie. I was pretty ticked at first, but now I realize that you were just trying to help in your own way. Besides, it wasn't only on you. Jake played a big part in it too."

"You've been really great about it. You are a kind person."

"I wouldn't go that far. But I guess I can be forgiving when I want to be. So don't worry about it anymore. You've given me a nice place to stay to make up for it. Now if we can just sell my house, all will be forgiven."

"I'm here whenever you're ready to list it. With all the repairs he's done, I think we shouldn't have that hard of a time finding a buyer."

"Thank you for everything you've done."

"That's my job."

"Well, that might be the case, but I wanted to thank you for overseeing the house for all these years. I really do appreciate it."

Funny how she didn't mind that she hadn't spent more than one night there. It didn't bother her that one of her reasons for coming back to Patience hadn't even happened. She didn't know what to feel about that. Or what exactly it meant.

Chapter Sixteen

A few hours later Anna stood in front of the mirror, admiring her look for the night. She wore high-waisted, wide-legged black pants that showed off her assets. She was beginning to like her hips and butt. They gave her shape, and with the recent looseness of her pants, she thought maybe she had lost a few pounds. All that walking and occasional running might have been paying off. She paired the pants with a white blouse tucked into them, its sleeves rolled a quarter up her arm. Instead of putting her hair in a ponytail, she curled it and left it hanging past her shoulders. Her face was starting to show some color so her makeup looked amazing on her semibronze skin. Overall, she was happy with her appearance for the evening. If she said so herself, she looked *hot*.

She gave her hair one final fluff before a knock sounded at the door. Her heart beat rapidly in her chest. She forced herself to take a calming breath, letting it in and slowly out. She wiped the palms of her hands on her pants and opened the door.

"Wow, sweetness, you look stunning. What did you do to your hair?" Jake's gaze, emphasized by his sparkling sapphire eyes, started at her feet and ended at her hair.

"Do you like it?" she asked.

"Yes, I do. I want to run my fingers through those

big, bouncing curls."

"Don't you dare, mister." She pointed a stern finger at him. "It took me an hour and lots of hairspray to get it like this. I will not have you messing it up already."

"The night is still young."

Her thighs ached at the invitation. She had awakened in his arms for the past two mornings, and she couldn't think of a better way to welcome the day. Never had she felt so rested and ready to fight what was ahead of her. Except it didn't feel like a struggle. Things were simple with Jake around. They talked about the easy stuff, leaving the complicated things for later. They had made love several times last night and early this morning, and he held her afterward—keeping the dreams that plagued her mind lately at bay for the most part. She felt safe with him.

Last night he'd saved her. When she'd needed him, he was there, taking care of her. He did it in a way that made her feel in control of her life. He'd given everything he had to her when he came to her rescue out of the blue.

Last night with him had been a pivotal point in her life. Jake gave her the control she desperately needed. And for the first time, she was taking charge when it came to her body and the way she felt about her sexuality. Jake had done more for her than he could've imagined. Not once did she flinch at his touch. Nor did she shy away from taking what she wanted from him. This was a major step.

"We'd better go." She grabbed her small red handbag and indicated that he should walk out of the door he had just barely entered.

"You not going to lock up?"

"No, I never lock the door."

"I've noticed that. Last night I just walked in, which I was thankful for at the time, but it's not safe."

"In all the time I lived in Patience, my mother never feared someone coming in while we slept."

"Well, y'all had Larry there to protect you for some of those years, and after that your mom should have locked the door," he said, not knowing his words were far from the truth.

And there it was. She was wondering when Larry would be brought up. Thus far she hadn't been confronted by that bastard's name. But she'd known that someone would bring him up sooner or later. Little did Jake know that Larry wasn't the protecting type. He was just the opposite.

All her previous feelings of being in control of her body diminished the minute Larry's name was mentioned. She gripped the doorknob to steady her uneasy legs. Why did Jake have to bring up that name right now? She and Jake weren't even together when her mom's boyfriend had lived with them.

Jake placed a gentle hand on top of hers. "You okay, babe?"

"Yeah. Just haven't heard anyone talk about Larry in years."

"I didn't know him personally. Did I miss something? Was I not supposed to bring him up?"

"You ready? If we're late, Em will kill us both."

"Then let's not get killed. After you." He extended his arm out in front of him to let her walk ahead. But there was no hiding the fact that before he closed the door, he reached around the knob to lock it.

The night air was cooler than it had been earlier. The temperature during the day had to have been close to ninety-five with high humidity. Now a slight breeze blew in, hopefully bringing a day with lower temperatures tomorrow.

"You care if we drive my truck tonight?"

"You expect me to ride in Python again?" She hadn't given the first time that much thought because the only thing she was concerned about then was getting to her place so she could finally be with Jake.

"Let me guess…Boston?" he asked.

"I named it that the day you tried to run me off the road. It reminded me of one of those damn green pythons."

"I thought we'd already covered this. I didn't try to run you off the road. And you just drive too damn slow. I don't know what I think about you giving my truck a name that represents everything you hate. Since your precious Sparks hate the Boston Pythons."

"Well, maybe you shouldn't have a green truck jacked up off the ground. Not to mention you drive recklessly."

"I can't help that the color of my truck is not blue like your little sports car. And I'm not reckless. I wish everyone would quit saying that. I love to drive fast on long country roads. Running up on you was pure coincidence. A good surprise, if I say so myself."

His wink caused her insides to tremble. He should come with a warning label: *Attention, ladies*. He might have bad taste in baseball teams, but, God, he surely could charm his way into a woman's bed.

****

After putting up a half-assed fight, Anna agreed to

ride in his truck. Of course, Jake demanded that she not call his truck Python when he was around, and her reply was "Python." He let out an aggravated sigh but dropped the subject. His brooding response made her smile.

Her own mood was a combination of jitters and concern over what the others would think about them showing up together. The town already buzzed at the knowledge of him having spent a couple of nights at her place. They could put two and two together and figure out what was going on behind closed doors.

She still didn't know what she and Jake were doing, but she did know it was destined to be short-lived. After the wedding and after making sure her house was ready to be sold, she would be heading back to Linden—not accomplishing everything she needed to. Her bad dreams were more frequent on the nights she wasn't with Jake, but that was to be expected with her being back where the nightmare began. Patience was a trigger for her. But she was making it through them. With the exception of last night, she was handling them pretty well.

She'd expected more anxiety, but it wasn't there. Of course, she hadn't been at her house very much. But the few times she had, she didn't panic and run out of the door screaming. The memories were still fresh, but her emotions about her past were different than she had expected. It was as if she didn't care anymore. She felt sorry for that six-year-old girl who had to live through the traumatic experiences, but the twenty-nine-year-old woman was starting to move on the best she could. She wasn't naive about her situation, though. The road ahead of her was going to be difficult, but she could handle it.

They pulled up at the church where the wedding would take place. Jake jumped out of the truck and rushed to open her door before she could do it herself. She had to admit he was charming.

"You ready for this?" Jake asked.

"I guess. You know people are going to stare and whisper."

"Probably. But there's no reason to. It's not like we're on a date."

"What? This is our third—and final—date. We agreed. I had dinner with you, went to watch a baseball game, and now I came here with you."

"We just happened to show up here together. You had to be here. I had to be here. Therefore, it isn't considered a date. When we go on a date, I'd like to have you all to myself, not share you with half the town."

"You're impossible, you know that?"

"I'm just playing by the rules, sweetness, just playing by the rules." He kissed her on the nose for good measure, and she couldn't help but smile. He reached over her, opened the glove box, and pulled out a small gift bag.

"What's this?"

"Open it."

She pulled at the tissue paper. "You got me a new iPod. I thought you would've forgotten about this by now." She then pulled out a navy-blue armband. "This is great, Jake. It'll really come in handy. And it's my favorite color."

"After you left that night we were at the track, I went back to where I thought you might've dropped it.

You were right. It was broken. I told you I would buy you a new one. I'm just making good on my promise."

"Thank you. I love it." And she did. It meant even more to her because he remembered making the promise. She showed him just as much by giving him a big, open-mouthed kiss.

****

"Anna, why haven't you come over for lunch, missy?"

Anna turned her back on the cheese-and-cracker tray to find Mrs. Bradshaw tapping an impatient high heel on the indoor/outdoor carpet. She instantly reached over to give Em's mother a big hug. The older woman returned the hug and held on a little tighter. She was like a second mother to Anna, and Anna regretted not calling and setting up a visit with her and Em's father.

"You look lovely like always, Mrs. Bradshaw."

"Thanks, girlie, but that doesn't help you any. I still want to know why you haven't come by the house. My daughter is demanding, but I know she hasn't kept you that busy, has she?"

"Well, I have been busy with Em, along with other things."

"I can see that."

Anna followed the woman's line of vision all the way to Jake. Leaning against a wall, he joked around with Tommy. As if he knew they were looking, his gaze turned in their direction, and he gave a wink. He wore light khaki pants, casual brown shoes, and a springy blue polo that brought out the sapphire in his eyes. She went wet in places she had no right being wet in while in a church.

"I see the way that boy looks at you. Not to

269

mention all the time y'all have been spending together. I haven't seen him look so happy in years. I see hope and love in his eyes. And that is a wonderful thing to have."

"You're mistaken. Jake and I are just friends. We've only been spending time together because he's been holding my house hostage. That's it. If he looks happy, it's all him, and it has nothing to do with me."

"For your sake, child, I hope you don't tell yourself that too long, because it would be a shame to miss out on love. And that boy loves you."

With that, Mrs. Bradshaw was gone, leaving Anna to stare at the cheese platter. Holding on to the counter, she took a deep breath in and let it out slowly.

Love?

There was no way Jake loved her. Falling in love was not part of the deal. She'd agreed to the three dates, and that was it. No love was included. Well, she couldn't forget about the amazing sex they'd been having. That wasn't part of the deal either, but sex was just sex. She was an adult who was having big-girl sex with an amazing lover. Nothing more.

No. There was no way he loved her. That was impossible.

"What's up?"

She was so inside her head that she hadn't noticed Jake leave his wall and walk over to grab her hand off the counter. She was forced to use his steadiness to hold herself up.

"What are you thinking about?" He bent down to peer into her eyes.

"What?"

"You've got that line running across your forehead.

What's going on?"

She tried waving him off. "Oh, it's nothing."

"You sure about that?"

He rubbed the top of her hand with the ball of his thumb. It was endearing, and at any other time she would've found it a turn-on. Right now, not so much. She was beginning to think everything concerning Jake was a turn-on for her.

"Yes, I'm sure. I would know if something was wrong with me."

"Fine. I'll let it drop for now, but you will tell me what's bothering you."

"I'm sick of you telling me what to do and making choices for me. I don't need you."

His scowl deepened. "That's not what you said last night."

Her cheeks flushed, and she exploded inside. She wanted to yell and throw the cheese cubes in his cocky face. But instead she stood there, frozen to the carpet. He was right. She had said she needed him last night. But he was taking it out of context. Yes, she needed him, but only for sex. That was it.

"Now slow down. I don't know why you're trying to pick a fight with me, but if you don't want to make a scene here, I suggest you take it back a notch and wait to discuss it until we get home."

He removed his hand, and she missed it being there. She couldn't tell him why she was so mad all of a sudden, because she didn't know herself. The emotion had snuck up on her and turned her once-happy spirit to rage within minutes. She wasn't deliberately trying to hurt him, but the words just started to flood out of her mouth. They were words that represented more than just their face value. She wanted to say more, but this was not the time or place to do it. So she held her tongue.

****

Jake pulled up to the apartment and after switching off the motor, he reached for his door handle.

"There's no reason for you to come in," Anna said dryly.

Ignoring her request, he got out of the truck and made his way to the front door. This time he didn't even attempt to help her out.

"Well, here goes," she muttered while carefully jumping from the truck.

She turned the doorknob but then remembered Jake had locked it before they left. She picked the right key and let them inside. He allowed her to enter first, but only so he could slam the door after he walked into the room.

"You're going to damn well tell me what's going on," he said before she had time to set her purse down.

Anna tossed her purse on the table and kicked off the high heels. "I don't have to tell you anything."

With his arms crossed, he leaned himself up against the back of the couch. "I think you do. When we left here earlier tonight, you were fine…great, even. Then sometime between then and the rehearsal dinner, something happened. And I think I deserve to know why I was the target."

"I'll tell you again—I don't have to tell you anything." She turned her back on him and hurried to the bathroom. She couldn't face him, not yet.

He gripped her arm, yanking her so she was facing him, before she could switch on the bathroom light.

"Let me go!" She tried to squirm out of his hold.

"Not until you tell me what's going on with you. And I don't want to hear you're fine or nothing is wrong, because I damn well know something is up. I've been around you long enough to see that much."

But even with his voice sounding harsher than she'd ever heard it and his hand tightly holding her arm, she was not frightened of him. Everything she knew about him and what they'd shared over the past weeks—or even before then—told her he would never do anything to bring physical harm to her. And just her recognizing that was huge.

"You know nothing when it comes to me."

"Honey, I know more than you think. We have a history, and you're forgetting that not only have we spent lots of time together, but we have shared a bed for the last couple of nights. Sex can bring people closer."

"Maybe for others, but for me, it's just sex. Nothing more."

"I don't believe that for a second. You're not the type who can make love and not feel something. I think you feel more than you want, and it scares the shit out of you."

"Like I said earlier, I don't need you, so if you can please let go of my arm and leave."

He let go of her arm, and she thought he was turning to leave, but instead he walked over to the open window and stared into the darkness that surrounded the apartment. She guessed he didn't want to show her how much her words hurt him. And she knew they did, especially if he did in fact love her. Maybe that was why she'd said them.

She sat on the edge of the bed, head down, looking

at nothing in particular.

He loved her? How had this happened? Mrs. Bradshaw had to be mistaken. Maybe Jake just liked having her around but didn't actually feel anything more. It could be that she was just a warm body to wake up to.

He raked an impatient hand through his hair and turned from the window to glare at her. "You know, Anna, I'm getting fucking tired of you telling me that. You might not want to need me, but you do."

"How so?"

"Let's see… For starters, you needed me to fix your run-down place. You were never going to be able to sell it because you don't have the time or skill to put the work into it—"

"You egotistical jerk. I didn't ask for your help."

"Let me finish. You needed me to show you what is so great about Patience and what you'll be missing when you leave again. You need me to give you multiple orgasms. You need me to be there when you have your nightmares. Should I go on, or is that enough proof?"

This was her life. No man was going to take that away from her. But she had a problem. She needed Jake, and it was nice having someone in her corner.

"I don't want to need you. I don't want any man to take care of me." She mentally gave herself a tongue-lashing for displaying weakness with her fragile voice.

"Dammit, Anna, that is the stupidest thing I've ever heard. I know women are independent and rule the world, but everybody needs somebody to lean on—and love. There's nothing wrong with needing those things. Why are you making this so difficult?"

"Do you love me?" She didn't really want the answer but couldn't stop the question from flowing out of her mouth.

"Yes." He said it so simply and with conviction, as if he meant it with his whole heart.

Crap. Now what am I supposed to do?

He moved to where she was sitting, bent his knees, sank down in front of her, and covered her hands with his own. "I love you, Anna Lynn Kelly. This is not how it was supposed to come out, but you give me no choice. I'm pretty sure I've loved you since we were sixteen, and after everything went to hell, I don't think I've ever recovered and stopped loving you. I know that I need you."

"You don't know me. You can't love me."

"I will be the judge of that."

She didn't believe her ears. "You just can't... It's impossible."

"We would be here all night if I named off all the reasons why I love you. But the main reason is because I think you are the bravest person I know. Something happened here a decade ago, something that still haunts you, but you faced it, and you came home anyway for your best friend. And well, call me selfish, but I love the way you make me feel alive. There is also the fact you haven't had many lovers, and I consider myself damn lucky that you trusted me."

"How do you know I haven't had many lovers?"

"Because you shy away from sex even though I know you harbor a fire deep inside you. You don't like to talk about it, and most of the time you like to be in control. Not that I'm complaining—the sex with you is over the top, and I hope to keep having it with you for the rest of our lives."

"You have no right to say that I'm shy about sex. I thought I was doing pretty well, considering."

"You are. You're wild and passionate, and I love to be inside you. But I can tell something keeps you a step back. You put guards up, and I can't seem to enter. When I wanted to go down on you, you wouldn't let me. You shut down when the talk of sex comes up, but you don't mind the sex. And you've had nightmares the few times you've been in my arms. Not so much like last night when I got here, but sometimes when I watch you sleep after we make love, I can see you're scared of something. I just can't figure that part of you out yet."

Tears filled her eyes. No one had ever said anything so loving to her in all her life. And what surprised her most was that he truly recognized her faults. He saw most of her, and he loved her for it. How would he feel if he knew the rest of her past? Would he still feel the same way? What if he knew why she shied away from all things relating to sex, especially about him putting his mouth between her thighs, and the reason for the nightmares? God, he knew so much about her. How did that happen? When did she allow that to happen?

He took his thumb and caught a tear before it slid down her cheek.

"You can't feel this way. It's only been two weeks," she said.

"I've loved you most of my life. That to me is not too fast."

"Jake, I can't do this with you. It's too soon, and I'm leaving Patience."

"You can trust me, Anna. Please tell me what's

going on."

He begged her to talk to him, to tell him the secret she'd been carrying all her adult life. Hell—not just her adult life, but most of her childhood. The secret that stole her innocence. If she told him, things would change dramatically. Forever. "I can't." More tears fell, and he went into the bathroom and brought back a handful of tissues. She wiped away the falling tears, sniffling at the same time.

"You can, Anna. It's just me, Jake. The boy you once loved, and maybe still do, even if you don't want to believe it. I will not hurt you again. I know what it feels like to bottle up your emotions. Before too long, they'll swallow you up, and you'll lose yourself to them. I would hate to see that happen to you even more than it already has. I would hate to see you not smile or laugh or just live your life because of the walls you surround yourself with."

He stood from his kneeling position. Sitting beside her on the bed, he took her hands and pulled her to face him. She gazed back at him and witnessed the concern and what she guessed was love. He really loved her. She didn't know how it was possible, but there was no mistaking the softness of his expression when he stared into her eyes.

Silence fell between them, but his eyes never left hers. "It's too hard, Jake."

"I can see that, baby. I'm right here, though. You can fall on me. I'm here for you, and you just have to start believing that."

"I do."

"Then you can tell me anything. I'm not going anywhere. I thought I proved that when you told me about the depression and sleeping meds."

Anna's defenses weakened. She was emotionally drained, and the hold she'd wrapped her feelings in began slipping away. "I don't know where to start."

He slid his thumb over the top of her hand. It was endearing and comforting. "Why don't you start from the beginning? Why did you break up with me and leave town?"

She remembered that day too well, and it broke her heart every time she thought of it. "I didn't think I was good enough for you."

He shot to his feet. "What's that supposed to mean?"

She flinched at the snap in his tone and rushed to defend her choices. "It's true. The scouts were looking at you, and we both knew you were going to be drafted. You were too good not to, and you would be off traveling city to city for six months out of the year, and I would just be here. I had nothing going in my life, and I would only be dragging you down. I wanted you to take your chance and run with it. I didn't want you to give up your dream for me."

"So you broke up with me so that I would be so furious, leave this town, and never think about us again? Well, that didn't work, because I thought about you every fucking day. When I wasn't training or on the field, I was thinking of you."

"I never meant to hurt you. You have to believe that. I was going through my own mess and wasn't thinking clearly. I know that's no excuse, but it's the truth." Her gaze fell to the floor. She couldn't stand to see the hurt in his eyes.

"Look at me," he said, and she brought her head

up. "What mess did you have going on?"

"It was like this town was closing in on me. There were too many bad memories here, and I couldn't get away from them."

"What memories? You had a mother who loved you, you had Em, and you had me. How is that a bad memory? Did I mean so little to you that you felt the only way to get away from me was to run?" He started roaming the room. "Did our relationship mean nothing to you—because it meant something to me?"

"You're right. I did have a mother and good friends, and you meant the world to me, but that was the problem."

He stopped in front of her. "How is that a problem?"

"I didn't want to have sex with you. There. Are you happy?" She clasped and unclasped her hands.

"Okay. Why not?"

"I just couldn't."

"I never pressured you to have sex. I think I was pretty considerate, considering I was a teenage boy with raging hormones and a girlfriend who, whenever she was around, made the front of my jeans a little tighter. I think most of my senior year, I had a zipper indentation on my cock."

Her mouth fell open.

"See, there you go, shutting down all because I mention you making me hard."

"Sorry, but I'm just not used to that kind of language."

"Well, get used to it. You'll be hearing it for years to come. But we'll talk about that later. Right now I want you to finish your story."

They were definitely going to talk about that later. Those comments were scaring her blind. Two weeks hardly equaled years to come.

"So you couldn't have sex with me. Is there a reason? Did I not do it for you back then?"

"No, I mean, yes, you did it for me. When we were in the back of your mom's old station wagon, I was very tempted more than once. I've always wanted you. That wasn't the problem."

"Then why didn't we do anything? I sure was willing."

"I wasn't comfortable with sex. It scared me to the point that I was having an anxiety attack."

"Most are terrified the first time, but I thought we had something special, that you trusted me to be easy with you. Take care of you."

"I know you did. I never doubted that. I just couldn't, okay?"

"Why?" A tick started in his jaw.

"Because I had a bad experience. Is that good enough for you? Can you leave me alone now?"

"No, I can't. What kind of experience?" An alarming combination of panic and anger passed across his face.

He was pushing her, but he also used a gentle and concerned tone while doing it. Probably from fear of scaring her again.

She used the tissue he gave her to blot her face. She couldn't control the flood of emotions. Her eyes slammed shut, and she was suddenly back there. Lying in that bed…in that room. Smelling the cologne he always chose to wear. She could feel the covers being drawn back and smell beer as he breathed on her skin.

She didn't want to be back there, but she couldn't escape the man who demanded the answers she kept locked away.

"I can't say it out loud," she cried. Jake went to her and wrapped a strong arm around her. She nuzzled his neck, finding a safe place. Her safe place.

"Sweetheart, you can tell me anything. You will feel better if you just say it. I'm here for you always."

Keeping her head on his shoulder, she whispered as if she were still that terrified six-year-old girl. "He touched me."

"I'm confused."

"Larry. He touched me."

"Larry? Your mom's old boyfriend. That Larry?"

"Yes," she sobbed.

Jake's entire body tensed. "What do you mean by *touched you*?"

Anna fell silent. When Jake bent down, she cut her gaze up at him, showing him everything he was too afraid to actually say and ask.

"Son of a bitch. The bastard touched you? Son of a bitch. Fucking bastard. Tell me what he did. I need to know."

She noticed he didn't quite know what to do with his hands. One minute he raked them through his hair to the point it was standing up straight, and the next they were balled in fists and punched the top of his thighs.

She raised her head off her safe place and looked into those blue eyes. Not only did fury reside there, but so did concern. It was an odd mixture, a combination that almost scared her. He was angry but trying not to show it and failing miserably. He couldn't hide the kind of anger he had at that moment. And it touched her deeply to see how concerned he was on her behalf.

"When I was six…" She trailed off, unsure if she was capable of saying it aloud. Around the people who actually knew her secret, the abuse was always the elephant in the room. She hadn't spoken about the details in years.

"It's okay. Just get it out." He rubbed the small of her back, but the heat of his fury radiated off him.

"When I was six, he would come into my room when he thought I was asleep, but I never was. He would pull my covers back and touch me in places. I lay there, helpless. I didn't do anything, Jake. I let him do that to me, and I never screamed or fought him off."

"I'm sorry, but I have to ask… Did he rape you?"

She shook her head. "No, he didn't. But…"

"I could kill the bastard. I have to find him first, but then I'm going to fucking kill him with my bare hands."

"Please don't be mad." She tried to calm him. She knew he wouldn't hurt her. She was more worried about what he was going to do. Going off in search of the man who'd taken her innocence wasn't going to help or change anything.

"Baby, I'm not mad at you. Nothing about what that animal did to you is your fault."

"But I let him." Knowing that she'd never once stood up to Larry stuck with her after all these years. At times it was what bothered her the most.

He petted her hair as if she were that small helpless girl. "That was not your fault. You were a kid who was scared and vulnerable. You thought he loved you. You had no way of knowing that someone you trusted would take advantage of you like that. Don't ever beat yourself up for not saying anything. He's the sick bastard who deserves a slow death, which then results in him going straight to hell."

"But I let him touch me," she cried.

"Baby, listen to me. You were a child. There was nothing you could've done to stop him. Where was your mom when all this was going on?"

"I didn't tell her until I was a freshman in high school."

"Good God. He lived with you for all those years, and your mother never knew?"

"Yes."

"How long did the abuse last?"

"About a year. All of sudden he just stopped. We never talked about it. When I became a teenager, I noticed him looking at me in what I thought was a sexual way. It might have just been in my head, but I never trusted him. One summer day it was just me and my mom at the house. He was at work. I couldn't hold it in any longer. I wasn't sleeping or eating, and I knew my mom could tell something was wrong. She was persistent that I tell her what was bothering me, so I told her everything. I remember being scared that she would be mad at me somehow, but of course she wasn't."

"What did she do?"

"After we cried together, she packed his stuff and had it waiting for him on the front lawn. He never gave a fight or asked why she was kicking him out. He just left us, and we never heard from him again. From that day on, it was just me and her."

Jake cuddled her in his arms. Her head fit nicely below his chin. "I'm so sorry. I wish I would've known.

It explains a lot."

"That's why I'm a little cautious about the sex talk, and I don't just let anyone in. It's not you personally. I just have a hard time trusting anyone. And it's why last night when we were having sex and you wanted to—"

"It's okay, Anna. I get it now. We can take things as slow as you need."

"Thank you," she said, relieved. "There was more."

"What do you mean more? How much worse could he do?" His fury was written all over his face.

"He wasn't just abusive to me. He pushed my mother around when he was drunk or just bored. He was also mentally abusive to her, which was worse. He treated her like dirt, and she began to think she was. She allowed him to belittle her. It took her finding out that he'd hurt me to finally take a stand and kick the jackass out. I was never prouder of her."

"God. How did I never know this? We might not have been dating at the time, but we lived in the same town. How could I not know something like this was going on? I feel like shit. And damn it, that morning back at the house when I shattered the dish. That must have brought up so many bad memories for you. I'm so sorry, Anna. If I had known—"

"No, Jake, it's fine. We were good at hiding it. There was no way you could have known. I won't lie and say that it didn't make me think about what was done to my mother, but I'm over it. Please don't feel bad about it any longer.

"Em and her parents knew, and I'm sure Ms. Edna knew too, even though she never mentioned it. Other than that, it was just a big family secret. After he left, my mom worked at the bank during the day and cleaned the bank at night to make sure we had enough money. I actually think she enjoyed all the work. It made her feel like she was worth something again and that she was finally taking control of her life." She smiled at the memory of her mom when she got her first check. Her mom had picked her up from school early that Friday, and they'd gone on a small shopping spree, which only included a new top for Anna and a new pair of heels for her mother. But to them it was everything. It was forty dollars well spent.

"I always liked your mom. She was a good woman, and I can see a lot of the good she had in you. I bet you don't know this, but I went to see her after you left. I begged her to tell me why you left, but she just said you needed to get away. She said if you wanted to talk to me, you would call, and for me to respect your decision. Before I left, she handed me a shoebox. It was filled with pictures, letters, dried-up flowers, and tons of other stuff that represented our time together. I was touched that you kept all those things. I think the box is still at Bradley's in the attic."

She and Jake sat there a moment, staring at the floor, thinking back on their past. They'd had some good times together. They had been truly in love to the point where it was overwhelming at times. People weren't supposed to find their soul mates at the age of sixteen, but she had thought she had. It had just about killed her when she'd discovered Jake's betrayal.

"No, she never told me. You were right about something you said earlier."

"What's that, sweetness?"

"Me not having many lovers. I've only slept with one other guy before you. His name is Chris. I took a business class with him. He was a sweet single father. Safe. We went on a couple of dates before I slept with him. I really just did it to see if I could. I needed to know that I wasn't as scared as I felt. It wasn't spectacular or anything, but it was an accomplishment for me."

An expression she thought was jealousy briefly passed over his face. He recovered and tried to downplay what he really thought and probably wanted to say. "So you didn't see fireworks?"

She laughed. "No, Jake, there were no fireworks. I only see those with you."

He laughed. "Nice. I do have a reputation to keep, you know?"

She should have been angry that this man knew her deepest secret, but she surprisingly wasn't. It was freeing to finally let go of all her crap.

"I still have one question," he said.

"What?"

"What brought all this on? I mean, did something happen at the dinner?"

"Yes. I was talking to Mrs. Bradshaw, and she said you loved me. I don't know how she knows, but she said she can see it in the way you look at me. I know you just said you did, but I need time to process it. I'm not ready for this."

"You process away. I will still be here when you figure out you love me too. I will always be here."

Chapter Seventeen

Anna woke just after midnight. After she and Jake had made love, she'd fallen asleep wrapped in his strong, safe arms. The steadiness of his breath warmed her skin. Their lovemaking had been slow and gentle. A different pace from all the other times. They were still learning each other's bodies, and she still got butterflies when he stripped her of her clothes. When he drew her into his arms, she relaxed into his hold. His hands roamed all over her skin, while his kisses ran from her mouth and stopped at the V of her breasts. He'd acted as if going any farther down her body wasn't even an option for him.

The man's body was magnificent. His endless series of curses when he was about to climax was becoming music to her ears. She loved that she could drive him crazy and make him lose himself.

She freed her body from his protective hold and tiptoed out of bed. After slipping on her panties, she pulled on the polo shirt he'd worn earlier to the wedding rehearsal—surrounding herself with his manly smell. It was just one part of him she wasn't ready to let go. What she was feeling was still somewhat of a mystery, but her heart felt as if it were about to explode. All she knew was that she was, for once in her life, happy. Happy and safe. It was a welcome combination.

How had she fallen in love with him? Oh, she just

needed to give it up. She'd never stopped loving the man.

But he'd hurt her all those years ago and hadn't even explained himself. She couldn't love someone who could so easily break her heart, could she? But, on the other hand, he was so caring and concerned. Was that enough? Did it make up for everything else he'd done when they were teenagers?

Knowing it would be useless to try to get more sleep, she padded across to her studio kitchen and brewed a pot of coffee. She'd been too preoccupied earlier to take her little blue pill. And the day had been too emotional for her to be able to just sleep pleasantly in Jake's arms. Now she would be up for the rest of the night, the night before Em's big day. Well, Em wouldn't have to worry about Anna outshining her. Anna could already see the bags forming under her eyes.

When the coffee was ready, she reached for a cup in the cabinet and was ready to wait out the night.

"Whatcha doing, sweetness?" Jake rested both hands on her shoulder.

She jumped at the voice coming from behind her. "Jake!"

"Sorry to scare you. You didn't hear me get up?"

"No, I didn't. Want some coffee?" She turned her head to the side so she could see him. *Oh. My. God.* "You're naked." Feeling brave, she turned completely around to face him, abandoning her interest in the coffee.

"Yeah, I was hoping you would be too."

It wasn't that she hadn't seen him nude, because they'd had sex more times than she could count over the past couple of days, but this was different. This was him standing comfortably naked in the kitchen. No intense kissing or stripping of clothes this time. He was just there in his birthday suit. "Uhh, I made coffee. Do you…umm…want some?"

"You already asked me that."

"Well, do you?" she said, aggravated with herself and the way she was acting around a naked man.

"There are much tastier things I want."

She let that hang in the air for a moment because she didn't have anything sexy to say back. God, she wished she did. If she was going to be a woman who had unattached sex with hot men—or a hot man—she was going to have to come up with some sex talk. Instead, she went with, "We've got to talk." Well, that turned the heat down in the room.

"Not the reaction I was expecting, but all right. What's up?"

"Can you please put some clothes on? I can't do this if you're standing here naked in front of me."

"You're tempted, aren't you?" A smirk was plastered on his face.

She couldn't lie. He would see right through it. Plus, she didn't want to hide her feelings. She wanted to feel free and wild. "A little."

"Just a little?" He held his index finger and thumb several inches apart from one another.

"Okay—a lot. Now will you please do what I say?"

"Bossy. I like it." He walked the few steps toward the bed, where his khakis lay and pulled them on. Since she was wearing his polo shirt, he just put on the white undershirt she'd pulled off him during the heat of passion. "Better?"

She poured herself a cup of coffee, forgetting about asking him again. If he wanted some, he could get it himself. She added her creamer, and when she was satisfied with the flavor, she took a place on the couch she rarely used. Jake sat in the oversized chair just opposite. She missed his closeness, but the distance made what she had to say, or better yet, ask easier.

She'd never been strong enough to hear the details of Jake's betrayal, but she was ready now. It was a night for answers.

"So what's got you up after midnight drinking coffee?" he asked. His hair was unruly, and sleepiness was still evident in his eyes.

"I need to know about Cara, Jake." There. She said it. It was finally out there. She couldn't take it back now.

"Oh hell, Anna. You want to talk about that right now?"

"Yes. I need to know, and I need to know right now. The not knowing is driving me crazy. I think I deserve that much."

"You're right. You do, but I don't see why we have to talk about it this minute. We have a wedding to go to tomorrow, and I don't know about you, but I need to get my beauty sleep."

"It's not funny, and I don't appreciate you brushing it off like it meant nothing. Maybe to you it was just another night, but to me it was life shattering, and I deserve more than a cute remark."

"You're right—"

"You've already said that, so get to talking."

"Okay. Sorry." He scrubbed his palms over his face. "It was the night after you met me in the barn to break things off. Bradley was having a bonfire party, and as you can imagine, he invited girls. Tommy was there, so was Em, even Tex."

"I get it. Everyone was there. I don't need the guest list. I need to know how you ended up sleeping with her."

"You breaking up with me blindsided me. I was in love with you. Tex had gotten one of his older friends to score us some alcohol, so I had more than a few beers. I was walking around the field by myself when I came up on the barn we met at the night before."

"You slept with her at the last place we were together? You sorry son of a bitch." She stood to walk off and leave the conversation and the old wounds that were surfacing. She'd thought she could do this, but she couldn't. Why would she want to know about one of the worst nights of her life?

"You wanted to know, so I'm telling you. Sit down and listen."

She paced the room before zeroing back on him. "You don't tell me what to do."

"Can you please just let me finish?"

She sat back down, but not because he demanded she do so. But because whether she wanted to or not, she needed to hear this, and it had been her idea to get it rolling.

"I don't know why I wanted to torture myself by going to the last place I saw you, but I did. I was trying to figure out what had happened and how things changed so quickly. I heard someone crying, so I called out. It was Cara. She was mumbling all sorts of things, but I was going through my own shit, so I just kept saying 'Yeah, yeah.' When she wouldn't stop crying, I did all I knew to do. I rubbed her back and told her it was going to be okay. Not that I believed anything was going to be okay for myself, but it seemed to work for her because she was finally making some sense." He stopped to rub his hands up and down his face again, this time not so hard.

"Well, aren't you just a knight in shining armor?"

"What was I supposed to do, leave her there to bawl her eyes out? I can be a son of a bitch, as you like to point out every chance you get, but I wasn't going to just walk away, leaving her to cry all alone. I watched my mom cry for a month straight after my dad died, and it broke me. I can't just leave a woman when she needs help. I'm sorry for a lot of things, but that I'm not."

"Fine, go ahead, even though I think it's obvious that there were other ways you could've handled things—like going to get one of her friends. But whatever. You can't go back and change what you did, so just tell me what happened next."

"I did ask if she needed me to go get one of her friends, but she said no. She didn't want anyone to know what had happened. She was embarrassed."

"About what?"

"Her boyfriend, an older boy she was dating over in Knight, had just broken up with her. She was supposed to introduce him to all her friends at the party, and all the girls thought it was cool that she had an older boyfriend."

"That's nothing. Em always dated older boys."

"I don't know, Anna. All I do know is she was embarrassed because he didn't come with her to the party. We were kind of in the same boat, so since she'd opened up to me, I decided to join in on the pity party.

Nobody knew about you and me. Bradley suspected, because he's my brother. He can tell when something's up, but unless you told Em, nobody knew."

"I didn't. That whole next day I stayed to myself. I remember her trying to call and probably invite me to that party, but I wasn't ready to talk to her. I didn't want to talk to anyone."

"Well, I had to get things out and sorted. I was trying to figure out what I had done for you to end things the way you did. Cara and I were talking, and then she came up with this plan. She was mad more than hurt. She suggested that we tell everyone we slept together."

"Wait. What?" She swore her heart stopped beating. The shock of his words paralyzed her.

"Cara and I never were together."

"You've got to be kidding me? Why would y'all do that?"

"She wanted to make her ex-boyfriend jealous, and I just didn't care anymore. You'd ended things with me. Nothing mattered after that. The next day when she told everyone…I just didn't deny it. It wasn't like I cheated on you because you had already broken up with me, so I didn't see the harm."

Her body went rigid as she processed his betrayal. "You didn't see the harm in breaking my heart?"

"You broke me too, Anna. I don't know what else to say."

"I didn't lie to you. Everything I said was the truth."

"That's the thing—you didn't tell me anything. You saying you couldn't do this anymore was a lame excuse for leaving. If you would've told me what was really going on, things would've been different. What did you expect me to do?"

"Nothing. I guess I should've expected nothing out of you. Get out."

"No."

"I said get out. I can't do this with you right now. Please go."

"Anna, you wanted to know, and I was just explaining how it all went down."

"I said leave!"

"Don't shut down on me now. Whether you like it or not, you feel things for me. And for us to work it out, you're going to have to start talking to me. If you want to yell, yell. If you want to slap me, I can't say that I would enjoy it, but I'll take it. Just do something besides shut me out."

There was nothing she wanted to do. She couldn't yell, and while slapping him would've made her feel good for the moment, it still wouldn't have changed anything. She would still feel hurt and lied to.

"Go."

****

Pulling down the long, curvy driveway, Jake felt as if he were coming home. And home was where he needed to be at the moment. He'd screwed up. He stopped his truck just behind Bradley's Jeep, grabbed his tuxedo for the wedding, and walked around to the back. When he was growing up, his house had always been one where friends entered through the back door. In those days he'd thought it odd, but over time he realized informality made the house seem more inviting. When his mom had been alive, everyone was welcomed in the Lawrence home. She was never one to turn a stranger away. God, he missed her.

Lucy, Bradley's basset hound, met him on the porch. He patted her head and gently moved the lazy dog out of the way so he could enter the house.

"Bradley, I'm here."

He laid his garment bag over the arm of the chair and made his way to the kitchen to get a cold soft drink out of the fridge. He popped the can and drank half. It was ice cold and took his breath away. It gave him a kick, but not the kind he needed. He needed a kick in the butt, and only one person could give that to him and live to tell about it.

"Bradley, where you at?"

"Right here, bro. Why aren't you dressed?"

Bradley had all the Lawrence good looks when he used his swagger and walked into the kitchen. He was already dressed in his tux. He reminded Jake so much of their dad. It hurt to look at Bradley and see his dad's eyes staring back.

"I brought my tux with me. It was too damn hot to ride over here in it."

"You look like shit today."

"Well, thanks. You look well yourself."

"No, really, what happened to you?"

"I didn't get much sleep last night." Jake's eyes were swollen and bloodshot, and his brother was only speaking the truth.

"Sexual frustrations?"

"Fuck off. We're not talking about that again. Last time we kicked each other's asses."

"Chill. I'm just trying to lighten your mood."

Jake slumped down in a kitchen chair. "I screwed up. Big."

"Screwed up how?" Bradley pulled out a chair, turned it around, and straddled it.

"With Anna. I told her about Cara."

"You what? Why would you do that? I thought things were going good between the two of you. After what happened at the bachelorette party, Cara is the last person I would've brought up."

"Things are good…they were, but she wanted to know, and I couldn't lie to her anymore. I told her everything."

"Which was?"

"That I never slept with Cara. That I never denied it when Cara told everyone at school that we did."

"You mean you never screwed her?"

Jake had been so out of his mind that he'd never even told Bradley what had happened between him and Cara. "That's exactly what I'm saying."

"You let Anna think all these years that you cheated on her? Why would you do that?"

"I don't know. Maybe because I was pissed that she broke up with me. She left me. What was I supposed to do?"

"Did she tell you why she broke up with you?"

"Yes."

"You want to share?"

"No." He couldn't tell Bradley the real reasons for Anna's departure. That was between him and Anna. She'd thought she was doing him a favor by leaving, and even though she was dead wrong, he couldn't dismiss her reasons. She had lived through a type of hell he'd never had to think about while growing up. Not for a moment in his childhood had he felt unsafe in his own home. His heart broke for her.

"I get that, but Anna seems like a levelheaded woman. I imagine she had a damn good reason for ending things."

"In her mind she did."

"Then you are just going to have to forgive her for that. But, man, I have to say, you lying to her about Cara is messed up. That's something I would do, not you."

"I know I screwed up, but I was in a bad place."

"I get that, but why are you just now telling her?"

"I brought it up several times since she got back, but she didn't want to hear it. Last night, well, it was actually early this morning, she wanted to know. You should've seen the way she looked at me. I thought she would be relieved."

"Come on, Jake. No woman is going to be happy that you've lied to them for what...ten...eleven years. You have to see that."

And Jake was realizing that. On one hand, he understood where she was coming from. She was hurt and had spent all these years believing the worst and hating him for something he hadn't actually done. But he thought she would in some way be relieved by his lack of action. There was nothing he could do to change it now. They both had made mistakes, and now they were paying for them.

"I know, but I don't know how to fix it."

"Talk to her. Don't let things end like this. You've been in a bad place since your accident and are just now getting back to a happy frame of mind. Besides, you've been waiting a long time for this."

"Huh? Long time for what?"

"Jake," Bradley said. But when Jake continued to

stare at him, still confused, Bradley continued. "You have to know what's been happening here. What all of this house business has been about. Don't you?"

"Yeah, I needed something to fill my time, a project to help get my head on straight."

"Okay, so that's why you decided to remodel a house. But why Anna's?"

He'd never put much thought in his reasons for choosing his ex-girlfriend's place. "Because it was available and needed it. I don't know."

"Think about it, man. So you just decided one day, when your life was already going to shit, that you were going to make life harder by surrounding yourself with memories of the girl who broke your heart? The one who got away. No, you did it because you knew she would eventually have to come back. You've been waiting for her. Now she's here. You can't let her go."

Jake's head spun. Was his brother right? Had he been desperately waiting for her return?

"Guess I never thought of it that way. I will handle it. Thanks."

"No prob. Now, are you going to get ready?"

"Yeah, but I have one question."

"What's that?"

"Who's going with us?"

"Whatcha mean? Nobody's going with us."

"You mean you don't have a date accompanying us to the wedding?"

"No. You know what they say about weddings. They're good places to find hot, available women."

"Why didn't I think of that? Give me a minute, and we can get to the church."

****

"Anna, I don't think I can do this."

Anna had never seen her best friend so scared. "Emilee, you listen to me. Tommy loves you. It's rare for any of us to find a love like the both of you share. Do you love him?"

"Of course I do."

"Then quit second-guessing yourself, put this dress on, and get ready to walk down the aisle."

She loved her friend, but Em had picked the worst time to start having wedding jitters. The ceremony was expected to start in minutes, which meant she had to get Em ready and calm enough to stand on her own two feet as well as put the last-minute details into her own appearance. Though the sun had been beaming all day and it was a good evening for a wedding, she couldn't shake the revelations from the night before.

But she didn't have time to think about Jake and his betrayal. This was Em and Tommy's day, and Anna's emotions would have to come later. And later they would come. After she'd turned her back on Jake and insisted he leave, she hadn't gotten much sleep. Zero sleep was more accurate. She drank a pot of coffee, emailed Liza, and tried reading, but nothing would help her forget Jake. Whether she liked it or not, she was going to have to feel the pain he'd caused all over again. And she didn't know if she could survive it for a second time.

"Do you need me to do anything?" Georgia thankfully interrupted her thoughts.

"No, I think we're going to be good now." Anna turned to Em. "Aren't we, Em?"

"Sorry, girls, I'm getting married. I do get the right to want to run, don't I? It's written in the wedding handbook or something."

"Em, thank you for letting me come to your wedding. You are a beautiful bride, and even though I don't know you, I can tell that you and Tommy have something others search their whole lives for. I, along with most, am envious of that kind of love. I wish nothing but happiness for the two of you," Georgia said, sounding full of romantic notions.

Anna saw a tear slide down Em's cheek. "No, there will be no crying. It took you almost an hour to get your face the way you wanted it. We don't have time to reapply." She shoved a tissue into Em's hand and forced her to gently dab at the falling tears. They were on a strict timeline, and crying wasn't an option. The tears needed to be saved for the actual ceremony.

Or in Anna's case, after the ceremony.

"Georgia, that is so beautiful of you to say. How long have you lived here?" Em still looked misty-eyed.

"I've only been here a couple of months. I haven't gotten to know a lot of the people around, but the ones I've met seem real nice."

"You are a good person. Why don't you, Anna, and I go down to Ollie's one night after I get back from my honeymoon? It can be just a girls' night out."

"That sounds like fun. I would love that," Georgia said.

Interrupting the girl talk, Anna chimed in, "Hate to be a downer on the girls' night, but I won't be here when you get back from your honeymoon. I plan on heading home in a few days." Or tonight, she wanted to add but decided to keep her mouth closed. Em would only pry, and they didn't have time for some drawn-out discussion. And they really didn't have time for Em to find Jake and beat the tar out of him.

"You trying to kill me or something? I thought you were staying a little longer so you can do some finish work on the house. What's changed?" Em took Anna's hands and brought them down, forcing her to sit in the chair beside her. "Tell me."

"We don't have time for this right now. You need to get your dress on. I will talk to you later."

"Promise?" Em asked.

"I promise."

She should have known that Em, even before her wedding, wouldn't let the conversation go unchallenged. And when the time came, what was she going to say? That she'd reluctantly come back to Patience, knowing it wasn't the best idea, but had decided her best friend came first. Now, standing in the bridal suite, Em's life was moving forward, and Anna's was standing still.

"Here we go. Georgia, if you could unzip the dress, then that way I can just step into it."

Georgia did as Em instructed, and before Anna realized, Em was zipped up tight in her wedding dress, looking amazing. The strapless taffeta flare gown was a perfect match for her body. The beautiful beading was stunning, to say the least. The open back showed off her tanned skin.

Anna stared at Em's reflection in the mirror. "You really look pretty," she whispered. More tears filled their eyes. They laughed and reached for more tissues.

"Well, I think I'm going to find me a seat. Good luck." Georgia gave Em a hug, careful not to mess up the bride's makeup, and left the bridal room.

"Now, what did you just tell me about crying?" Em

eyed Anna in the mirror.

"I know. I can't help it. Just look at you. You're stunning. Tommy's jaw is going to drop to the floor when he first sees you. It just really hit me that you're getting married. You're going to have a different last name after today."

"Can you believe it?"

Anna turned Em around to face her and gave her a fierce hug. "You ready for this?"

****

After seeing the gleam in Em's eyes, Anna pushed aside her feelings for the day and forced a smile onto her face. In the process of walking down the aisle, she made sure not to let her gaze drift to Jake's. While she stood at the altar, holding her friend's bouquet as well as her own, she could feel his presence.

When the ceremony was over, she took Jake's arm as they walked back down the aisle, but she kept her head forward and put one foot in front of the other until she could free herself from his hold. She would not let him tempt her with his glorious smell. The same scent that made her reminisce on all their nights cuddled together. She couldn't afford to lose focus just because his hand accidently grazed her hip when she looped her arm into his.

She needed air. They reached the outside steps, and she let go of his arm and turned her attention to straightening Em's dress.

"Quit, Anna. It's good, I promise. Your duty as maid of honor is over. Go have fun. I love you."

Anna couldn't ignore the way Em's eyes shot up to Jake when she told her to go have fun. She didn't want to go have fun. What she really wanted was to shut herself into the powder room and free the tears she'd been waiting to shed.

"You sure you don't need anything else?" She practically begged for one of Em's chores.

"No. Now go, and don't forget we never had that discussion about why you look so down today. We can't talk right now, for obvious reasons, but we will. In the meantime, don't think so much. Live life and stop trying to control everything. I love you, but you've got to stop trying to plan out everything. Just be happy."

Throughout the reception she tried to stay in the present and positive for Em's sake, but she couldn't stop her mind from going back to the night before. She had laid out her painful past to the one man she might only ever love, and he didn't judge her. He was concerned but didn't look at her as if she were some damaged product. They'd made love, and he was so gentle. Everything had been perfect until she'd had to open an old wound.

Would it have been better not to have asked? Things might've been different right then. Instead of her feeling depressed at her best friend's wedding and watching everyone enjoy the perfect day, while she only wished for the day to end, she and Jake could be dancing, stealing kisses, having wedding sex in the downstairs bathroom. But not now. Everything had changed so quickly.

She made her way to the powder room. Despite Em's reasoning, she had to think. She entered the small bathroom and stared at her pale face in the mirror. She craved her bed and sleep. Maybe she would do that. After the reception she would go back to the apartment, take her little blue pill, slip between the covers, and not come back alive until sunrise.

The door swung open, and in walked Jessie. Her lavender dress fit snugly to her waist and then flared out. The coloring looked radiant against her bronzed skin. Against Em's demands, Jessie had opted to keep her hair down. Em thought it was only because Jessie loved to do the opposite of what she said. Whatever the reason, she looked amazing.

Jessie checked under the two bathroom stalls to ensure that they were indeed alone. When she confirmed they were, she asked, "What's up with you?"

"Nothing. Why?"

Jessie put both hands on her hips and eyed Anna. "Don't give me that bull. We haven't known each other long, but I can tell something is bothering you. You have the same look you had that day at Cut and Curls. I have a pretty good idea of what it is, but I want to hear it from you."

Anna's gaze fell to the new heels cramping her feet. "Did Em send you?"

"No. I've been watching you mope around here all day. When I saw you make tracks to the bathroom, I followed you."

Anna believed her. Jessie had no reason to lie. Anna had learned quickly it wasn't in Jessie's nature to do anything other than tell it like it was. She admired so many things about her new friend, and one of them was that she didn't take any crap from anyone. Her backbone could hold up against a Navy SEAL.

"It's Jake."

"Figures." Jessie rolled her eyes. "What did the asshole do this time?"

"I don't want to keep you from your brother's wedding."

"Do you honestly think I want to be out there fighting for a bouquet? Hell to the no. Spill." Jessie stood in front of the swinging door as if standing guard.

Anna let her body sag against the sink. "He lied to me. Again."

"About what?"

"Last night I asked him about Cara—"

"Shit," Jessie said. "Did you really want to know about all that? I thought y'all had gotten past it."

"That's the thing. We never did. I could never bring myself to hear the gory details. But last night I was strong enough to tackle the hard questions that had to be asked. I needed him to tell me everything, and he did."

"So if he told you what happened, then how did he lie to you? I'm not following."

"He never slept with her."

Jessie threw her hands in the air. "What? Now you've really lost me."

"It was a hoax. It was a way for them to get back at Cara's boyfriend for breaking up with her…and me too, I guess—even though he didn't come right out and say that last part. When she went back to school and told everyone they had been together, he never denied it. They never had sex."

"Isn't that a good thing? I mean, that he was never unfaithful to you?"

"Yes, it's good that he never slept with her, but he let me go on for eleven years believing he had. He let me think he couldn't care less about our relationship, and that it was easy for him to find someone else."

Anna couldn't control the mist turning to full-blown tears.

Jessie left her spot guarding the door and wrapped her arms around Anna. Her new friend had a standoffish posture, and while Anna knew she was trying to be supportive, she could tell Jessie wasn't one to give out many hugs.

She wiped at her tears. "I'm sorry. You probably didn't know what you were walking into. Ever since I've been back, I've been emotional."

"Don't apologize to me. You have every right to be upset…angry even. But I still can't help but be confused at why you seem to be angrier at Jake now than you did when you thought he had slept with that woman."

"Isn't she related to you somehow?"

Jessie waved her hand in front of her face. "Way down the line."

"I know it might not make sense, but I can't get over the fact that he kept that big piece of information from me. I've lived with the ache that he slept with someone else, especially since he and I were never together. It made me feel that because I never put out, he was ready to be done with me and move on. It stung. I just don't think I can forgive him."

Forgiveness was one of the major reasons for coming back to Patience, and it was something she considered overrated.

She didn't know if she could forgive any of it. Her past abuse, her mother for not knowing what was going on in her own house, or Jake for lying to her for eleven years.

Damn forgiveness.

"I didn't know you two were never together. I can see how you would feel that way. Men can be dicks sometimes, but I was around Jake after you left. He was at my house a lot then because of Tommy, and he was heartbroken. About two weeks after you left town and my parents had gone to Savannah for a little weekend getaway, Jake stayed at our house for the night. He broke into my dad's liquor cabinet and found the hard stuff. Tommy had already gone to bed, leaving me with Jake. He got to rambling on about past mistakes and some things that didn't make much sense. He said he never meant to hurt you and that all he did was miss you. He actually cried."

"He really must have been plastered if he allowed himself to break down in front of you." Did Jake remember the night Jessie was referring to? He had always been a prideful person. If by some chance he did, it probably pissed him off knowing a woman as strong and capable as Jessie saw him during a vulnerable time.

"I was a little weirded out, but I felt sorry for the guy. I took the alcohol away and put him on the couch to sleep it off. The next day he never mentioned the conversation, and I never brought it up. I guessed he didn't even recall us having it. I could tell he loved you to the point that it almost killed him. I'm not saying what he did was right, because it was downright shitty, but he was hurt and confused about you breaking up with him. He wasn't in his right mind, and I believe at the time he was doing what he had to do to cope."

Jake had lost her in the same way she'd lost him. But she wouldn't have lost him if she'd never let him go in the first place.

Was she wrong after all these years?

Had she caused all the heartbreak?

"I never meant to cause him pain. I thought I was doing what was best for him. I like to think I ended things for good reasons, but maybe I was wrong."

"It sounds like both of you made some life-altering mistakes, but you are here together now. And the way I hear it, y'all are setting the nights on fire."

Anna gave Jessie a questioning look.

"Don't look at me like that. What do you expect the nosy citizens of Patience to do in their spare time?"

"I guess Jake and I walked into that."

"Yeah, you did. You should've known that you and Jake would be the highlight of the town gossip."

"What do I do now?"

"What do you want to do?" Jessie asked.

Anna knew what she had to do to make things right between them. She couldn't leave town until she did. She and Jake both deserved that much. Those teenagers who were so in love and never knew their lives were going to be anything but simple deserved closure.

"If I don't get to see Em before she leaves, will you send her and Tommy off with my best?"

"I will. Oh, and Anna, forgiving Jake doesn't necessarily have anything to do with letting him off the hook. Forgiveness is more about you and not letting the situation control your life anymore. You have to let it go if you ever want to move on. Jake is a good guy."

That deserved another questioning look.

"What?"

"Don't take this the wrong way, but when did you become so insightful?"

"I must have heard it somewhere. Don't tell

anybody."

Anna shook her head and laughed. "Thanks, Jessie."

"Go kick some ass, girl."

Chapter Eighteen

Anna searched the fellowship hall for Jake, but he was nowhere to be found. She ended up waving Em and Tommy off before leaving the reception. What reason was there to stay? Em was gone, living her life with her new husband, and Jake was missing.

She needed to talk to him and figure out what was going on between them. She needed closure before she left Patience again.

When did Jessie get to be so deep? But she was right—forgiveness was about her and her need to move on and not let her past define her life anymore. That could be said for her past with Jake as well as not being defined by the abuse any longer.

She decided to go back to the apartment, change out of her bridesmaid's dress, and go to the house to wait for Jake. He would have to show up there sometime.

The town seemed quiet, probably because everyone was still at the reception. She would miss her hometown, she would miss Ms. Edna, she would miss Em and their girl talk, and she couldn't deny she would miss Jake. He'd become such a big part of her life again.

She turned the corner to Garrett's apartment, and for a quick moment her body went rigid. There it was, Jake's giant green truck. Her heart beat like a drum, and the mere sight of him sent a hot tingle rippling down her spine. He had shucked his jacket, his tie was loosened, and his sleeves were rolled up his forearms.

She parked behind him and stepped out of her car. "Jake." His name came out as a faint whisper.

"Hey, sweetness."

"What are you doing here?"

"I had to see you. I had to make things right with you. I feel like shit after last night, but you wanted to know the truth, and it was time to finally tell it. I know I should've handled it better, but I can't change the past, no matter how hard I wish I could."

"Jake—"

"Don't interrupt, please. I need to finish."

She nodded. Maybe he, too, was trying to find closure.

"It was killing me at the wedding when you would barely touch me. You wouldn't even look me in the eye. All I could think about was pulling you hard up against me and kissing you forever and showing all of Patience you are mine."

When he rocked back and forth on the heels of his dress shoes and stopped talking, she asked, "May I speak now?"

"Go ahead."

"I was going to do the same—at least the setting things right part. I forgive you, and in some way, I understand why you did what you did. Not that I agree with it, but you were shattered, and I know how that feels. I also realized that I love you, probably never stopped." She paused because she wasn't being completely honest. She stood tall and welcomed the moment of vulnerability. "No, I know I never stopped loving you. You are the only man I have ever loved and felt safe with. I wanted to tell you all that before I left."

"*Left*? What do you mean *left*?"

"I have to get back to my life in Linden."

"What about the house? Are you leaving because of your nightmares and memories of the house? If that's the case, it won't help if you run from them."

"No. I also realized I don't need the house to let go of my past. Revisiting this place had nothing to do with the house, maybe not even this town. Of course I wanted to be here for Em, but I also had to prove to myself that I could come back here and come out okay and that the innocence taken from me didn't define my life. I'm strong enough to handle what I was dealt, and I'm in the process of finally being able to face it. You had a hand in that. You showed me that I could make love and not be terrified. A wise friend also told me it was about forgiveness. I see that now and am ready to embrace it."

"That's great, Anna." His voice came out in a soft murmur.

"And as for the work you're doing to the house, you're handling that all by yourself, and I don't mean that in a bad way. I appreciate the work and time you've put in it. You were right in saying I needed you. I could've never done what you did for it. So thank you."

"Is that the only way you need me? I know you don't like to believe you need anyone to care for you, maybe even someone you can lean on, but you do. You need me, and I know for damn sure I need you in my life."

She was a little dizzy, and it had nothing to do with

the heat. The raw emotion in his voice ripped a hole in her heart.

He left the side of his truck and made his way to her. Now that her breathing was becoming irregular, she felt faint. She longed for his touch but didn't know if she was prepared for the feel of his hands on her skin.

He reached out and ran his palm along her arm.

"Jake, don't."

"I love you. I can tell you that all day long. Every day, if you need me to. I want to spend the rest of my life with you."

"I have to go back home."

"You are home. This has always been your home. Don't you see that? I want to be your home, the place you find comfort. Please don't leave me again."

"Don't put this all on me. I told you my reasons for leaving the first time, and that has to be good enough for you. I have a life. I fulfilled my obligations here, and I like to think that I accomplished my personal goals, so I'm free to leave now." She had come here for her best friend and to free that six-year-old girl, and she'd done those two things.

"So I was just someone on your to-do list?" He took a step back. A combination of fury and pain flashed in his eyes.

"Of course not. I meant the stuff from my past. But while I didn't come back here for us, I feel I will be leaving with peace between us. It lightens my heart to know we're in a good place. But I feel you've helped me more than I helped you."

"Do you know what kind of man I was before you came into my life again? I was a moody son of a bitch. Just ask anyone. After my injury and my mom's death,

I shut down. I told you most of it at the ball field, but what you don't know is that my life changed when you entered it. I found love and hope again. I don't just want you—I need you, Anna." Moisture filled the corners of his eyes. "I don't have to have other women, alcohol, or bar fights to feel something—or even baseball. You're it for me. Nothing in my life makes sense without you in it."

He took that last step between them, and his mouth took possession of hers. He kissed her so hard she had to tilt back her head to take in all he was giving. A groan escaped through his chest as he placed both hands on her hips.

When he pulled back, his fingers grazed her arm, and she couldn't stop the sudden gasp and shudder that overtook her. He had a way of throwing her system off balance.

"Don't even say that you can't stay here, because I know it's a lie. I was young and stupid before and made a terrible mistake, but I'm a grown man, and I won't make that mistake again. You run again, and I will just come after you. I should've done that eleven years ago. I want to build a life with you here. I want us to have our own wedding with all our friends and family around us. I want us to buy a house with a big backyard so I can teach our kids how to play baseball." He put up a pointing, warning finger to stop her before she interrupted. "And I won't stop until I have all those things."

"You want to marry me?" Her voice cracked.

"Don't forget about the kids." A boyish grin split his face.

She pulled out of his grasp and turned away from

him, needing a moment. And looking at his boyish charm wasn't helping the situation. He wanted to marry her? Love was one thing, but making a family was something totally different.

And what about the plea in his voice when he expressed how much he needed her in his life?

"Why do you want to marry me?"

"Do you really need an answer to that?" he asked.

"I want one."

"Okay. Because you are the most amazing woman I've ever met. I've loved you my entire adult life. Because you are brave, because you know how to knock me down a peg, because my life seems empty without you in it. Do you need me to go on? I want to be your safe haven. I just love you, simple as that. Isn't that all that matters?"

She searched his face and found only truth. She could see the respect he had for her. He really loved her, and why would she want to leave that, turn her back on him? Did she really want to return to Linden and run from love? No, she didn't. She wanted this man who stood before her.

She jumped into his arms, wrapping her own around his neck but not kissing him just yet. She gazed down at his face. He had the dearest face she'd ever seen.

"Do you love me, Anna?"

"Yes, I told you I did. I love you so much it scares me."

"Then stay here with me. Live here. Start a family with me here in our hometown."

"I'm terrified, Jake. I'm just finding my strength."

He set her down on her feet and cupped her face.

"I'm not asking you to give up anything. In fact, I refuse to let you. And if living here is the problem, then forget the whole hometown thing, I'll go back to Linden with you."

"You would do that? You would leave your home and your brother for me?"

"My home is anywhere you are, and as for Bradley, he's a big boy, and I can come back and see him anytime. Don't you get it? I just want you."

"Oh God," she whispered. "I don't think I've ever had anyone say such things to me. I'm so lucky to have you back in my life. I can hardly breathe because of the love I feel for you. I need you too, Jake."

"So is that a yes?"

"That would be a yes, slugger. I want to stay here with you, marry you, and then we can talk about kids. I would like some time with just the two of us. We have a lot of wasted time to make up for."

"Thank the Lord." He sighed. "All that sounds good. Just so long as you want me."

"I definitely want you." To show him just how much she wanted him, she rose up onto her toes and planted a kiss on him. An eternity later, Anna pulled back and stood straight on her aching feet. But that didn't matter. Nothing mattered except her and Jake. They were finally going to get that second chance. All because of love—and surprisingly, forgiveness.

Epilogue

Two months later

"I can't believe you brought me to a Sparks game." Anna couldn't wrap her mind around the fact that she stood in Spark Stadium, a place where traditions ran true. She had dreamed of coming here for years, but New York was an expensive place to visit, and she just couldn't find the money to spend on such an elaborate trip.

"Just so you know, I brought you here because I owed you a third date. Don't get any wild ideas that this will be a yearly trip, because no sirree, it won't. One New York game is about all I can handle in this lifetime."

"If you plan to marry me, Lawrence, then you have to marry my baseball team too. You don't get me without them. So you might as well get your butt over here, sit down, and be prepared to watch the best team in baseball."

Jake made a *uuummhh* noise that resembled a complaint, but she let it go. The guy was being a trouper, considering he refused to be a part of anything related to New York. He was just going to be stuck dealing with it. She'd fallen in love with the Sparks many years ago, and she put her foot down when it came to them. Just because she and Jake were back together didn't mean she would be abandoning her team. Once a New York fan, always a New York fan.

They took their amazing seats, courtesy of contacts Jake had. He'd taken some major crap asking for the tickets, but he did it for her. He did it to make her happy and to make one of her dreams come true.

They sat right next to the home dugout. In just minutes, she would see Jax Dalton take the field.

"I see you over there drooling. You just remember that you're my woman, and Dalton can only look."

Anna threw a handful of popcorn in Jake's face. "Oh please, don't tell me you're jealous. I'll tell you what. If he asks me on three dates, I will go. But that's it. How's that sound?"

"Real funny, sweetness. You are my woman now. I'm sure number two over there can get any woman he wants."

The crowd started to buzz, and Anna screamed at the top of her lungs when the home fans chanted Jax Dalton's name. Dalton held up his glove to show acknowledgment. The atmosphere was jumping. She had always wondered how it would feel to see a game in New York. And so far it was better than she expected.

Three outs, and it was the home team's turn at bat, which meant Dalton would be up first because he was the team's leadoff hitter.

"Do you know that you look like some little giddy schoolgirl right now?" Jake asked, sounding way past annoyed.

It was only the first inning, and she didn't know if he was going to make it through the entire game without exploding. "You embarrassed?"

"By you? Hell no. I just find you damn cute and feel really sorry for Mr. Dalton."

"Why's that?"

"Because you'll sit here the whole game idolizing his every move, drooling over him. But after nine innings, I will be the one taking you home. I will be the one curling up with you in bed tonight." He gave her a southern boy wink. "Maybe we can do a little more of what we tried last night?"

"You're a bad, bad man, Jake Lawrence. But for you—and only you—I think that can be arranged." It had taken two months, but Anna had finally gotten up the nerve to let Jake touch her in that very delicate part of her body with his mouth.

He rubbed the top of her arm. "Are you sure you're still okay with it?"

In the past twelve hours, he'd asked her three times if she was okay. It was sweet, and his concern touched her. "Yes, Jake, I'm perfectly fine. In fact, after I have my fun here, we can go back to the hotel, and you can make me forget all about Jax Dalton."

"I've got something else to make you forget," he said with a sexy grin that always melted her heart.

"What are you up to?"

"This." He dug into his jeans' pocket and pulled out a small black box. "I know it's correct protocol to get down on one knee, but it's a tight fit in these seats." He placed the box in her hand and waited for her to respond.

Her eyes kept darting back and forth between the box and Jake. "You bought me a ring?"

"That's usually what men do when they want a woman to marry them."

They had been so consumed with finishing up the remodel on her house and their nightly lovemaking that even though she'd already agreed to marry him, a ring hadn't been thought of—at least not on her part. He must have had this planned out for some time. Maybe he'd brought her there so he could propose again, but this time with a ring.

She opened the tiny box and stared at the princess-cut diamond ring. "Oh, Jake, it's beautiful."

"So that's a yes? You like it?"

They were simple words, but they didn't take away from the impact they had on her heart. This man wanted to marry her. Build a life with her. How had she become so lucky to find Jake again and have him still love her after all their years apart?

"Yes, of course I'll marry you. And the ring is perfect. I'll never take it off."

The people around them clapped, and at any other time, she would have been embarrassed by the attention, but not now. Right now she was too happy to be concerned with such little things.

She spent the next three hours in pure bliss. She was in the process of closing the arrangements on the house next to Garrett's office and couldn't have been more thrilled at the thought that in the next few months, she and Jake together would be remodeling the house to make it a better fit for a coffee shop downstairs and a small bookstore upstairs. Liza was planning to come for a long visit when the shop opened, and although she didn't think Jake was looking forward to meeting Liza in person, Anna couldn't wait to see them together. While Liza was cautious about Anna getting back together with Jake, she admitted it didn't surprise her any.

Jake had talked her into not selling her childhood home just yet. He suggested that she give herself more time to make a decision since she was moving back to town. She knew for sure she didn't want to live in it. Her reasons were not because of her past, but because she wanted to find a place with Jake. A place that was perfect for them. So they'd decided to stay at the apartment until the remodel was finished and they had more time to find a place with Garrett's help.

Em was over-the-top thrilled. Anna had waited until after the honeymoon before telling her best friend that she and Jake had made up. But then she remembered Em never knew about the argument the night before her wedding. Em didn't care. She had just been happy to hear Anna was staying. Anna couldn't wait to tell Em about the ring Jake just placed on her finger. But she was glad for the time. She wanted to be able to savor the moment with Jake and all the Spark fans surrounding them.

With the score tied at one in the bottom of the ninth, the cheering crowd was wound up like a rubber band when Dalton walked to the plate.

"I love you, Jake—love like I never thought was possible for me. You make me so happy."

"I hope me bringing you here proves how much I love you."

"Shut up, slugger, and kiss me."

Tugging on his Atlanta Rockets T-shirt, she brushed her lips over his. She was so wrapped up in *her* man that she didn't even care when number two, on the first pitch, hit a walk-off homerun.

A word about the author...

Jennifer has always been an avid reader, but it wasn't until she became a stay-at-home mom that she started to read romance. Her passion of reading romance turned into another passion she had as a child—writing. One late night of writing about sexy heroes and strong-willed heroines turned into two nights, until seven months later she had written her first novel.

She lives in a small Tennessee town with her supportive husband (whose dream is to be on the cover of one of her books), a beautiful daughter, and two dogs who can't seem to get along. If she's not writing, you can find her reading, hanging out with her family, or cheering on the New York Yankees.

http://www.jennifersimpkins.net

Thank you for purchasing
this publication of The Wild Rose Press, Inc.

For questions or more information
contact us at
info@thewildrosepress.com.

The Wild Rose Press, Inc.
www.thewildrosepress.com